Long Empty Roads
The Survivor Journals, Book Two

Sean Patrick Little

Spilled Inc. Press
Sun Prairie, Wisconsin
© 2018

This book is a work of fiction. Names, character, and incidents are the products of the author's imagination or are used fictitiously. All characters in this book have no existence outside the imagination of the author and have no relationship to anyone, living or dead, bearing the same name or names. All incidents are pure invention from the author's imagination. Any resemblance to actual events or persons, living or dead, is entirely coincidental.

Published by Spilled Inc. Press
Sun Prairie, Wisconsin
Email: spilledincpress@gmail.com
On Twitter: @SpilledIncPress

All rights reserved.
ISBN-13: 978-1-387-41636-3

Cover Design: Paige Krogwold, © 2018

November 2017

Printed in the U.S.A.

Long Empty Roads
The Survivor Journals, Book 2

By Twist

For anyone who understands loneliness,
And anyone who has cured someone of it.

It's Thursday, I think. I'm not sure.

Honestly, it doesn't even matter. The apocalypse wasn't a cruel dream. The Flu was real. Everyone I have ever known is still dead.

The world is still a vacant and barren place. I am still alone, heading south-by-way-of-the-East-Coast looking for any possible survivors of a catastrophic viral apocalypse who might want to help me rebuild civilization.

This is the continued journal of my daily life.

My name is Twist (it's a nickname, actually). I'm eighteen. I miss Big Macs, television, human contact, and going to the movies.

And I am still alive.

CHAPTER ONE

Still Alive

I dreamed last night. I don't often remember my dreams, but this particular dream I did. In the dream, I was surrounded by friends. Not particular friends, mind you, just faceless, voiceless shapes that my subconscious brain recognized as friends. That was something that I haven't known in over a year. All my friends are dead.

In the dream, my friends and I were bowling. What bowling has to do with anything, I'm not sure. I was never into bowling when everyone was still alive. I have no desire to go bowling now. Bowling was something Wisconsin kids did on Friday or Saturday nights when there wasn't anything better to do. A small group of us would go get some cheese curds, a few Mountain Dews, and roll balls at the Prairie Lanes until midnight. It wasn't exciting. It wasn't even fun, really. It was just something to do while we hung out, something to break the monotony of sitting around and talking. It was easier to talk to girls if every so often you had someone to laugh at or some silly new way to roll the ball.

Anyhow, I dreamed I was doing well. This is highly unusual. I'm lucky if I break a hundred. I'm a lousy bowler; it's just not something I was raised to do. In Wisco, there are families who take bowling very seriously. Their kids start in leagues when they're four or five. The parents bowl every weekend. My parents were from outside the Bowling Belt, originally. My dad was not into playing sports in the least; he was an occasional hack golfer, but that was it. My mom would never have worn shoes that other people also wore, so we never went.

In the dream, I'm a strike king. The ball is hooking like I'm some PBA tour pro. The pins are scattering like playing card houses in a tornado before the might of my throws. All the girls in those faceless, voiceless shapes are watching me in awe. I have no idea how I knew they were in awe—my brain was taking great liberties. Anyhow, after I throw my final ball and seal the 300 game, one of the girls approaches me. There's sexual tension between us. She moves in to kiss me. I can feel her form, the softness of her curves. I don't know what kind of girl gets turned on by someone who is really good at bowling, but it's a dream so I roll with it. She parts her mouth slightly, and I lean in. We're almost touching. I feel electric. My lips almost touch hers, and I catch a whiff of her breath. It is foul, like tuna and old socks. I start to gag.

And like that, I'm awake. The dream world dissipates in an instant. I'm in bed, curled into a near-fetal position. There is a large black-and-white cat an inch from my nose. He is curled up like a furry burrito with his feet tucked under him, and his rank stank-breff is assaulting my nasal passages.

"Seven hells, Fester." I rolled away from him. "I'm brushing your teeth as soon as it's morning." I tried to bury my head under my pillow and return to sleep, but it was too late. I was awake. Outside the thin plastic windows in the back of my trusty Jayco Greyhawk RV, I saw the pale pink sky of the morning sunrise. Somewhere, birds were beginning to stir. I could hear their first tentative chirps. It was morning.

I lay in bed a moment longer, staring at the white plastic on the ceiling of the RV. It was bumpy, like the surface of an orange. It reminded me that I hadn't had an orange in well over a year. I wondered if I'd find orange trees in Louisiana. I thought about making a detour to Florida, first. If I harvested some oranges, maybe I could plant some orange trees in Louisiana if I didn't find any. I shook off the covers and sat up. It was the middle of summer. Already the air was thick with humidity, and I could tell that it was going to be an aggressively hot day.

I was parked on the desolate Interstate Highway 90 just outside of South Bend, Indiana. When I'd stopped for the night, I'd just thrown the RV in park in the middle of the eastbound lanes. It wasn't like I was going to cause an accident or any delays. That's one of the few bright spots of the apocalypse: No more traffic jams. I could also say that it was nice that no police officer was going to roll up on me and write me a ticket, but after a year with barely any human contact, I would have welcomed any amount of ticket-writing or general questioning from someone in a blue uniform.

I threw open the RV door and stepped into the thigh-high weeds along the side of the road to relieve myself. Fester watched from the doorway. When I finished, he meowed impatiently, one of those long, drawn out whiny meows. I don't speak Cat, but I'm certain it translated to something like, "Feed me, stupid human."

Fester has only been with me two days. He climbed into my RV while I was parked on the highway outside of Rockford, Illinois, and has been largely disinclined to leave it. He's an adult shorthair, as far as I can tell, one of those common, everyday types of furballs that tended to populate animal shelters and Facebook photos. He was super friendly, and he was fixed at some point in his life, so I assume he was owned and loved by someone before the Flu. He claimed the shotgun spot in the RV as his own. As far as travel companions go, I could have done worse.

I left the door of the RV open while we ate. The morning air was thick and humid, perfumed heavily with wildflowers along the side of the road. It was nice. I drank in deep breaths of it even though I knew it would probably set off my allergies. It was moments like that: me sitting at the table and having a bowl of instant oatmeal, Fester chowing down on some canned cat food, with the birdsong and summer air almost overwhelming me that I felt normal, like this was what life was meant to be, that I might actually enjoy being in this new world.

It was the rest of the time that I confronted the oppressive, depressive, and stark reality of being constantly alone.

It has been a year and a few months since the Flu struck and killed everyone. Already the Earth was beginning a vast reclamation project by slowly erasing human existence. The highways, without constant traffic, were given over to frost heaves in winter and heat buckles in the summer. What was once a smooth blacktop highway became a mostly semi-smooth highway with the occasional bump that would jar my suspension and knock the teeth out of my head. (*I only had to hit one of those before I started really concentrating on the road.*) Weeds were beginning to grow rampant from the new weather-made cracks in the asphalt. The more they grew, the faster the asphalt began to break down. The occasional highway signpost, uprooted by weather and time, lay across the highway like roadblocks. Wind-blown debris from homes and dumpsters was scattered in the ditches slowly being swallowed by a choking growth of unchecked weeds.

The highways were devoid of human existence, though. The Flu hadn't hit suddenly. It was fast, but it had waylaid people for a few days before claiming them. There were no cars along the sides of the road. No one outran the Flu. People died at home alone or with their families, or they died crammed into standing-room-only hospitals that couldn't help them, that couldn't even make them feel comfortable as they died. It had culled the primate genus from the face of the Earth with wicked efficiency, save for a few lucky schlubs like myself who somehow had a genetic immunity to the virus.

In the year I was alone, I was struck by how much I'd taken for granted. When I drove my parents' car before the Flu and I hit a stretch of bumpy road, I used to curse the government and the lazy road crews that couldn't keep that tiny section of highway in decent working order. Now, I understood the scope and gravity of their job and marveled that they were able to do as much as they did.

Entropy was an ugly, daily reality in my world. I was confronted with it constantly. I was fighting a losing battle against time. Just because I dodged a bullet by being somehow immune to the Flu doesn't mean that I was immortal. Eventually, something would get me, I would die, and then I would break down just like the roads. I was alone and fending off Death until the Grim Reaper decided it was my time. I refused to lie down and die, but I also had to wonder what the point of being so stubborn was. I was alive, and I told myself that I had to go on living for the sake of those that died, but *why*?

When I tried to find a reason for *why* I continued to live, I could never come up with a decent answer. I felt like I was having a mid-life crisis, and I was only eighteen. I was in constant battle with feelings of futility. I knew what lay at the end of my road because it was the same as everyone else's road. I just wondered why I had to keep driving it. Like Jim Morrison said: "No one gets out alive."

Depression and breakfast: a winning combination!

Fester and I set off for South Bend after we finished eating. I made sure to dress myself in a presentable fashion. This was important. Getting dressed everyday forced upon me a meager sense of normalcy. It also would help if I happened to stumble upon another survivor. I knew for certain that three other people besides me had survived the Flu, even though all three were dead now. The Laws of Probability would say that there had to be others. It wasn't a matter of *if* I would find other survivors; it was a matter of *when*. I was always actively looking for any signs of life. If I happened to find another person, I certainly didn't want to look like a deranged lunatic or something, unshorn, wearing three-day-old boxer shorts and a single sock because my right foot tended to get cold while I was driving the RV. It's not a good look. I kept my hair scalp-short and practical with battery-powered clippers, giving myself a boot camp buzz every two weeks or so. I shaved every four days to stay neat. I made sure I dressed every day as though I were going out amongst living people in a regular society. I forced myself into these routines. Routines were how I kept from losing my mind and giving up.

During my first day on the road, I made up a rigid schedule in my head and vowed to stick to it. I had a wind-up alarm clock in the RV. It went off at what I assumed was around seven every morning, just in case my tuna-breathed traveling companion chose not to wake me at dawn. (At this point, Greenwich Mean Time was non-existent. I set the clock by guessing dawn was somewhere around 5:30 AM.) By eight, I was fed, dressed, and on the road. I only stopped for the day at dark. No point in trying to go on hucking through the night and getting sleepy. That was just dangerous and stupid. I had a queen-sized bed literally twelve feet behind the driver's seat. Moreover, in the dark I might miss some tiny sign that someone was still alive in the area.

I'd gone through the northeast corner of Illinois and crossed into Indiana. I'd found no signs of life in the areas of Rockford, Des Plaines, Chicago, or Gary, Indiana. It didn't mean there weren't people alive in those cities; it only meant I hadn't found them. I worried about that. How many people was I missing? There was no way I could ever know. I'd ventured into smaller towns along the way, using the highway as a guide, but exiting frequently to roll through the smaller burghs and villages five or ten miles off the main path. It was difficult to assume where some living person might be hiding. Would they stay in the city because the looting for supplies was easy? Would they retreat to the country because it would be easier to grow food and harvest wood for burning? Are they traveling around, like me, looking for other people? Would I never find them because they're busy looking for me? I shoved those thoughts out of my head and exited the highway at the signs pointing the way to the University of Notre Dame.

I wasn't a huge sports fan. I'm awkward and relatively nonathletic. I was a decent wrestler, but I lost as often as I won. That was about the extent of my physical abilities. I couldn't hit or throw well. I wasn't particularly fast. Wrestling was a good sport for me. My dad wasn't athletic, either. He had been an accountant. He played golf maybe once a month when clients insisted. He wasn't good at it. He didn't have a team loyalty outside our general proximity to the Wisconsin Badgers, Milwaukee Brewers, and Green Bay Packers. However, my dad was a Notre Dame fan. He wasn't Irish or Catholic, and his own alma mater was Colorado State, so I have no idea why. He said it was a throwback to his dad. I didn't know my grandfather too well; he died when I was young. Apparently, when my dad was a kid, they'd always watched Notre Dame on Saturdays, so the tradition just continued. Saturday afternoons in the fall at my house were reserved for Golden Domer football. When I was a kid, I had a Fightin' Irish jacket. I had been steeped in the lore and glory of ND football since I was a fetus. I just wanted to see the stadium in person once before I settled in the south. Just once. Just once before travel possibilities reverted to pre-internal combustion engine times.

That was the most haunting part of this journey: I knew that gasoline wouldn't stay viable forever. Already I was starting to see breakdowns in the fuel reserves I was finding. I was operating wholly on the knowledge that I would never venture back to the north again. I would never see my old hometown of Sun Prairie again. I would never see any of the towns I was driving through again. Once I made it Louisiana, that was it; I would be done traveling. Forever. I would build my life there. I would die there, eventually. The rest of the country, the rest of the great open space of America would be dead to me. My whole world would be the little bubble of land where I carved out a daily existence. Everything I passed, I tried to make sure I locked it deep into my memory banks. It would be all I would have in terms of knowledge of the world for the remainder of my life.

I rolled the RV slowly through the streets toward the campus of Notre Dame. Cars were parked haphazardly on the sides of the roads. I occasionally glimpsed some dogs. Most of the dogs that were surviving had gone feral and become dangerous, returning to that necessary pack-hunter mentality that they had locked away in the back of the wolf-part of their brains. Maybe some of them would welcome a human master again, but it was hard to trust a pack of them when they growled and barked at your arrival. A single blast of the shotgun into the air would send them scattering. Silly dogs. Still scared of the boom of fireworks.

I parked the RV on the edge of campus, the stadium in sight. I geared up: a mostly-empty Army-issue rucksack for hauling back anything worth taking (*I also carried a couple of tools in the bottom of the bag for breaking locks when necessary*), a Remington shotgun on a shoulder sling that I threw across my back apocalypse warrior-style, a slim, black semi-automatic handgun in a leather holster on my right hip secured with a tactical gun belt that I'd taken from Cabela's back in Wisconsin. Please do not think for an instant that I'm some sort of badass post-apocalyptic warrior god. I am not. I'm rather the opposite. I don't like guns; I barely touch them. I just know their value in this world-gone-wild. The shotgun is there to scare away the dogs should they start to think about attacking me. The SIG Sauer is there for my own mental health. I don't want to use it, but I don't want to not have it there if I have to use it. Prior to the apocalypse, I wasn't anti-gun, but I wasn't pro-gun, either. I was gun indifferent. Now, I am all for guns. Totally pro-weapon. I know they have their place. They are tools. They are insurance. I both fear and respect them. I just do not like them or enjoy them, and I wish I did not have to carry them.

I addressed Fester before leaving. "Don't drain the battery playing CDs the whole time I'm gone, okay?" The cat was curled up on the secondary bunk, the one situated over the driver and passenger seat in front. He squeezed his eyes shut at me. I worried about him in the RV. In the heat, it could get dangerously hot inside the RV. I opened every window, save the ones without screens on them. It was enough to get a thick, sludgy breeze moving through the cabin. I made sure he had a big bowl of water. I was parked under a large, leafy oak. Between the shade and the breeze, it shouldn't be dangerous. At least, I hoped. I'd buried one pet already since the Flu struck. I'd only had Fester two days, but he'd been a welcome companion. I didn't want to lose him, too.

I shut the door behind me, locking it. I know that's probably a stupid superstition. I always locked doors when everyone was alive, and now that everyone was dead, it seemed needless. I think it had something to do with my own sense of paranoia. I somehow still assumed that someone is nearby despite all evidence to the contrary, and if I don't lock the doors, that person will come and steal my RV. I also don't want to ever open the door and find someone rummaging through my stuff. I don't know how that scenario would play out. Would I shoot them? Hug them? I just don't know. If I lock the doors, my mind rests easier.

Notre Dame's campus was everything I hoped it would be, save for the sidewalks and grassy areas teeming with students and faculty. There was a darkness to the campus now. All the buildings stood silent and empty. The residence halls were probably littered with the moldering bones of the dead. (The Flu began in early May, before most campuses were done for the year. Many students never made it home, too sick to travel.) As I walked, I kept expecting a face to be peering at me from one of the windows. I tried not to look at the windows because of that. It gave me that weird, hollow feeling in my gut and groin, that same feeling you get when you're in a haunted house at the amusement park and know you're about to be scared out of your pants but you just don't know when the costumed worker is going to jump out at you.

The planet was working hard to reclaim the buildings. The grass was thigh-high everywhere. Ivy growing up the sides of some buildings was unchecked and swallowing the buildings in green leaves.

I had no desire to loot any of the buildings. I knew from the experience of going through the campuses at the University of Wisconsin-Madison, UW-Oshkosh, UW-Milwaukee, UW-Platteville, Marquette, and UW-Whitewater that I wasn't going to find much worth taking. The residence halls might have some food (plenty of ramen noodles) and water, but I wasn't desperate at the moment, and there would be more food and water in other places down the road. I just wanted to see the stadium.

When I was in Madison, I broke into Camp Randall once. I walked out to the fifty-yard line and pretended to run a fly route to the north end zone. In my mind's eye, I caught the pass and scored the touchdown. I ran to the student section and started to celebrate it (everybody Jump Around!), but stopped when only the empty aluminum benches stared back and the cheers in my mind gave way to overwhelming silence. There would be no pass patterns today. Just memories.

The stadium was locked well. There were thick, heavy padlocks on the gates, but I could climb over those. The double-doors to the stadium were bolted. I used a lock-pick master key to jimmy the lock and open one of the doors.

Beneath the stadium was utter darkness. I had to use the small LED light I kept in the rucksack to light my way to the field. Once I got to the field, though, it was all worth it. The stadium that I'd seen so many times on TV loomed larger than life. The field turf field was still green, still looked like a field should look, despite the weeds beginning to grow around the edges from cracks in the concrete. The painted field lines were still faintly visible. For a second, I wondered if I should root around in the locker rooms and storage rooms and take a helmet with me as a souvenir. I decided against that. I had no use for it, and it would be a pointless trophy.

I walked to the middle of the field and stared at Touchdown Jesus on the building behind the stadium, memorizing every detail. I climbed the stairs to the press box and sat on the benches on the fifty-yard line. From the stands, I could see the golden dome of the Notre Dame administration building and the Basilica of the Sacred Heart looming over the edges of the stadium. My heart swelled. My dad would have loved to have seen a game here. He went to the occasional Badger game when he needed to entertain a client for his work, but it was only one or two a year at best, and usually one of those pre-conference tune-up games where the Badgers would pay a half-million for some sacrificial lamb school like Akron or Western Illinois to come to the Camp and then decimate them 70-13. If we had lived in South Bend instead of Madison, I think he would have splurged on a pair of season tickets. No—I *know* he would have.

Reminiscing about my dad hurt. I didn't cry, though. Part of my brain thought about it, maybe even wanted to cry. My dad should have been here, but it was over a year since I buried him and my mom in the backyard of our house in Wisconsin. I think I had grieved him enough in the past year. Now, I just wished he'd been here with me to see the stadium he loved. If I closed my eyes, I could almost imagine my dad next to me. It was a sad, melancholy day, but I like to think that it helped me heal, helped me put memories of my family to rest so that I could concentrate on my future. In a way, I left my dad in that stadium.

Eighteen months ago, I would have snapped off thirty cell phone photos of this and then never looked at them again except to show friends as proof that I was there. Now, I appreciated the moment. I lived in the present and committed the experience hard into my memory. I breathed in the smell of the stadium and the thick South Bend summer air. I stared at Touchdown Jesus until I was certain I would never forget what it looked like from the stands. I spent at least an hour thinking about watching Notre Dame playing games. I tried to replay some of my favorite plays in my head. When I exhausted my mental reserve of key big-game plays, I strolled around the stadium once more and left.

It was a silly little side trip. I wasn't expecting to find anyone hiding on campus. I wasn't expecting to find supplies. This was a stop just for me. It made me remember my dad. That was enough. It was the final stop of my farewell to the past. I had spent my tears and grief, and now I had to look to my future. Whatever life I have left in front of me, I had to plan for the possibility that I might be hacking it alone. These were my memories for the years ahead.

CHAPTER TWO

The Small Towns

I made a lackadaisical stroll around campus, letting the summer heat dictate my pace. By the time the sun was directly overhead, I was ready for some water and some food. I walked back to the RV and found a sleepy cat waiting for a treat.

I made canned tuna for lunch. I added some salt and pepper to mine, and then mixed it with a few fast-food packages of mayo. The fast-food squirt packs could keep a long time. I scavenged a whole box of them from a McDonald's where I used to have an after school job. I don't know if I trusted any of the stuff still on the shelves in stores anymore. Fester liked his tuna plain.

I missed bread. All the bread in the world was spoiled now. I could learn to make some, I suppose. There had to be flour somewhere in the world that wasn't spoiled, but it seemed like a lot of work to try that in the tiny RV kitchen. It was easier to go the prepackaged route while I was traveling. Still, a big stack of hot French toast with cinnamon butter and syrup would really have hit the spot. Once I got to Louisiana, bread would be high on my list of things to make. In my head, I had an on-going checklist of plans for things that I would have learn once I settled Down South. Learning to cultivate, harvest, and mill wheat would have to be one of them. I don't know if I could live the rest of my life without bread.

I was kind of proud of myself for living without a lot of things for the past year. If the Flu hadn't happened, if life was still proceeding as normal, I would never have given up TV, pizza, the Internet, cell phones, or hanging out with friends. In the face of having no other alternative, it was easy enough to do all of those things. It wouldn't have done any good to cry or throw a fit about it (although to be honest with you, I often felt like doing both of those things), so I just put my head down and muddled through, pressed on. Like the Wisconsin State Motto says: "Forward!"

When I was younger, if I got upset about something and started to freak out about it, my dad would always step in and ask me a question: "Can you control this?" This was his way of centering me. If I couldn't control it, then no amount of throwing a fit would change it, therefore throwing a fit was a waste of time and energy. If I could control it, then it was my fault it wasn't working and instead of throwing a fit, he would tell me to channel my energy into fixing the problem that was upsetting me. If I got upset at Super Mario because I wasn't good at the game, I could practice and get better. If I got upset at the TV because a show I wanted to watch was preempted by the local TV station because a severe thunderstorm was rolling in, then I needed to redirect my anger.

I was still grieving the world even though I tried to think I was not. It was impossible to not do it. I couldn't control the Flu. I had no say over who lived and who died. I could control my life, in theory, and that was where my energies needed to focus. It was easier said than done. Often, especially in the evenings after I stopped for the day and I'd eaten, I'd be trying to get comfortable with a book or writing, and I would get overcome with a wave of nostalgia or depression that would just deflate me. It was those moments where the "why me" would start, and the "why bother" would follow it. The self-doubt would creep in. Little voices in my head would remind me that I didn't have to be alone. I could choose the easy way out. It would be fast and painless. I would try to ignore them, but those voices were pretty persistent.

Why was I still alive? Why me? I asked myself this a lot in the past year. It made me think of a scene in the movie *Grumpier Old Men*, when Burgess Meredith tells Jack Lemmon that God forgot him. In a way, that's how I felt. I could find no sane reason for why I was still alive, why I was still on the Earth. I won the worst possible prize in the genetic lottery. I was an abomination, still alive in pure defiance of the Earth's plans. My parents created a being with a unique combination of cells that, for whatever reason, granted him an unusually healthy immune system and kept him from contracting the worst virus the world ever created. You might call it luck, but it sure as hell hasn't felt like luck to me. That's why I tried to fill my days with routines. The routines kept me on a schedule. The schedule prevented downtime. The downtime was when the voices began to whisper. Don't think about them, I had to tell myself. Ignore the existential dread. Keep moving. Keep ignoring. Just keep being.

The highways, while the fastest and most convenient way to move through the country, were also one of the biggest reminders of what happened to the planet. The roads stretched out before me to infinity, a lifetime of endless space converging to points on the horizon. Barren spaces filled with a lot of no one and nothing. Four lanes of ghosts going nowhere. I moved on the highways to get from point to point, but I made sure to deviate from those as often as I could.

Each morning, I looked at a map. Before I left Wisconsin, I'd taken a travel atlas of the United States and Canada from what was left of the local

Walmart. I used that map to figure out where I would go for that day. I would figure out where I wanted to be by nightfall, and then I would circle a few small towns along the way that I wanted to visit and search. I like small towns. The town where I grew up was technically a city. It had a population of more than 30,000 people before the Flu, moving closer to 40,000 actually. It felt like a town, though. It was small enough that you could walk from one end to the other if you wanted to, and many of the people knew each other. It was friendly. I always wanted to live in a really small town, though. When I read the Little House books by Laura Ingalls Wilder as a kid, I thought that living in a town such as De Smet, South Dakota in the late 1880s would have been cool. There were maybe fifty or sixty people in town, tops—men, women, and children. Everyone knew everyone and they all depended on each other to some degree. They looked out for each other. I liked that idea.

When I deviated from the highway, I wanted to find the little towns that were isolated out in the countryside. I didn't want those towns that made up part of a megalopolis, where you could go through three suburbs without realizing one ended and another began. I wanted to find towns that were little bastions of civilization surrounded by fields and forest. In central Indiana, it was easy to find the towns surrounded by fields--but forests, not so much. I chose the towns by names, not locations. I liked to find the towns with the silly or unusual names. Names that popped up on my radar were places like Wakarusa (which made me laugh because I thought it sounded like the name of a Pokémon), New Paris (which was astonishingly nothing like old Paris), and Shipshewana (which I liked because it sounded like what the back-up singers sang during the chorus in a 50s pop song).

The thing I liked most about the small towns was the sameness. The houses were all similar to the houses in every other small town. You could tell the different eras of the town's growth by looking at the construction of the homes. Every small town had a nucleus of houses built around the turn of the 20th Century, large boxes with simple designs and giant porches. The homes of the 30s, 40s, and 50s bookended the big homes. The post-Depression Era homes were smaller and more humble. They had one-car garages and postage-stamp lawns. Beyond that were the homes of the late 60s and early 70s. The design became more ostentatious, and the garages expanded to two cars. The newer homes, the ones built in the 80s, 90s, and early 2000s were all stamped out of the same design playbook, cookie-cutter construction, aluminum-sided beiges and grays, big lawns, and large windows.

The main streets were all lined with old buildings that once housed stores and services like barbers and dentists. Maybe the old local diners or cafes were still there. Maybe they were long shuttered. There were always gas stations in these towns. Some newer, some older. There was a Subway in most of the towns. Some of the larger ones might have a McDonald's or a Hardee's, or even a Culver's (if they were lucky).

Outside town, farmhouses stood like dark sentries against the coming entropy. They couldn't stop the march of time. They were all two-story and square, built in the National style that was so popular. Some had added garages or porches, but many stood untouched from their original construction. Next to the blocky farmhouses, weathered wooden barns were in disrepair. Some of the older barns were gone entirely, replaced by modern dairy operations with corrugated steel finished in a factory red that would never blister or peel.

Every small town in Iowa or Illinois looked just like every small town in Wisconsin. There were subtle differences, but at their core they were just alternate-dimension versions of each other. This trope was continuing in Indiana, so far. There might be fewer trees in some of the towns. There might be more grain silos in some of them, but at their heart, small towns were small towns. I enjoyed that sameness. It was comforting.

In every town, I cruised along the streets slowly letting the impulse power of the engine creep me along the streets. I would occasionally honk the horn of my RV. I was hoping the noise would draw survivors, if there were any. In the post-apocalyptic landscape of America, the lack of industrial noise was deafening. Without cars providing a constant din of engine noise and rubber-on-road, without the semis pulling trailers, without drivers having the occasional fit of road rage, a pristine silence lay heavily over the countryside like a wet blanket. If you have ever had the chance to go camping somewhere fifty miles away from any sense of civilization, you get a sense of what I mean. If you haven't, then I'm not sure I have the words to do the silence justice. If there's a wind, then that fills your ears with static. If there are crickets, grasshoppers, or locusts, then you hear chirps and a buzzy drone. If there are birds, you hear the occasional birdsong or chirp. However, in between those noises is a profound lack of *anything*. In that lack of anything, something different, like the noise of an RV horn, was as good as a tornado siren. It was a bomb going off. It was someone screaming at the top of her lungs in the middle of a funeral mass. Before the Flu, I'd grown deaf to the sound of humanity. There were always cars on the highway that ran through Sun Prairie, and there was always the sound of tires on pavement. I grew so numb to it that I stopped hearing it unless someone suddenly jacked his brakes and the squeal of rubber pierced the hum and reminded me that it was there. Now, there was only silence.

I would drive to the center of whatever town I was in, creep the main street, and blow the horn often. Sometimes I would do long on-off blasts. Sometimes I'd do three short blasts and then listen for a reply. Sometimes I would just lay on the horn for a solid ten or twenty-second burst. After I blasted the horn, I would shut off the engine of the RV and stand in the street waiting for a response. I would strain my ears trying to pick up any sound no matter how faint. I would wait there at least a half hour.

I would spend that whole time hoping.

When I was satisfied that no one was going to respond to my calls, I would take an empty rucksack with my tool kit in it and a shotgun. Then I would go to the town grocery store and pharmacy. In the grocery store, I would plunder any bottled water that was still available. Given how much I needed to drink in a day, not to mention a need to bathe occasionally, I was going through a lot of water. In many of the stores, the shelves were cleared of anything like water or non-perishable canned goods. Sometimes I could find secret stashes in the back, hidden from the prying, desperate eyes of customers. It took the Flu about a month to render the planet dead. In that time, most stores succumbed to the panic of those who had not yet gotten sick. I knew that I was going to eventually break down and start going into private homes to restock. I didn't want to do that. I knew I'd have to deal with the decaying corpses of those who passed on the year before. I had already seen enough desiccated corpses to know that I wanted to avoid them, if at all possible. They didn't faze me anymore. I just did not like seeing them.

In the pharmacies, I took drugs. --Wait, that doesn't sound right. I didn't take drugs like a junkie. I mean I put drugs like antibiotics and similar pills into a bag and took them back to my RV in case I needed them later. I wasn't a pharmacist, but I knew that antibiotics and painkillers had their uses. At the very least, an industrial bottle of ibuprofen could go a long way. I also went to the pharmacies because I figured that if someone had been there recently, it would show. I figured that pharmacies and grocery stores would be the places most likely for survivors to stop and try to resupply. I went to those places hoping to find signs that someone else was still alive.

One of my hidden fears was that the drugs that currently existed would all go bad and I'd have nothing. I know that pharmaceuticals have expiration dates, but I didn't know if those were just a safety thing, or if that was a hardline "take-this-and-you-will-die" warning. I survived the Flu, but I knew I wasn't immortal. Infection could kill me. A good virus could kill me. Stupidity could kill me. How many people died because of a stupid accident in the days before antibiotics were commonplace? I made a mental note to plunder a book of natural remedies from a library before too long.

Shipshewana, Indiana was a town of about 700 people before the Flu struck. As I entered the town limits now, it was abundantly clear that none of them made it. Grass towered in every lawn. Branches had fallen in storms. A thin patina of dust coated every surface. I slowed the Greyhawk to a crawl and crept through the empty streets.

There was a single, tiny pharmacy in town. I pulled to a stop in front of it. A plain sign over the door read "The Shipshewana Pharmacy." It was a small building, an old-timey looking little place. It was a rural pharmacy, no real frills, but still quite nice and quite necessary. The store's name was emblazoned on the building on a vinyl sign made to look like a red-and-blue pill. A tattered *OPEN* flag hung in front of the store. The door was still intact. I hoped there would be adequate stores of medicine inside.

I slipped out of the Greyhawk, grabbing the Remington shotgun and my rucksack with supplies as I did. "Stay," I told Fester. This was another private joke. I knew he wasn't going anywhere. He knew how good he had it.

I walked to the door and pulled the handle. It wasn't locked. It swung open easily, and I strode inside. Light from the glass door provided decent illumination in front of the store. The rear was dark. The store was narrow, the shelves still relatively stocked. The cold and flu medicine aisle was decimated, of course. I had yet to find a pharmacy with a well-stocked supply of Tylenol Cold & Flu. The first couple weeks of the Flu had caused a massive run on anything that might alleviate any symptoms. I slipped behind the counter and pulled my LED flashlight from the bag. I scanned the rear for any drugs that I might recognize or take for later. The antibiotic Z-packs were easy enough to find. The painkillers, too. Most medicine, though--I had no idea about what it was or what it did. The technical names were long and confusing and meant nothing to me.

I did notice that one section of the store was picked over. Bleomycin. Cisplatin. Etoposide. Ifosfamide. In each of the spots labeled for those particular drugs, the shelves had been picked clean. No idea what those things were. It seemed strange, too. Why that one section of the store? I found a guide to pharmaceuticals and looked them up; they were all cancer drugs—specifically, testicular cancer. I checked the shelf again. In the light of my LED, I noticed marks in the dust. Fingers had left trails. Boxes had been moved after the dust had settled.

AFTER the dust had settled.

My stomach immediately twisted into a weird knot of hope and fear. Someone had been in here relatively recently. Maybe yesterday. Maybe not this week. Maybe not last week. But at some point in the last month at least, someone had been in this pharmacy. Someone was still alive and they were in or near Shipshewana, of all places. Forgetting the need to pilfer proscriptions, I ran out of the pharmacy. Part of me was elated that someone else was alive. Part of me was terrified that they'd be deranged and might shoot at me.

I ran back to the RV and started it. Should I lay on the horn? Should I hide the truck? I had no idea what to do. I wanted to laugh, cry, and scream all at the same time. I pulled the RV down a street next to the pharmacy and threw it in park. I leapt out with the shotgun. I went back to the pharmacy and tried to find clues. There were faint footprints in the dust around the store. There was no record of whom, obviously. The footprints were faintly visible in front of the store, now that I knew to look. They looked like they left the store and headed slightly to the left. I guess that was as good a place to try as any. I started walking in that direction.

I only made it half a dozen steps when I saw him. He was walking toward the pharmacy leaning heavily on a pair of metal canes, the kind with the braces that ran up the forearms. He was elderly, at least early 70s, maybe a little older. He was stick-thin, a slow-moving skeleton in green runner's shorts and a black t-shirt with the rainbow prism from Pink Floyd's *Dark Side of the Moon* album cover on it. His head was bald, fringed by a shock of wiry, white hair, and complemented with a long, stringy white beard.

I couldn't help myself. Joy welled up in my chest like a spring. All sense of cool or concern left me. I started waving like a maniac. I yelled out, "Hey! Hey there!" I started to jog toward him.

The man froze, his head whipping up. His jaw dropped open, and he looked at me with wide, terrified eyes.

I realized I was holding a gun. "Oh. No, man. I'm...sorry." Stopped, dropped to a knee, and laid the gun on the ground. I held up my hands to show I wasn't armed. "I'm not going to shoot you. I'm a friend!"

The man sank to his knees, slowly, painfully. He covered his face with his hands. I could see his shoulders twitching. He was weeping.

I ran to him, stopping three paces back to give him space. "Sir? I'm sorry about that. I wasn't going to shoot you. Honest. I'm not a violent guy."

The old man wheezed and sobbed. He looked at me with watery eyes. He couldn't speak. Sobs wracked through his body. I don't know why, but I started crying too. I stepped forward and sank to my knees in front of him. He reached spindly skeleton arms toward me, and we embraced. His arms felt like sticks around me, as if a strong wind would snap them in half, but there was a desperate strength in them. We held each other and sobbed for several moments. Neither of us could find words.

When we finally separated, the man's trembling hands grasped my shoulders. His fingers kneaded my flesh as if to make sure I was real. He held me at arm's length. He blinked away tears and swallowed hard. Then, in a thin voice he asked, "Are you him? Are you the angel I've been praying for? Did you come to finally let me die?"

CHAPTER THREE

The Hermit of Shipshewana

What do you say to something like that? I had no witty comebacks. I did not even have anything comforting to say. I was stunned. My mouth opened and closed several times as I fought for words. Finally, I was able to muster, "I'm Twist." I didn't know what else to say. "I'm just a kid." Technically, I was an adult, but I still felt like a kid. I didn't know that I would ever feel like an adult, really. I stood frozen like a deer in headlights waiting for the old man to stop crying. Each second took an eternity.

The old man wiped his eyes with trembling fingers, and he gave a coughing laugh. "Well, it's good to see you, Twist. Damn good to see you. Good to see anyone, really." He pulled me in for another hug, and we both started laughing. He clapped my back several times. The dull, hollow thumps felt good. It made me feel like I was real, like I wasn't dreaming anymore. I returned the favor for him, careful not to hit too hard for fear of breaking him.

When we finally separated, I got to my feet and helped him to his feet. Standing, he drew me in for another hug. I let him because it felt good to have friendly human contact again. I could feel his ribs with my forearms. I could feel his vertebra poking out in the skin on his back. It was abundantly clear that he was not well at all, and probably not long for this world. It had to be cancer.

He stood there for a moment, his hand on my shoulder to steady himself. Tears continued to leak from his eyes. He swiped at them with the back of his wrist. "Well, where are my manners? My name is Fisk. Doug Fisk. And it's damn, *damn* good to see you."

"Twist," I repeated. "It's really good to see you, too."

"What kind of a name is Twist?"

"Nickname. My real name was Barnabas."

Doug smiled widely. "I like Twist better."

"Me, too."

"It's a lot more *Mad Max,* a lot more *Road Warrior*, if that makes any sense to you. Fits better in the apocalypse."

I was surprised that Doug knew his Australian apocalypse films. "That's what I said!"

Doug shook himself as if he was trying to wake from a dream. "Well, look at this—my first guest in more than a year, and I don't even offer you a drink. Why don't you come back to my place? I have food. I have water. Are you hungry?"

"No, I'm fine. I have food, too. I'm well stocked."

Doug bent down to pick up his crutches. I kicked myself, mentally. I should have picked them up for him. My mother would have been mortified if she'd been there. She's probably rolling in her grave. Doug didn't seem to think ill of me, though. He said, "Well, what in the name of all that's good and pure are you doing in Shipshewana?"

I felt no fear, no deception in the man. I felt safe with him, strangely. I did not, for one second, think he was going to steal my RV or try to kill me. I told the truth. "I was looking for survivors."

Doug looked around at the empty streets in the tiny town that once held 700 people. "Here? In this town?"

I shrugged. I know that I looked sheepish. "Well, anywhere. I just came here because the name of the town made me laugh."

The old man gave a short bark of a laugh. "I get that. I like that. You and me, Twist, we're gonna get along just fine." He started limping back in the direction where he'd been coming from. "C'mon, good sir. C'mon back to my place. I will put us out a feast! I'd kill the fatted calf if I had one. Chicken will have to do, instead."

I started to follow. I didn't want to break the protocols of new friendships and first conversations, but I knew I had to bring up the drugs. "Were you headed to the pharmacy?"

The smile ran away from his face. He hesitated, and then nodded. "Yeah...I...." His voice trailed away, and he laughed again. "I'm dying. Got the big C." He stood in profile to me. "You can tell, right? I was diagnosed just before the Flu hit. Did two radiation treatments, and then the world ended. I went from making plans to leave all my things to my family, to watching my family die. Isn't that a kick in the dick? Everyone died, and I was still there. Ironic, isn't it?"

"You were getting drugs to treat the cancer?"

"I was getting painkillers. I used up all the cancer drugs a few months ago. Maybe that's why I lasted so long. Now, it feels like I got lightning in my crotch and it hurts. I have been making myself walk over there once a day to get a day's supply of painkillers." Doug looked at the crutches. "Maybe today will be the last time I do that."

"Why not just bring the whole supply? You don't look like you walk too well. No offense."

Doug waved off my comment. "None taken--I don't walk too well at this point. But, I leave those drugs where they are. If I brought them all back with me, I might just decide to take all of them at once. Plus, this forces me to keep moving. It's not much, but at this point, it's my whole day. It keeps me going. It gives me a reason to get out of bed. The day I can't do it anymore, I know that I'm short-timing it. I figure I've got time enough for lying around and not moving coming soon enough, so I better do what I can while I can." He gave me a smile. It wavered for a moment, but he bit back the sadness. "Enough about that! Let's go back to my place. We can talk and eat. It will be good to talk to someone."

"I have an RV—" I started.

"Bring it!" Doug called over his shoulder. "It's the white house, just over there." He pointed to a simple white rambler. No frills. It was the type of house that I'd seen at least a hundred of in every town. The lawn grass was overgrown and all the windows were dirty. It was the type of place I wouldn't have looked at twice if I had only been passing through town. It made me wonder if I'd accidentally passed other survivors.

"To the feast!" Doug called. There was a spring in his crutch-aided steps. As I moved to the Greyhawk, I realized there was a spring in my steps, too.

I parked the RV in Doug's driveway. There were no shade trees in his yard, so I cracked all the windows for Fester, even the two front windows. I knew Fester wasn't going to jump out, and I was certain that no one would happen by and snatch him. I still locked the doors to the RV, though, despite the fact that anyone could reach through the window and hit the power lock. Dumb, I know. Old habits die hard.

Doug's house was much cleaner than I thought it would be. The living room was simply decorated, a brown couch and recliner, and a large, flat-screen TV with a thick layer of dust on it. There were old pictures hanging on the walls. I saw Doug as a much younger man, a family man posed with a wife and three children in the cheesy Olan Mills-type family portraits done for church directories. There were pictures of the three kids as high school and college graduates, and pictures of weddings. Around those bridal photos and altar shots were pictures of grandchildren, school portraits with bright, excited smiles and fresh-scrubbed faces.

"All gone now." Doug's voice startled me. I twitched. "Sorry," he said. "It's strange to hear someone else's voice, isn't it? I'm used to hearing my doddering old voice and that's it." He held out a glass for me. "Well water. Better than that bottled stuff you've been drinking, I bet."

I took the glass and took a long drink. He was right. The mineral tang on the tongue was a pleasant change to the sterilized, tasteless bottled water I had been drinking for the past year. Plus, it was much colder than the bottled water I'd been drinking all summer. It wasn't refrigerator cold, but it was much colder than room temp or RV-in-the-summer-warm. Nothing beats icy cold water when the temperatures climb, but this was an acceptable second place drink. "It's very good."

"Had to hook up a hand pump to the well when the power went out, but it's been worth it. I pump up a couple of buckets in the morning and it lasts me all day." Doug gestured to his kitchen. I followed him, taking a seat at his kitchen table. There were stacks and stacks of word puzzle magazines on the table.

"It is how I passed the time," he said with a sheepish grin. "I'd go through one of those things in a week. I ran out of my own supply, used up all the ones at the stores in the area, and had to take to rooting through my neighbors' places for magazines with empty puzzles."

"I read a lot of books." I told him about holing up in the Sun Prairie Public Library for the past year and tearing through their collection, sometimes reading two or three books in a day—depending on the length and how badly my winter depression had been affecting me.

"Smart man," Doug said. I don't know why, but hearing him call me *man* made me feel really good. There was something easy about his nature, something overwhelmingly paternal. In the few minutes I'd known him, I already felt endeared to him. He was one of those old guys who felt like *everyone's* Grandpa. I wanted him to take me fishing, for some reason.

Doug had a wood-burning cook-stove in his kitchen. It had not been there originally. Part of his kitchen wall had been cut so the heavy exhaust pipe could be threaded to the exterior. The stove was cold now, though. The summer days made it far too warm to bear cooking indoors. "This is how I survived the winter." He patted the old stove's flattop. "Pretty much sat in here all day, every day. Kept this place nice and toasty. I had a bunch of neighbors with wood-stoves. Stole all their wood. I cook outdoors in the summer, though."

Doug sat at the other vacant chair at the table. He rested his crutches against the wall next to him. He leaned forward and gave me an earnest, friendly smile. "So, Twist—tell me everything."

"Everything?" When someone asks you to tell them everything, where do you start? I hesitated.

"Tell me, how did you survive the past year? You're a young guy. You must be mighty resourceful. Did you carve your existence out of the wilderness *Iron John*-style?"

"I don't know about that." I've never read *Iron John*. I had no idea what he was talking about. I took another long drink of water, and then I launched into my tale. I told him about burying my parents and my girlfriend, and then waiting to die under the big tree in my yard while reading Stephen King's *The Stand*. I told him about realizing I was immune to the virus, and finding my dog Rowdy in the neighbor's house, and then moving to the library. I talked about raiding stores and taking cars from the local Chevy dealership to explore the countryside. I talked about storing wood for the winter in the community room of the library. I rambled on and on, telling him every detail—except for three things: I didn't tell him about how I almost put a gun to my head and ended myself, I didn't tell him about finding two other living people, and I didn't tell him about suffering hallucinations due to depression and isolation. I didn't think I needed to start off our friendship by letting it drop that I might be nuts and that all the other survivors I'd met had died shortly after meeting me.

The whole time I talked, Doug never looked bored. His eyes sparkled. He smiled. He laughed in the right places. He was the best audience. When I finished my summary, at least a half-hour had passed, maybe more. I paused to finish the glass of water he'd given me. Doug leaned back in his chair like a man who'd just finished a Thanksgiving feast. He smiled broadly. "Man, it's good to hear someone else's voice."

"It's good to have someone to listen to me," I told him. I meant it, too. I hadn't realized how badly I'd needed to just talk to another human, just be heard by someone. Fester was a fine listener, but he wasn't really what you would call an "active listener." During the long days driving, I tended to make up Fester's part in the dialog by filling in his commentary in a silly posh British accent, which is how I think Fester would sound if he did have a voice.

I tried to be a gracious guest and afford Doug the same opportunity to unload his past year's activities. "What about you? What have you been doing?"

The smile was chased from his face. He shrugged and waved a hand at me. "Ahh, what I've been doing isn't important. I've just been waiting to die. Literally. That's it."

"No exploration? No nothing?"

Doug's mouth curled into a half-smile. His eyes took on a wistful sheen. "Went into South Bend once in the first month after everyone was gone, probably early June. I stole a Viper from the Dodge dealership—you know, one of those showroom models. I pushed it out, reconnected the battery, and then put the hammer down on it on the Interstate. That was fun for an hour, but after that, I realized I was kind of immune to the rush, you know? There were no cops, no traffic to dodge. It was just sort of empty, you know?"

I did know. I'd considered doing the same sort of thing at one point, but my own cowardice chased me away from it. I didn't want to get in a wreck and die a slow, painful death bleeding out on the side of a road. "How fast?"

"Got it up to a hundred and forty before I chickened out and eased it back to a hundred." Doug chuckled. "Hey, I'd like to show you something, if you don't mind."

"Lead the way," I said.

Doug stood up from the table and grabbed his crutches. He limped toward the screen door in the kitchen. "C'mon."

We walked out onto a flagstone patio in his backyard. Weeds were creeping through the gaps in the gray-and-brown flagstones. The backyard was not overgrown, though. It was definitely shaggy, but Doug had mowed the yard a few times this summer. It must have been a real chore for a man in his state. I know why he'd done it, though. It was much nicer to look at a well-manicured lawn than the shaggy wild growth everywhere else in the neighborhood.

There was a row of tall lilac bushes along one edge of the yard, a sort of natural fence line. In the rear left corner was a large chicken coop with at least a dozen hens running around an enclosed wire-mesh yard. He paused at the edge of the flagstones and pointed to the rear of the yard. "I did this last year."

There were two graves. One was filled in and covered with large stones to prevent predators from digging into it. There was a crudely constructed cross hammered into the ground at its head. The other grave was empty. It had been dug deeply and a large, weathered pile of earth sat next to it. Grass was sprouting in spots on the hillock of dirt.

Doug pointed to the covered grave. "That's my wife Miranda. Lost her in the third week of the Flu, after they were telling everyone there was nothing to be done. Buried her myself. Only dug the grave a few feet down, though. It was rough going." Doug started to limp out to the other grave. "I figured I was going to go too, so I dug my own grave. I didn't think I'd actually get to use it, though. It was more of a metaphor, really. It was representative of my intent to lay by my wife's side forever. Sounds corny when I say it out loud, but that's how it is."

I didn't know how to reply to that. I'd buried my parents and girlfriend in similar shallow graves. I buried my dog Rowdy, and my friend Meri, too. I never dug my own, though. Was I secretly optimistic, or was that just effort after foolishness. Doug wasn't talking, so I sought for something to break the silence. "It doesn't sound corny," I said. "It looks like a nice grave."

Doug nodded. "Took my time on it. The first two or three feet was pretty easy going. After that, it was all a war of attrition against the ground. Rocks, roots—you name it. Had to use a pick, a shovel, and a chainsaw to get it to where I wanted it. I got it to six feet, though."

"Impressive."

There was a pause. Doug reached out and put his hand on my shoulder. "I need you to bury me in it, Twist."

"Now?"

Doug laughed, his voice ringing out through the neighborhood. "No, not now. Although, I wouldn't put up much of a fight. I'm not long for this world. The way I feel, I figure I could check out at any time."

Doug limped back to the patio and sat in a weather-beaten plastic chair. A grim look chased the smile from his face. "One of my biggest fears, and this goes back to my childhood, was dying alone. I'm scared to go, Twist."

"I don't blame you," I said.

"It seems silly, doesn't it, after being surrounded by death for so long? Dying alone was something I have had to work really hard to accept, and in some ways I've even been able to coach myself up to the point where I'm almost looking forward to it." Doug gestured to his legs. "Feels like I got lightning hitting me in the ass half the time. Feels like there's fire in my balls. I got no appetite anymore. I spend half my days in a drug-induced sleep. It's no way to keep living. Death has its benefits, I guess. The pain will end, at least. That's the only part of it I'm looking forward to, though." Doug swallowed hard. Tears were brimming in the corners of his eyes. "I'd retired the year before I was diagnosed with the cancer. Almost forty-five years of selling houses, coaching youth baseball and basketball, doing a little residential painting on the side here and there for extra money—I'd worked hard. My wife, she was a school secretary. Worked the same job since she was twenty-three. Good job. A State job. We both retired and were finally going to travel to all the places we wanted to go. England, France, Hawaii, Japan…you name it, we were going. You know where we went?"

I shook my head.

Doug leaned toward me. "Canada. That's it. We went to Banff. It was glorious. Beautiful, beautiful city. I wanted to move there. But, that's all we got to do. The summer after I retired went by too quickly. One of my daughters had another baby, so we didn't go anywhere that winter. Next spring rolls around, and my doctor says I got cancer. No more travel plans anywhere. Just treatment. Even with the treatment, the doc said it didn't look good. It had spread pretty quickly. Told me three years, at best." A single tear slipped down Doug's cheek. "You know what was bad about that? I was selfish enough to be glad I was going to die before my wife. I knew she was strong enough to go on without me, but I knew I wasn't strong enough to go on without her." Doug buried his face in his hands. His back shuddered as he sobbed for a few moments. I said nothing, but I felt very uncomfortable. I had no mechanisms for dealing with something like this. My only defense was to stand there silently and let him cry.

Doug's head snapped up, and he laughed. He wiped tears from his eyes with his fingers. "Life has a really bad sense of humor, you know? I had to bury her, and here I still sit, wasting away a centimeter at a time." He used the edge of his t-shirt sleeve to wipe his cheeks. His stomach was wasted, pale, and sickly thin, and his ribs were showing through his skin. "It just doesn't seem fair."

There was a long silence. I was still standing on the edge of the flagstones. I hate to say it, but I had thoughts about running to my RV and leaving. All this time, I wanted to meet other survivors, I wanted human contact, but I'd come upon a man with days, maybe weeks left to live. He was right; it wasn't fair. I cleared my throat. "Why didn't you…"

He looked up at me. "Suicide?"

I nodded. "If you dug—" I nodded toward the grave. "Weren't you going to?"

Doug blew out a long, slow breath. "Thought about it, sure. I had all the painkillers I could want. It would have been easy. I even went so far as to uncap the bottle of morphine tablets. It would have been *really* easy."

"So why…"

Doug shrugged. He fell back in the chair, shoulders slumping. "I don't know. Maybe because seventy years of Catholic upbringing told me suicide is a Mortal Sin. Maybe I was just too scared." Then he flipped the question. "What about you? You must have thought about it, too." I hesitated. He already knew the answer. At that moment, I realized that anyone who survived the Flu must have thought about it. I know of one man who had done it back in Wisconsin. It was only natural. Why keep living if no one needed you to keep living? "How were you going to do it?" he asked.

"Gun," I said.

"Simple. Quick. Smart. Why didn't you?"

"Because a tornado almost killed me. I was getting ready to do it, and a tornado swept through my neighborhood. It destroyed several houses, but left mine standing. I figured it must have missed me for a reason, and who was I to argue why. I guess I wanted to know why I was still standing after surviving a tornado and the Flu."

Doug chuckled. "Yeah, that's as good a reason as any, I guess."

I crossed the patio and sat in a second weather-beaten chair facing Doug. "After the tornado missed me, I figured I owed it to all my friends and family who died to keep on living, for their sakes. Maybe part of me considered it a big middle finger to Fate or something."

"I like that." Doug smiled. "A big middle finger to the universe. Did you go stand in the storm and yell at the sky? Really let God have a piece of your mind?"

"Not really, no." I thought for a second. "I should have."

"Me too." Doug gestured at his yard. "Instead, I just sat back here waiting for my clock to run out." He sniffed. "I'm ready to go now, Twist. I didn't want to die alone, and I prayed to every god I could think of to send an angel to watch over me. God, Allah, Zeus, Yahweh, Odin—I begged them all for someone. And then you came. I don't know which one of those crazy bastards sent you, but Twist, I'm begging you: Please, please stay. Please bury me after I'm gone. Can you please grant a dying man a last request?"

How do you say no to that?

CHAPTER FOUR

Waiting for the Inevitable

We had a fine dinner that night. Doug killed one of his hens and roasted it spatchcocked in a cast-iron pan over the fire pit at the edge of his patio. Fresh meat was a treat. It was the first time I'd had fresh chicken since before the Flu. Doug had a can of small potatoes, and we made that our side dish along with some baked beans from my own stores. After dinner, we sat in the cooling summer night slapping mosquitoes and talking about life before and after the Flu. In the few hours I'd known him, and despite our age differences, Doug had quickly become one of the best friends I'd ever had. Maybe it was because of the situation. Maybe if there were still people on the planet, there would have been no reason for us to bond that quickly. I couldn't tell you. I was just glad to be there.

Doug was a great talker, one of those guys who could just *talk*, not ramble—*talk*. Conversation, true conversation, was a dying art form before the Flu, and now it was almost deceased permanently. It was nice to be in his presence and absorb some of his gift. I suppose a career in sales had helped him, or perhaps that's why he sought out a career in sales. He spoke easily of his wife and three children, of life in Shipshewana, of selling houses. He didn't dominate the conversation, and knew the intricacies of give and take when two people are speaking. I could never be as slick as he was when talking to people. When I told him about Sun Prairie, and what I'd done before the Flu, he listened intently, asking questions and nodding along. I felt important when I talked to him. I felt like he was valuing me as a person, maybe even as a fellow adult. In high school, I was never one who really joined into conversations. I preferred to sit around the edges and listen. It was easier. Maybe it was because I was worried about what other people might think. With Doug, there was none of that fear. We sat by the fire, joked, and told stories for hours, well into the dark of night. I even let Fester out of the RV and he hung out with us in the backyard, picking meat out of the leftover chicken bones while doing that oddly charming threat-growling *narm, narm, narm* noise that cats do when they think you're about to steal their food.

When we finally decided to call it a night, Doug tried to offer me a bed in his house, but I declined. I had a bed. Even though I'd only been in the RV for a couple of nights, it was my home. He understood and told me that his doors would be unlocked if I needed anything.

In the morning, I walked into his house and found it quiet. My stomach plunged. I hoped he hadn't died that night. I walked down the hall toward the bedrooms and found his room empty. I felt relieved in that moment.

Doug was on the patio with a pot of coffee. He was still wearing the Pink Floyd t-shirt, but the green shorts had been replaced with khaki cargo shorts that were too big on his decaying body, so he'd belted them tightly at his waist with a thick, black belt. The sun was rising, flooding his yard with morning light. There were houses in the neighborhood blocking the view of the sun at daybreak, but after an hour or two it climbed above the offending homes. He offered me coffee. I declined, never acquired the taste for it.

"I like to come out here in the mornings when the weather lets me. The sun feels good on these old bones," Doug said refreshing his mug from an insulated plastic thermos.

We talked more. I told him about driving through most of Wisconsin looking for other survivors. I told him about trying to free as much livestock as I could by cutting down fences and opening barns. I told him about the dog packs that started roaming Sun Prairie by the time I'd left. He listened and nodded along.

When I finished my stories, he got to his feet. He stretched and coughed. "I don't have long now," he said. He rolled his shoulders forward. "I can feel it, Twist. Getting old is hell. You know the bitch of it? I never felt old until the last couple of weeks. That way you feel in your head right now? That never went away for me. In my head, I'm still seventeen, eighteen years old. I look in the mirror and think, who the hell is this old man looking back at me?"

"At least you made it to old age," I said. "A lot of people didn't get to. Hell, I might not get to. Think positive!"

Doug chuckled. He scratched at his wiry beard. "I suppose that's true. I always figured if you made it to fifty, that was a good life. Anything past that was a gift. Then, I turned fifty and thought, I want another fifty years. We never get enough time, do we?" He picked up his canes. "Hey, I want to show you something. It's just down the road. I could use the walk." We strolled to the end of his block. There was a cross-street at the end of it, and then there was a large cul-de-sac with only three houses on it beyond the cross-street. Doug walked toward the middle house, crutching along on wobbling legs. "That house there was my neighbor's. Fella named Jim. Good guy, but he was one of those conspiracy guys, you know? Always thinking the government was coming for him. Always thinking that the sky was falling. He was always talking about aliens and the Illuminati and the Bilderberg Group."

"I'll bet he had a field day when the Flu started," I said.

"Oh god, yes. Said it was a government conspiracy, a manufactured virus to purge the poor and save the resources for the wealthy. The first week of it, he was on his porch shouting to the heavens that we were all doomed. For the first time in his life, he was right, I guess." Doug walked to the front door and opened it.

The house had a lingering smell of decay. It wasn't unpleasant, though. No one had died in this house. It was just the start of the house's eventual collapse, water stagnating in the basement, walls taking on mold, and support timbers rotting behind the drywall. The house was messy, as though it had been abandoned mid-task. I could see a lot of survival gear scattered around the living room and kitchen. Doug pushed through the main floor of the one-story rambler and out a sliding patio door at the rear of the house. The backyard was overgrown. A garden shed stood in one corner of the fenced-off yard.

"Jim was one of them—what you call 'em? The guys who think the world's ending tomorrow?"

"Preppers?"

"That's it." Doug limped toward the garden shed. "He's been talking for years about economic collapse, Russian nukes, and the super-volcano under Yellowstone. About eight years ago, he and his wife went whole hog and had a military-style bomb shelter installed beneath their backyard. Oh, it was a whole thing with the city. Took him two years just to get the permits. No one wanted him to do it, but he did it anyway." Doug opened the garden shed, and instead of a lawn mower and some tools, there was nothing. The shed was empty, save for a metal cover on the floor of the shed. Doug cast the cover aside and revealed a heavy steel hatch with a push-button combination door.

"I don't know why, but Jim decided he liked me," Doug said. "Gave me the combo to that door *just in case*. That's how he said it: 'Here, Doug—*just in case*.' Then, he winked like he was letting me in on some grand secret."

I knew why Jim liked him. It was probably because Doug listened to Jim's stories of the apocalypse like he'd listened to me. You gravitate toward people that make you feel important.

"Combo's six, three, six, eight, nine, zero, zero. Punch that in for me, would you?"

I did as Doug asked, and the door clicked. I twisted the handle and the latch gave way. I pulled it open and a metal ladder awaited me.

"Go on down," said Doug.

I arched an eyebrow. Something in my gut said it was a trap. Doug must have known. He chuckled. "Don't worry about it. I'm not going to lock you in there. Here, if you don't mind waiting up here for my crippled self to get down there, you can come down after me." It took him about five minutes to climb down the twelve steps, but he did it. "Trust me now? C'mon down."

I climbed down after him. By the time I got to the bottom, he'd turned on some sort of battery-powered lighting system. There were two slim rooms buried ten feet below the ground, probably made out of industrial shipping containers. One was a basic shelter with a kitchen, complete with a hand-pump well water system, a working latrine and shower, a large room for dining and relaxing, and a series of bed-racks in the rear reminiscent of the racks in a submarine. The other container was there for storage. There were large plastic shelves on both sides and two sets of the same shelves down the center, back-to-back. All the shelves were stocked with cans and boxes, or toilet paper and feminine products, or bottles of water and cans of soda. It looked like the most boring grocery store in the world, a subterranean CostCo where everything was in bulk. At the rear of the storage container was a water purification system, and what looked like a hot water heater.

"'Bout a week after I figured I was supposed to be dead, I thought about Jim. Figured he was hiding in his shelter with his family. I came out here, punched in the code, and came down. No Jim. No nobody." Doug sat on the couch in the main area of the shelter. It was a small, but functional piece. No frills. It didn't look very comfortable.

"He put in all that work for this shelter and didn't use it?" I was staring at the shelves of supplies. It looked like three years of food and supplies. "Seems wasteful."

"That's what I thought, too." Doug walked back to the ladder and dragged himself out of the shelter. He climbed faster than he'd descended. "Then I found him."

I climbed out after him. Doug pointed to the garage. "Lined his wife and two kids up in the garage and shot 'em all in the head. Then, he did himself in."

I was a little dumbfounded. No, a lot dumbfounded. All that, the digging, the rigging, the supplies—and he chose to kill himself. All I could think to say was, "Why?"

Doug shrugged. "Tells you something, doesn't it? Here's a man who was prepared for the apocalypse, dead-on, one-hundred percent prepared. He knew it was coming when we all laughed at him, and yet when it showed up on his doorstep, he chose to end himself and his family. Only thing I can think, they were all showing signs of the Flu before they could retreat to the shelter, and rather than poison the shelter with their germs, Jim and his wife exited in the fastest method possible. Once you see your neighbors gasping to death and choking on their own fluids, it's pretty easy to not want to go out that way."

"Why did you bring me to see this?"

Doug looked at his feet. After a moment, he looked up again. "Twist—Barnabas—" it was weird hearing him invoke my given name. "I like you," he continued. "You seem like a good boy. You remind me a lot of my

34

youngest son, Clark. He was a good boy, too. Sweet natured, kind, a good father. You strike me as being just like him. I've known you less than a day and I can tell your heart is in the right place."

"Thanks."

"I brought you here because I just wanted you to see it. I wanted you to remember it. You have—God willing—another sixty years on this planet, maybe seventy or eighty, if you get lucky. You're going to go through a lot of ups and downs. I just wanted you to see that even the best laid plans of mice and men can go awry. I wanted you to see what Jim and Nancy did, and know that sometimes, even in the best case scenarios, even when you think you've covered all your bases, you haven't."

"I know that," I said. And I did, or at least I thought I did.

Doug held out his hands defensively. "I'm not saying you don't. I'm just reminding you of that."

We started to walk back to Doug's house. "I spent a lot of time thinking in the past year. I suspect you did, too."

"It was all I did, really."

"Well then, there you go. Did you come up to any realizations? Any truths?" He looked at me out of the corner of his eye.

I had to shake my head. I hadn't. I knew less now than I did a year ago.

"Well, I came up with one truth. Only one."

"What's that?"

Doug sucked in a big breath of air. "When it comes to life and how to live it, none of us know shit-all about it. However, I learned that when it comes to life, all the planning in the world can't save us from dumb luck and chance. Jim and Nancy, they were a nice enough couple. They had two nice kids. They were active in the school. I liked them, liked them a lot." Doug paused. He looked over his shoulder at their house. "But they got so wrapped up in preparing for doom, I think they forgot to enjoy being alive. Don't do that. Whatever happens, whatever you do with yourself after I'm gone, promise me that you'll enjoy being alive. If not for yourself, for me. My time is up, but you can fit a lot of enjoying life into the next sixty years. Do that for me."

It seemed like a small thing to ask. I started to tell him that yes, I would, but I stopped myself. Did I even remember what joy was anymore? I couldn't lie to a dying man. "I don't know if I know how."

"You're young. You'll figure it out, I'm sure. Just promise me that you'll find a moment or two where you can look around and think to yourself, 'I'm glad I'm here. This has all been worth it.'"

"I'm glad I'm here now," I said.

"Not really what I meant." Doug stopped crutching forward. "Look...I look around here, and I see my life. My kids played on these streets. I celebrated Christmases, birthdays, and baptisms in my house. This is where I'm glad to be. You need to go out and find your own place to be happy."

"My own happy place."

Doug started walking again. "You say it like that, and it sounds stupid…but, yeah. You need to find your own happy place. Keep that in mind, Twist. Don't get so caught up in *surviving* that you forget how to *live*. There isn't much point to surviving in this world if you're not actually living."

We spent the rest of the day talking, eating, and drinking in Doug's backyard. He killed another hen (*"Not like I'm gonna need them,"* he joked), and we made fried chicken with oil in the cast iron skillet and a bag of flour he had sealed in Tupperware. Doug's fried chicken was amazing. The Colonel *wished* he could do what Doug did with a simple piece of chicken. I ate most of the chicken at Doug's insistence. He wasn't very hungry anymore, he said, and it's not as if he had a fridge to keep them from going bad afterward. I easily destroyed most of the bird in a single sitting. It was the most food I'd had since last winter, when I'd had to put a cow out of its misery and feasted on the beef afterward. My stomach bowed pleasantly. Fester laid beneath my chair, his own belly full, as well. That night, we turned in earlier than we had the previous night. It had been fun, Doug told me, but he was tired. He looked tired, too. The dark circles around his eyes were thick and heavy.

The next morning, I ventured to the patio to greet the sun with Doug, but he wasn't there. I crept into the house and found him in his bed. He was propped up with an extra pillow behind his head and shoulders, and only a sheet covered his legs. His eyes were baggy and swollen. "I think my clock is winding down, now," he said. I saw a set of Rosary beads in his fist.

"I could get you some pills," I said moving toward the bathroom.

"No! Please, I'm ready to go now. I'm ready." He sighed. "I don't know what kept me alive this long, but I figure it's because I was just waiting for you. Maybe you needed to know other people are out there somewhere. Maybe this is all part of some grand cosmic plan. Maybe it's not. I wasn't going to get better, either way. It's time for me to go, Twist."

The bedroom was cluttered with clothes, magazines, and books from a year of living with no thought to company or cleanliness. The smell of time and age was thick in there. The light in Doug's room was colored to a pale blue by thin curtains over the two windows. I opened the curtains and cranked open the windows to get some light and cross-breeze in the room. Doug blinked a bit at first, but quickly accustomed himself to the light. He looked around the room and smiled. "I haven't pulled those curtains since last year. I forgot how this place looked in the light."

He looked even older than he had the day before. His hair was still wild from sleep. His eyes looked even more tired. He grimaced and clutched low on his stomach. "Find me some painkillers, would you?"

I grabbed pill bottles from the small pile on the nightstand. Most of them were empty. I plucked them by the lids and shook them until one rattled. Hydrocodone. That would work. I opened the bottle and gave him a pill. He held it in his hand and looked at me with a raised eyebrow. "I look like a baby to you? I've been taking this crap daily for half of the past year. Let's pretend we're playing blackjack, and maybe you hit me again. Pretend I've got a three and five showing. I'm gonna need a few more cards, dealer."

I shook two more pills into his hand. He popped the pills into his mouth and crunched down on them. I passed over a half-full glass of water he'd had on his nightstand. He drank and swallowed the pills. He grimaced again. "It's getting worse. It takes about twenty or thirty minutes for those pills to kick in. I considered shooting this stuff, but I hate needles."

"Liquid medicine spoils faster than pills," I said. "Liquid stuff might be bad by now. Maybe lethal."

His head fell back against the pillows, and he inhaled slowly through his nose. "You won't go anywhere, right?" He closed his eyes. "I don't know how long this takes, but I can promise you that it won't be too long."

"Hey, somebody has to bury you, right?"

Doug smiled at that. His eyes popped open again. "You have no idea how much it means to me that you showed up." He reached out a hand and patted my forearm.

How do you respond to a comment like that? *Thanks* doesn't cut it.

Once the pills kicked in, Doug slept. I brought Fester in from the RV. He immediately found a sunbeam crossing Doug's legs and made it his own. I brought a chair from the kitchen to the corner of Doug's bedroom. I picked up a book from Doug's floor, a pulp spy thriller from the 1960s, sort of like James Bond, but not nearly as slick.

Doug woke around noon. I made us a lunch of eggs from the hen house. Doug only ate a few bites. "Waiting to die isn't fun, man." He stretched his arms over his head and arched his back. I could see the hollows of the gaps between his ribs through his shirt. "The worst about dying slow is the pain. It's not like a cut, where there's a localized pain, it's all just a constant dull ache that slowly intensifies until you can't handle it. I'm tired of the pain, man. I guess it's just a matter of deciding what's worse: the pain or the fear of death." He was quiet for a moment. "What do you think happens when we go?"

I'd considered this many times over the past year. I vacillated between the two extremes of Nothing and a classical version of Heaven complete with angels, harps, and all my dead relatives waiting for me to arrive. I envisioned every sort of thing in between, too. I even considered different concepts of Hell, but I didn't like to think about what could be worse than being left alive after the apocalypse killed everyone I knew. "I don't know," I finally said. "I hope, whatever happens, we get to see the people we loved that died before us and make up for lost time."

"Miranda. I miss her. A lot." Doug reached out an arm and stroked a picture of a woman next to his bed. "Do you know how I knew she was the one?"

"Tell me," I said.

"She had huge boobs." He held his hands in front of his chest. Then he broke out laughing. "Nah, just kidding. I loved her because she wouldn't let me get away with anything. If I fed her an empty line, she just rolled her eyes. She was immune to stupid romantic gestures. She wanted honesty and openness. She wanted an equal partner. I bought her roses. She liked them, but it didn't impress her. I took her for a walk in the hills near our college, and while we were walking, I told her a story about my childhood. *That* she liked. I'd dated girls in college. She was a woman." He smiled at the memory. Then he winked at me. "The boobs helped, though."

Fester woke up and crawled up Doug's legs to demand attention. Doug idly stroked the cat's head. The cat twisted under his touch. "I miss my kids, too. They better be waiting for me on the Other Side. And my grandbabies." He reached for a handkerchief on his nightstand and wiped away his tears. "My oldest grandchild, Serena." He pointed at a small picture on the wall. "She was only eleven. She was the first of my family to pass. Died at a hospital in Indianapolis during the first week of the Flu." His voice cracked. "None of them got to grow up. They didn't get to have dates, or fall in love, or marry, or…" He trailed off. A sob wracked his body, but he bit back any others. He sniffed and wiped his nose with his wrist.

After a prolonged silence, I asked, "What do you think happens after we…" I couldn't say the last word. It felt too heavy for the small room.

"After we die? You can say it. It's not news to me." Doug mopped at his eyes with the handkerchief.

"Where do we go when we die?" I asked him.

"Heaven." Doug said it in a plain, matter-of-fact voice. "We go to Heaven." I started to open my mouth to ask him why he was scared to go if we go to Heaven, but he continued. "Maybe if I keep saying it, I'll start believing it. We go to Heaven."

"What's your version of Heaven?"

Doug thought for a second. "Oh, I don't know. I want to see my family. A perfect Heaven has a golf course and a movie theater. How about you?"

"I'd like to see my parents again. And Rowdy, my dog. I'd like there to be an awesome roller coaster, too. One with no line that you can ride over and over again."

"Oh, that's good. Can I put your roller coaster in my Heaven, too?"

I smiled. "Go nuts. Maybe I'll take a vacation from my Heaven, come over to yours, and we can ride your roller coaster together."

"I'd like that. I'd like that a lot. You do that. When you get to your Heaven, you come find mine." Doug groaned and breathed through gritted teeth. "Find me some more pills, would you?" I handed him four more hydrocodone pills. He tossed them back and drank more water. He nestled into his pillows. Fester curled up on his chest. "Tell me something."

"Like what?"

He shrugged. "Doesn't matter. I just want to hear someone's voice. Read to me from those journals you say you're writing. Tell me your story, Twist. I want to hear your story in your words."

"They're in the RV."

"Go get 'em."

By the time I got back in from the Greyhawk, Doug was asleep. I read from the journals, anyhow. I figured he just wanted to know someone was in the room.

We were both waiting for the inevitable. For Doug, it was a slow journey from constant pain to constant, debilitating pain, and further on to pain that reduced him to a barely-conscious, pill-dependent husk of a former human. For me, I was stuck in a limbo between waiting for him to finally give up the ghost and pass away so I could bury him as he asked, and getting back on the road to continue my journey to the South. I wasn't going to abandon him; I didn't have that sort of cruelty in me. However, after three days of reading to him in the ever-shrinking moments of his lucidity, I sort of felt the way I did when I visited my grandma's house—there's a sort of comfort of being there, but I couldn't get comfortable the way I *wanted* to be comfortable. I didn't want to venture too far from Doug's side in case he passed, but I was quickly growing tired of sitting in a chair in his room. Geez, I feel guilty about even thinking that.

It was the truth, though. He was a fellow human being, a good guy. A family man. He was suffering. I wasn't going to just ditch him, but at the same time, I wanted him to move on. I hated seeing how much he hurt when he was awake. I had to help him to the toilet, which was in the backyard. I eventually broke down, went to the hospital in nearby LaGrange, and got a bedpan to make his life easier. I had to help him clean himself. It was humiliating for him. He hated his dependence, I could tell. His moments of wakefulness were becoming shorter and shorter. When he did wake, it was usually because he was in pain. We'd chat for a bit, I'd help him in any way I could, and then he would dope himself into a narcotic coma again.

The Flu was horrible, but the period from health to symptoms to death was usually less than five days. It was an efficient, brutal killer. Cancer, on the other hand, was sloppy and lazy. It murdered people in increments, robbing them of seconds of their life instead of leveling a single, painless blow. I hated Cancer before the Flu, and I hated it even more now. Watching Doug waste to nothingness was making me realize that if I ever got to a point where I was stuck in bed dying slowly, I was going to have to somehow end it quickly, take as many pills as I could and hope I never woke up again. As much as I didn't feel like dying, I really did not feel like dying slowly.

In the middle of the night halfway through my second week with Doug, I heard him gasping. I was sleeping on an inflatable camping mattress in the hallway outside his door. I woke up immediately and rushed to his side, flipping on the small camping lamp at his bedside.

The light made him blink his eyes. They were wide open, scared. He was gulping for air, his mouth opening and closing like a fish. His hand twitched. He tried to raise an arm off the bed, but didn't have the strength. I gripped his hand. "I'm here." I saw his face relax slightly, but he couldn't breathe. He was going, and there was nothing I could do about it. There was nothing I wanted to do about it, either. It was time. He needed to go for his own sake.

I put a hand on his forehead. I put my head near his so he could feel my presence. I whispered into his ear. "Relax, Doug. Relax. It's natural." That didn't seem to help. He was still panicked, still tense. "Think of your kids. Think of your wife." I plucked Miranda's picture from the bedside table and held it in front of his face. He instantly went slack, his stress breathing reduced. He rested his head back against the pillow, and the tension fled from his neck. His eyes closed halfway. His head lolled to the side and we looked at each other. I heard a strained gurgle in his throat, as if he was trying to say something, but he was too weak to form words.

"It's okay," I told him. "You can go. Rest now."

He exhaled, a long, slow breath that must have been every last molecule of oxygen in his chest. He sniffed a slight inhale, and then that was it. Doug Fisk left this world. I was alone again.

The next morning, just as dawn was breaking, I carried the skin-and-bones body of Douglas Raymond Fisk to his grave. I took time to wrap him in the sheets of his bed like a shroud. I made sure his Rosary beads were wrapped around his fist as I had seen at Catholic funerals in the past. I didn't want to drop him haphazardly into the grave, although he'd told me once that I could just drop him at the edge and kick him in with my heel; he wouldn't mind. Instead, I laid him on the edge of his grave, right next to his wife's grave, and then climbed down into the grave so I could drag him down with me. It was awkward, trying to get him situated in a narrow grave while my big feet were in it with him, but I managed to do it. I had to grab the edge of the grave, pull myself up as far as I could, and then brace my feet on either side of the hole to keep from falling back into it.

I used Doug's shovel to toss the whole pile of dirt back on top of him a shovelful at a time. It took a good hour and change to fill in his grave. Then, I placed a pile of fieldstone over the grave to prevent scavengers from digging into it, not that they would with him being so deep. I just wanted it to match his wife's grave. I made a crude cross out of wood in Doug's garage and hammered it into the head of his grave to match Miranda's. Then, I sat back at the foot of the graves to rest. The sun was over the neighbor's roof and the backyard was bathed in light. It was going to be unbearably humid that day, as it had been since I'd first entered Indiana.

I didn't know what to say. Doug had been so easy to talk to when he was alive. Now that he was finally gone, I was speechless. I stabbed the shovel into the dirt and left it standing. I wasn't raised in a religious house, so I didn't know anything Catholic to say over the grave. I stood there for twenty, maybe thirty minutes just staring at the dirt. I hoped Heaven was real, and that Doug had found Miranda. Anything less would an injustice to a man who deserved eternal peace with his family.

I was alone in the world again, but I was glad to have had company for the last week and a half, even if that company was barely awake for most of the last five days. It was comforting to have had human contact again. I felt complete again, or at least as complete as I could feel. I thought about what he'd told me about there being a difference between living and surviving. I was definitely surviving. I don't think I was sure how to live anymore.

I opened the chicken coop and released the remaining hens to the wild. I couldn't take them with me, but I hoped they'd be okay. They could return to their coop at any time, if they wanted. I made a mental note to raise chickens when I finally settled. Having eggs would be a good thing. I didn't know how to catch wild chickens, but I'd have to figure it out. I plucked the few eggs from the nests in the coop for my own supply. I didn't have refrigeration (I'd unplugged the tiny RV fridge because it took too much power to maintain), so I'd have to eat them soon.

I took the RV over to neighbor Jim's house and raided his shelves of water, food, and toilet paper. *(You can never have too much, am I right?)* It took forever to carry cases of bottled water one-at-a-time up a 12 foot ladder. I filled the Greyhawk's storage holds and stored extra in the overhead bunk.

I started to consider the future. At some point, would I run out of toilet paper? What then? Corncobs? Newsprint? People like Jim and Nancy, these "Doomsday Preppers"—what were they actually preparing for? So they survive the apocalypse. What then? They bought themselves an extra ten, twenty years? So what? What do they do, next? What's the point? Do they just live like pioneers for the rest of time? Do they ever start to try to rebuild civilization? If so, how? There is an existing blueprint, sure. But where do they start? If a toilet paper factory wasn't high on the list, I'd want to know why.

I wasn't hungry, so I skipped lunch. I treated myself to a Coke from Jim's stash. There is nothing better than an ice-cold Coke. A lukewarm Coke is acceptable, but not nearly as life affirming. Right after the toilet paper factory, I'd want someone to bring back refrigeration.

CHAPTER FIVE

Days into Days

I put Shipshewana in my review mirror and continued east. I tried not to look in the side mirror too often as the little town dwindled behind me, but I did. I could not stop seeing it. It's hard to describe my feelings leaving there. On one hand, I was terribly excited to get back on the road. It felt good to feel the air moving through the window of the Greyhawk again. It felt good to see Fester sleeping on the top of the dashboard again, his furry body wedged against the glass. I felt more optimistic again. I had found four people who had survived the Flu in my travels. Granted, all were dead now, but the sheer odds meant there had to be more. I was more optimistic that I would find them, too. On the other hand, I was alone again and the tiny taste of companionship left a deep and painful want for more of it. Fester was great and all, but it wasn't the same as someone actually responding to my stories. I just hoped the next person or people I found would be younger and last longer than thirteen days.

While I drove east winding through the small communities looking for signs of life, I tried to piece likelihoods together. Where would there be people? Where would I want to go? Obviously Disney World was the first place that I thought of because it made perfect sense. I could hear the announcer's voice on the TV commercial: *Hey, Twist! You've just survived the apocalypse! What are you going to do now?* And I would look at the TV camera with my biggest, cheesiest grin and tug on my Apocalypse Survivor Championship ball cap and say, "I'm going to Disney World!" Just the thought of that image made me smile. Disney World might be the happiest place on Earth, but I'll bet in the post-apocalypse landscape, it was creepy as hell.

I thought about New York City. I wanted to go there. There would be cool buildings to go through. There was a massive population of people. If someone was going to survive in an urban setting, I had to believe it would be in New York. I also thought that if survivors were going to conglomerate after something like the apocalypse, it would be in places like New York City or Washington, D.C.

Thinking of D.C. made me think of the White House. I *had* to go there. I could sleep in the Lincoln Bedroom and steal a portrait of Martin Van Buren from the wall. I had no reason to want a portrait of Van Buren, but I just thought it would the most illogical choice. Most people would go for Washington, Adams, Jefferson, or Lincoln. The pranksters would probably go for Nixon. I'd go for Van Buren because the dude had some awesome windswept hair.

I know there's a secret bunker somewhere in Virginia beneath a mountain where the Secret Service will hide the President of the United States during a crisis like the Flu or a nuclear attack. I wondered if he was in there. A lot of the conspiracy nuts went crazy during the first days of the Flu, claiming it was a government plot to erase humanity so they could start over, and that the best and brightest of Americans were being hidden in bunkers around the United States and were given anti-virus shots to counteract the Flu. It was so far-fetched that it might even be plausible. I decided to go looking for the bunker, but then changed my mind. I was content to let politicians stay underground as long as possible. They could do less damage that way.

I thought about the major landmarks and cities I wanted to see. As far as I knew, calendar-wise, it was late July. I had at least two or three months to hit them all, no problem. Four months if I wanted to stretch it. That was plenty of time to get around to everything and still be in Louisiana before snow flew in the north, typically late November or December.

In the meantime, I was still struggling over the decaying roads, hunting supplies and survivors along the road, and keeping the RV running.

Filling up with gas was a chore. I had a bicycle pump that I'd rigged to tubes so that it could be used to siphon gasoline from holding tanks outside of stations, but it was always a chore that could take a half-hour of pumping to fill the RV, and it was always a chore to get into the holding tanks in the first place. There was a heavy-duty metal lid that had to be pried away, and then I'd have to get past a secondary seal. Sometimes, I'd find the tank was dry. That happened more than you'd think. There was no shipping the final two weeks of the Flu. A lot of gas stations ran dry. When I did find gas, I'd have to put a filter on the end of my siphon hose. The gasoline in the storage tanks was slowly starting to break down, and it was starting to get slightly gelatinous as the liquids evaporated over time. The filters helped keep the engine of the RV from gumming up too badly, but I still worried about it. How much longer would I have gas? It made me more aware that there wouldn't be any coming back from this trip. When I made it down south, I wouldn't be visiting Wisconsin again. That part of the world would be dead to me.

After I pumped gas, I was always exhausted. My arms would be tired. My back would hurt. The RV wasn't the most fuel-efficient vehicle on the planet, either. It drank gas pretty well. Too well. I was filling up at least once a day, minimum. It was just part of the routine, an unavoidable inconvenience like shaving or using the bathroom. It just had to be done. I would always go into the gas stations and poke around when I finished. If their doors were locked, I'd just let myself through the glass with a brick or something. In almost all of the stores, almost everything was picked clean. Smokes, booze, and adult magazines were always gone. Most of the candy, too. I could understand the smokes, booze, and candy—but why the adult magazines? I couldn't see people actually breaking into these stores thinking, *Welp, I'll be dead in a few weeks. Better see what Miss February's likes and dislikes were before I go,* but that must be what happened. I couldn't imagine being horny in a dying world. I'm eighteen and virile, but I have not had a single bodily urge like that since the Flu hit. And just thinking about that now made me worry about myself. Was I okay?

I shook off that thought and reminded myself that all previous definitions of "normal" and "okay" were no longer applicable in the apocalypse. I was dealing with undiscovered country now. Any rules were rules I would set myself, and I decided that people in the apocalypse didn't have sex. This was easy for me to do because there was no one with whom to have sex.

I hit the Ohio border and prepared to move through the three jewels of Ohio's north side: Toledo, Sandusky, and Cleveland. I'd been through Ohio with my parents years ago. It took about three-and-a-half hours to drive through the state at highway speeds. However, I was estimating that it would take me a few days to get to Cleveland because of the gas, because of searching towns, and because of the condition of the roads. The humid, summer days just kept melting into more humid, summer days. I hardly noticed the nights because I would lapse into uneasy, exhausted sleep. I just kept myself going, though. What else was there to do? Survive. Just keep surviving.

Outside of Toledo, I was exploring the suburbs around Maumee. I turned down a road and followed it out of town for a while. I hit a stretch of road where to the left was a wide, flat plain of tall grasses. There, I saw something so amazing that I was forced to simply stop the Greyhawk and gawk. There, in the wild countryside, just wandering as natural as you please, was a small herd of elephants, I kid you not. A large bull was leading four cows, and at least one of them had a small baby elephant trailing after her. They were wandering near a grove of trees, stripping leaves from branches with their trunks.

A family herd of elephants was not something I anticipated seeing in Ohio. I was amazed they'd survived the Ohio winter, first of all. I guess they're a pretty hearty beast. They must have been released by a zookeeper at the Toledo Zoo when that keeper realized the writing was on the wall for primates. I wonder if he/she had been able to release other animals, too. Were there lions and tigers roaming the countryside right now? Were there hippopotamuses in the Mississippi River? If other zookeepers across the country had followed the same lead, it meant that there was a strong possibility that a whole mess of introduced critters were now roaming around the countryside. I could come face to face with a fully-grown male lion. There could be camels, ostriches, emus, and who knows what else scavenging over the countryside. In that instant, the world suddenly got more interesting. I always carried a gun when I went scavenging, even back when I was in familiar territory. It was never to kill, though. It was a tool, like any other tool. I anticipated using the gun to scare, mostly. Maybe use it to wound. My biggest fear wasn't even animals. I knew there were bears and wolves in Wisconsin—mostly in the northern half, but they had been starting to move south after the threat of man diminished. I knew there were a few cougars and bobcats, too, but most animals weren't keen to attack. If I'd made enough noise, most animals would have run scared. Now, I had to consider the chance that there were strange predators in the country, zoo-raised African and Asian predatory animals that might not have ever developed the skills to hunt. They would be hungry. They would be highly opportunistic feeders. A gawky young man with big feet who couldn't run too fast would be a lot easier to eat than something that might fight back.

I made a mental note to always have a weapon nearby.

I spent a full day roaming through Toledo. I didn't find anything worth noting, but it was worth noting the weather. Oppressive was the only word for it. The humidity, even that close to Lake Erie, was a sauna. It felt like there was something physical about it, something tangible. It felt like if I'd tried, I could have cut out a donut of moisture from the very air and eaten it.

With no more television and no more weather forecasters, I'd had to become very good at reading clouds and noticing slight changes to the winds. For days, the winds had been pushing up from the south, from the Gulf Coast. It was bringing excessive heat and humidity. That day in Toledo was the worst of it. Sweltering, miserable heat. Even that night, when I was camped outside a rest stop along the interstate on the eastern edge of the city, it was too hot to sleep. The RV was stifling. I considered letting the engine idle for the air conditioning, but decided against it. It was too hard on the engine, not to mention the wasteful gas consumption. If I was moving to the Deep South, I was going to have to learn to live with heat and humidity.

It was too hot to build a fire. It was too hot to be in the RV. It was too hot to sleep. I stripped naked and sprayed myself down with mosquito repellent. I busted out my battery-powered clippers and buzzed my hair down to the scalp. I ate a can of tuna and slugged back bottles of water before pouring several bottles over my head and body to help the faint breeze cool me. I didn't necessarily *enjoy* being naked. It felt very exposed, and I always got that creepy sensation that someone was watching me even though I was certain there wasn't anyone for miles. I'd looked for signs, hammered the RV horn, and traipsed over the city for hours. No response. I was certain I was alone.

I thought that maybe ghosts were watching me. I didn't know if I believed in ghosts, but I was willing to entertain the idea of them. I'm sure that two years ago, the idea of ghosts would have scared me. Now, I found it somewhat comforting. I imagined the ghosts were my parents watching over me, or maybe the ghosts of all my dead friends coming to see how I was doing. I was standing naked in a pair of Adidas flip-flops, dripping wet, at a rest stop in Toledo, Ohio. I don't think that's quite the wild, glamorous, party-all-the-time lifestyle my friends would have hoped I would have adopted in a world free of rules. If I were them, I'd probably be disappointed in me, too.

I have developed strange habits being alone. One of the strangest is that in these moments where I'm exposed and uncomfortable, I start to sing "Under Pressure" by Queen and David Bowie. I don't know why. It just fits moments where I'm stressing out where I have no reason to stress out. I hope you have the whole image in your head now: naked, sweaty, wet teenage boy in flip-flops singing "Under Pressure" to a darkened Burger King sign. I'm not proud of it. Things like this just happen. This was not Hollywood's big-budget version of the Apocalypse, clearly.

While I was belting out that second verse, the wind shifted *ever so slightly.* Looking back, I should have noticed it. However, I was really feeling the Freddie Mercury jazz fills that night, so I ignored the shift. The air cooled slightly. A low-pressure system was dropping out of the north and colliding with the high pressure from the south. You don't have to be a meteorologist to know what that means.

My parents weren't big outdoors people. I went through that phase as a kid where I wanted to go camping. I went through outdoor magazines in the school library and looked at outdoor goods ad circulars and catalogs when they came to the house. I talked incessantly about going camping as a family. Eventually, I wore my parents down. We borrowed a big tent from a guy my dad worked with and headed up to Devil's Lake State Park in Wisconsin for two days of hiking and cooking over a campfire. The first night was fine. I was having fun. The second night, a thunderstorm swept through the region, and I thought we were all going to die. We had to abandon the tent in the early stages of the storm. We had to rush back to my dad's SUV and just watch as lightning struck so often that we could have read a novel by the incessant blasts of light. Hail pelted the campsite. Dad's

SUV suffered a few dents. The tent was leveled. After that night, I'd had my fill of camping. So had my parents. We never went again.

I was in an RV now, but RV's aren't armored trucks. The material that makes up the shell of one has to be durable, but lightweight. Ever see what a tornado does to a trailer park? Same materials, more or less. When I was back in Wisconsin, I used to watch for storms with diligence. It helped me plan my days. I never thought about watching for them while on the road. It hadn't occurred to me.

Jump ahead to four hours later. I am passed out on the bed in the back of the RV, Fester curled up next to my head. We are not touching because it's too hot to have a furry mammal on any part of my body. I have every window in the RV open, the roof vent open full. It was miserably warm, but I was also exhausted. I'd had to fight the Sandman to give up the magic dust that night, and I was just touching the edge of Dreamland.

The storm started with lightning in the distance, but I was out. I didn't see it. The first rumbles of thunder were low and distant. They weren't going to bother me, either. I woke up when there was a crack of thunder near enough to rattle the RV from tires to roof. It made me jump out of sleep. Winds had picked up to alarming speeds and were whistling through the screens of the Greyhawk with force. The air had cooled thirty or forty degrees. Before I could pull on a pair of shorts, hail started pelting my home; thick, heavy balls of ice smashed into the RV. One of the plastic side windows cracked. A swell of panic rose into my gorge.

I leapt to the driver's seat and started the engine. It had barely roared to life when I slammed it into Drive and stepped hard on the gas. The RV lurched, spun its tires on a few chunks of hail, and then caught pavement and launched ahead. I ripped the RV onto the highway, but then realized that was a stupid move. What was I going to do? Outrun the storm in a bulky RV? Not likely.

Lightning dotted the sky with frightening frequency. All around me were streaks of angry, blue-white light. The thunderclaps slammed above, each one sounding like it was just outside my car. I used the electric window controls to roll up the driver and passenger windows, but the side windows and the roof vent were still open. Nothing was muffled, nothing lessened. The winds were getting stronger. If you've never driven what is, in essence, a gigantic box with zero aerodynamics during a windstorm, you can count yourself lucky. I don't know how semi drivers deal with it. The wind was surging off the driver side of the RV. It was a constant fight to keep it on the road. Every blast of the wind would push me at least a foot or two to the right, and I would have to yank the wheel left to compensate.

I knew that being on the wide-open highway in the middle of a painfully flat prairie area was probably the worst place to have the RV at that moment. I needed to get off the highway and find shelter. I needed to be away from the hail and wind. I had no idea how much longer the next exit along the highway would be, and I wasn't going to turn around and drive the RV into the storm. Hail continued to pelt the Greyhawk. It sounded like someone was attacking me with baseball bats and crowbars, just sharp, hard cracking noises. I saw a highway overpass ahead. I remembered seeing television footage of people hiding from a tornado in the ribs of an overpass bridge once. I also remembered seeing many articles afterward telling people *not* to do that. I didn't see a lot of other choices, though. I needed protection from the wind and the lightning. I brought the RV to a stop under the overpass. The noise from the hail decreased immediately, although the rear panel was still being touched-up pretty good. I grabbed Fester, but he freaked out. He clawed and kicked at me, struggling to get away. He slashed my wrist badly with his rear claws, and I dropped him. He bounced to the table, and then leapt to the overhead bunk and hid behind the wall of water bottles. I couldn't get to him. I didn't want to leave him, but I didn't see any other choice. I sprinted out the side door of the RV and charged up the paved hill to the underside of the bridge. I clambered to a spot where I was protected from winds and rain, and braced myself against the concrete to wait out the storm.

When a storm hit back when I lived sheltered in a house, and had TV weathermen to tell me how fast the storm was moving and a helpful radar image to show me where the storm was, it was almost disappointing how fast a good storm clipped along. Often, before I could really get to a point of enjoying the lightning and thunder, the storm had passed by leaving a curtain of dull, gentle rain behind it. Now that I was pressed against concrete slabs and hearing wind howling only feet from my head, the storm seemed to last forever. In the frequent lightning, I could see the hailstones piling up like snowfall, a carpet of lethal, icy chunks ranging from quarter-sized to softball-sized. I was at Nature's mercy. There was nothing to do but ride it out and hope it didn't get worse.

I could hear the winds surging in the distance. A familiar freight-train noise was building. Tornado. I'd survived a tornado over a year ago in Wisconsin. I remembered it too well. It sounded far away, but I knew how a tornado could travel. I knew how it could dance through the countryside beholden to no one, save its own whims. I closed my eyes and hunkered down. A tornado coming close to the bridge would likely destroy the RV.

An eternity passed. The winds eventually died down and a simple rain followed the storm front. I was still alive. The RV was still intact. I left my hiding spot and returned to the RV. In my haste to find shelter, I'd left the stupid thing running. I walked around the Greyhawk and inspected the damage. The right side and the roof were dimpled like a golf ball from hail damage. The rear side had taken a dozen direct hits from large chunks of ice and the large plastic window in the rear was cracked in a corner, but not broken. All in all, I got off lucky. It could have been much, much worse.

I slept in the Greyhawk under the overpass the rest of the night. In the morning, my wind-up alarm dragged me from my bed. I considered sleeping in that day, but I was anxious to see if the countryside had suffered damage. I wanted to see if I could find a tornado's path and judge how close I'd come to serious misfortune.

I fed Fester dry cat food and skipped breakfast myself. I had no appetite. The temperature had cooled somewhat, but it was still summer, still hot, and with the new rainfall the humidity was going to rise even higher.

I found the path of the tornado. It had come pretty close to getting me, geographically speaking. The twister had touched down in the middle of an overgrown field just outside of a little blip of a town called Stony Ridge. There was a wide swath of turned-up grasses and fallen trees leading into the collection of houses that made up the town. I drove into town to survey the damage.

What is it about human nature that makes us love and fear images of destruction? Any time there was a storm that destroyed a barn or took down a tree, my friends who lived near the fallen object would post pictures on Facebook. If there was a flood in Florida, we'd all be glued to video footage of people kayaking through streets. When I was a kid, a tornado took out a single house just north of Sun Prairie. My mom and I got into a car to drive out to see the splintered wreckage for ourselves. Even in a world of entropy, I was still drawn to the majestic damage of storms.

I drove into Stony Ridge. It was one of those loose collections of older houses that was entirely forgettable, even more so now because most of the houses in town were obliterated. The tornado had done its best to erase the town from the map. Nothing remained except wild piles of splintered two-by-fours and concrete footings. Home goods and assorted debris were scattered across the streets. I spied at least two desiccated corpses tossed among the wreckage. They looked like thin, gray-green paper pulled over a skeleton frame, hollow skull-eyes staring and vacant.

The rain was little more than a drizzle, and curiosity got the better of me. I shut down the RV, got out, and started poking through some of the wreckage. Whenever I entered someone's home, it made me feel like an archaeologist. I was learning things about people, people who had lived and died before me. I could learn about their religious practices, what they ate, what they did for fun, and sometimes, if I opened the wrong drawer in a bedroom, I could learn about their sexual practices. I didn't really enjoy that part of it. It always felt a little skeezy.

In one of the homes, in what remained of the basement, I found a horde of bottled water and canned goods on a bunch of steel racking. On one of the shelves, I found twenty small, thin bars of pressed gold in a steel lock-box. No lie. I suppose it would have been something like $100,000 back when society still functioned, maybe more. I could only imagine the guy who had the gold anticipated the collapse of the markets and dissolution of currency. He must have invested in it well before the Flu, though. Judging from his basement stores, he looked like one of those guys who had been preparing for the fall of society. Fat lot of good it did him. He was dead. The gold was worthless. I left it where it lay and got back on the road, heading east into the rising sun.

CHAPTER SIX

Nighttime Visitor

The rest of Ohio was uneventful and, to be honest, extremely dull. Western Ohio was flat, almost as bad as Indiana was. There were empty, flat moonscapes of green fields and unending views of nothing, interrupted only by the occasional town. Eastern Ohio got to be a little more interesting, but still—not much going on there.

I went to the Rock and Roll Hall of Fame in Cleveland. It was destroyed. It looked like at some point during the end of the Flu, someone, or a group of someones, figured it was time to live out all their wildest Keith Moon fantasies. Most of the display cases had been smashed. Guitars had been broken. Drum kits had been smashed. Stage outfits were scattered. It was depressing. I walked around and used my flashlight to look at some of the photos of bands I'd liked. Genesis. Cheap Trick. Queen. I had some CDs in the RV, but I never listened to them anymore. It felt blasphemous to play them. Silence felt more appropriate, or the sound of the wind in the window. That was my world now. I didn't play any instruments. I couldn't read sheet music. I would be too busy farming, or whatever the hell I was going to do in the south, to learn to play. Maybe it was right that the Hall of Fame was trashed out and wrecked. It was a fitting end to those instruments. Music was dead.

I spent almost two weeks in Ohio. You wouldn't think you could spend two weeks in Ohio, but if you spent enough time driving through the cities and scavenging, two weeks goes by in a hurry. An hour here. Four hours there. Another hour of driving. Four more hours scavenging. It added up quickly.

I spent a couple of nights sleeping inside the city limits of Sandusky and Cleveland. That was a lot different than sleeping on the outskirts. If someone had survived the Flu and was roaming around the cities, they could easily have found me while I was sleeping. I wouldn't have known if they were friend or foe. I didn't sleep well those days. It was nerve-wracking. I kept two guns in my bedroom in the back of the RV those nights. I also kept most of the windows closed and locked despite the humidity. I also pulled all the curtains, even the big one that blocked out the cab windows. I hadn't pulled that one at all until that first night in Sandusky. Turns out, I didn't need to worry; no one found me, and I didn't find anyone.

The whole time I was in Ohio, I didn't see one sign of anyone surviving. Many of the stores had been ransacked before the final week of the Flu, but they were undisturbed since then. Dust was settled on everything in the stores, and I could see the footprints and scat of various vermin. Mold was starting to grow on walls that had suffered water damage. I could smell rot. For as much optimism that meeting Doug had put into me, Ohio was sucking back out of me.

Ohio: The Pessimism State. That probably would not look good on their license plates.

I crossed into Pennsylvania and headed east on Highway 80. Almost immediately, things started to get better. It didn't take long for the relatively flat prairie of Ohio to give way to tree-covered hills and vales of northern Pennsylvania. It was a wonderful change of scenery. The hills and vales didn't hold onto humidity as the prairie did, either. The weather became more pleasant. Still warm and humid, but not unbearably so, just standard summer weather. I started to gain optimism again. I went into the little towns and villages off the highway hopeful that I would see signs of life.

My first night in Pennsylvania was spent in a tiny town off the interstate called Clintonville. It was a nice, simple little town, nothing fancy. I parked outside of a local supermarket in the late afternoon. The market looked like an old house converted to be a small convenience store. It was primitive, but I liked it. There was a small parking lot where I could park the RV. I was getting burned out on the scavenging grind. Just by glancing around the town, the dark windows and overgrown lawns, I knew no one here had survived. I didn't even feel like looking for signs of life. I just wanted to spend a night relaxing and goofing off. Maybe it was because of what Doug said about actually *living*, or maybe it's because I had a burst of teenage slovenliness. Despite the desperate, driving need to survive, I was still eighteen; I had more than my fair share of laziness and lack of motivation.

I found a nice deck chair on the porch of a nearby house and set it up near the RV. I built a fire on a nice, sandy place next to the parking lot of the little mart. There was plenty of wood to be found around the town. Many of the residents had their own stores of cords of wood for their potbelly wood heaters or fireplaces. It only took twenty minutes of work to gather enough wood to last me the whole night. After I had enough wood for the fire, I took a walk. Fester wasn't really a hiking cat, so he stayed with the RV.

I don't know what got into me that night. Maybe I was possessed by a demon of curiosity or something. Up until that night in Clintonville, I hadn't wanted to go into anyone's home. I'd done it in Wisconsin a few times, but I didn't like it. I never knew which houses were completely empty, or which ones might have decaying corpses. Either way, going into private homes always felt a little like grave robbing. I ignored that sensation that day, though. I started walking up to random homes and trying the doors. Most were locked. Any locked doors, I let be. I wanted to find one that was empty and unlocked. There was a simple, nothing-special home along the main street, just a plain white box with a postage stamp yard and an open-air carport off the side of the house. It looked exactly like the house of the woman who used to babysit me when I was a little kid in Colorado. My parents both worked a lot when I was first born, so I spent a ton of time in that woman's house. Her name was Mary, but I called her Aunt Mimi because I couldn't pronounce Mary correctly for some reason. She was a sweet old lady, very no-nonsense and old school, but very loving. Seeing that house made me feel nostalgic. I decided I wanted to know what that house was like on the inside. I wanted to know if it had the same interior layout of Aunt Mimi's home.

I trudged through the overgrown grass and tried the door handle. The door was unlocked, but it was clear that no one had disturbed the home in some time. When I cracked the seal on the door, I sniffed the air. I'd learned that houses tended to have a funk to them when there were decaying corpses inside. A year of drying had mummified many of the dead. The effluence and vital organs had dehydrated and most of the really bad smells you'd associate with a recently dead corpse had gone with it. However, those nasty, nose-wrinkling smells would work their way into drywall and carpet padding, sheets and blankets, and just taint the house forever. You could tell the second you walked into a house if there were bodies inside. This house didn't have any rot smells, though. The fact that there wasn't a car in the carport or driveway hinted that whoever had lived here had gone to a hospital and died there, perhaps. Maybe they'd gone to the home of a relative to die. It didn't matter. They were gone, and they hadn't died in the house. The lack of a body in the home made me feel better about trespassing.

The house held its own smells, though. Ever notice when you go over to someone else's house the first time that it has a weird smell? Like, my buddy David—his house *always* smelled like soup. I never once saw anyone in his family eat soup, but the house had that smell of chicken stock, chopped vegetables, and bay leaves. I don't know why. I was smell-blind to my own house, so I couldn't tell you what it smelled like. My mom liked a particular scent of potpourri called *Nightmist* and there were little satchels and bowls of it everywhere, so I think it probably smelled like that. This little house had a stale smell. I could tell there had been standing water in the basement at some point in the past year. Might still be standing water. It had that scummy water funk.

The house was laid out exactly like Aunt Mimi's house. There was a large living room at the front door, a little kitchen and dining area just beyond it through an archway. There were two bedrooms to the right of the living room and kitchen and an old, cramped bathroom. I figured the house had to have been built in the late 1930s or early 1940s. Post-depression, there wasn't a lot of heavy spending, and houses were built small and tight. Easier to heat, that way. Efficient.

The decor in the house was nondescript. Simple. Brown. Dark woods and fabrics. Nothing noteworthy. The living room was clean. The kitchen was completely clean, scoured even. No dishes around the sink. No scraps anywhere. The fridge was full of spoiled food, but that could hardly have been the owner's fault. Clearly, the owner had been a neat freak. Either that or he/she had known something was up before they went to the hospital or wherever they went, and had cleaned thoroughly—sort of the home-based equivalent of making sure you're wearing clean undies in case you're in a car accident.

There were no pictures of humans on the walls. I found that a little strange. In every house I'd been in—*every one*—there were always pictures on the walls. Wedding photos, kids' school pictures, family reunion photos, and vacation shots, there were always images to give me insight into the people who lived there. This house had none. There wasn't even art on the walls. The living room had a strange, ornamental metal sculpture that looked like a double helix accented with squares and lines, but that was about it. Not even a crucifix or other religious symbols. The walls were perfectly bare. Or so I believed until I walked into the spare bedroom.

The master bedroom was as simple as the rest of the house. The bed was made with crisp corners and the top coverlet folded over and around the pillows like a hotel does. The closet was arranged neatly, men's clothes hanging from hangers and stacked in squared piles. There were no women's clothes. It was a bachelor's home. Judging from the style of the clothes and the few DVDs scattered around the TV, the owner was more likely a younger man. Outdoorsy.

I went into the second bedroom and froze. I hadn't expected what I found in there. All over the walls, as complete as any wallpaper would be, were newspaper clippings, articles printed from the Internet, and dozens and dozens of photographs. There were two six-foot bookshelves and every shelf was stuffed with books and binders. Everything had the same topic. Everything in the whole room concerned Bigfoot.

Sasquatch. Bigfoot. The Old Man of the Hills. Swamp-Ape, The Ohio Grassman. All the various names for the creature were represented on the walls. A dusty laptop computer was open on a desk in the room, the owner's research station. I made a casual survey of the articles. Many of them had to do with sightings in Pennsylvania. Whoever lived here had been a Bigfoot hunter, that much was clear. I played Dungeons & Dragons and spent a lot of time reading fantasy novels—so, I couldn't fault his hobby; at least he went outdoors and did some hiking.

It was fascinating to go over the articles. Many of the articles had highlighted lines marking sightings by police officers or multiple witnesses at the same time. There was a map of Pennsylvania on the desk with the spots where there had been Bigfoot sightings marked with an X. There were two marks just outside of Clintonville.

Great. I had to fear feral dogs, escaped apex predators, any gun-wielding psychos who watched *Mad Max* too many times, and now Bigfoot. The Flu had affected all primates the same. Man, monkey, and ape were all eradicated—myself and perhaps a few select others being the exception. If there were any apes with the virus immunity, they might have been freed from their zoos or even escaped on their own, and they might be building a life in the woods or plains around America. I like that idea. I liked the idea of the apes being given a chance to build their own community in the plains of Texas or something. It would be like *Planet of the Apes*, but hopefully without me being chased down by some apes on horseback and netted like a fish. I could not do a decent Charlton Heston impression, so if that did happen, I feel like a potential great moment would be wasted. Damned, dirty apes.

After finding the Bigfoot hunter's headquarters, I didn't feel like being in that house anymore. It didn't feel like Aunt Mimi's house anymore. I didn't even go check out the basement. I just continued my walk through town. As much as I tried to laugh off that guy's Bigfoot room, I found myself looking into the hills around town more than I would have otherwise.

When dark came, I had a good-sized bonfire roaring. I usually only burned enough wood to ensure I could cook a decent evening meal. Anything more felt wasteful. This was a vacation day, though. I was trying to have fun. I racked up a pile of dried hardwoods and stacked it in a pyramid shape. It went up quickly, the flames growing exponentially until the blaze was shooting ten feet into the air. Tongues of flame and ember leapt into the sky and fizzled to nothingness in the night wind. The heat and the smoke helped to keep the ravenous mosquitoes at bay. I rooted through the shelves of the grocery store and found marshmallows. They were a little hard, but still toasted nicely. I also found a few bars of chocolate and some graham crackers. Outside of being alone, it was fun to be a little irresponsible with my fire, and it was also fun to eat fifteen S'mores for dinner, but I imagined I'd regret that in the future. I still brushed and flossed obsessively after dinner, but giving in to some base impulses for a little while was incredibly enjoyable.

When I felt sick from hogging on S'mores, and the fire had died down to a respectable level, I sat in the deck chair with my feet propped on a log in front of me warming in the heat of the flames. The warmth of the fire was causing me to drowse. My eyelids were heavy. The book I'd been reading was forgotten on the pavement of the store parking lot next to my chair. I was halfway asleep, hovering in that twilight state where part of my brain just wanted to sleep and the other part wanted me to get up and do responsible things like making sure the fire was extinguished and putting on pajamas for bed. The Fall Asleep-part of my brain was winning the battle.

And then I heard the crack of a branch.

Nothing propels you from sleep to wakefulness like having had a snootful of Bigfoot articles earlier in the day and then hearing the sound of a nearby branch breaking. A branch breaking meant someone stepped on it. A branch breaking meant that an excessively hairy ape-man with size 27 feet was rounding the corner to feast on man-flesh. I launched out of my chair and had the shotgun in my hands. My heart went from a sedate, sleepy-time slow-bongo rhythm to the opening drum solo of "Sing, Sing, Sing" by Benny Goodman.

When I get scared, I tend to freeze. I tend to not want to hide. I think it's the same fight or flight response that rabbits have. They hope the coyote won't see them if they don't move at all, and when they know for certain that they're seen, they bolt and hope their speed can carry them faster than the predator. I was standing, half-blind from staring into the flames of the fire, with my senses on overdrive. The crack sounded like it had come from behind me, from somewhere near the grocery store. I didn't want to check it out, but I knew I had to. I knew that was part of being an adult, of defending myself and my possessions. No matter how much I didn't want to do it, no one else was going to do it.

I made a wide arc around the corner of the store. Whatever was there, I didn't want it to get an easy jump on me. I kept the shotgun at hip level. If it was a Bigfoot, I didn't want to scare it. If it wasn't, I didn't want to kill whoever or whatever it might be, but I certainly didn't want it to kill me, either. I moved well outside the circle of light made by the fire. My night-sight returned slowly. I was spot-blind for a while, blinking away afterimages of the flames.

I moved to the side of the grocery store and saw nothing. I froze again and listened hard to the night. There were no sounds outside of crickets and the spitting crackle of flames on wood. I continued around the store, moving behind it. Highway 280 ran along the side of the little mart. I walked down the middle of the street, moving as quietly as I could manage with a slow heel-to-toe step. I couldn't hear anything fleeing. I couldn't hear any footsteps.

I relaxed. I must have imagined the branch. Or maybe in my drowsy state, one of the logs in the fire cracked and echoed off the building behind me and threw me off. I was just about to turn around and go back to the RV when I heard *something* moving through the grass behind one of the houses.

My heart began to race again, and I felt a cold sweat break out across my body. I moved toward the sound. There was *definitely* something moving through the grass, something *big,* something *heavy.* My throat felt tight. I moved across the asphalt and toward the sound. Whatever was moving started to pick up speed. It must have heard me. I ran after it for a few steps, but stopped. Whatever had broken the stick was moving away from me at speed. I wasn't going to catch it, whatever it was, and I was certain that I didn't want to. It was moving faster than any human person would or could outside of an Olympic sprinter.

I backed away from the houses to the road. I didn't want to stay in Clintonville anymore. I didn't want to stay anywhere anymore. I hate to say it, but at that moment my eighteen-year-old burgeoning man/adult-self wanted my mommy. I wanted to be safe and warm and protected. I ran back to the RV, made sure Fester was inside, and got the hell out of Dodge. I hated driving through the dark, especially when the quality of the roads were in constant question. I was on edge, my eyes straining to watch for animals along the roads, sweeping constantly for buckles and upended chunks of highway. I drove as fast as I could to the next town, a place called Emlenton. There, I stayed on the highway and shut down the RV.

The second the RV was shut down, I pulled every curtain in the thing. I'd never done that away from the city before, but I was shaken. Badly. It felt like the night had eyes. The skin on my body was creeping. What little hair I had on my head was standing on end. I sat down at the table of the RV and turned on a little LED lantern. I didn't want to be in the dark. I couldn't find Fester. He was hiding. He only did that when he was scared. Did I scare him, or was it something else? Was he picking up on my fear? I would never know.

I had to talk myself down. I had to tell myself that Bigfoot wasn't real. It was a deer, I told myself. Or an elk. A moose. Maybe even a bear. It could have been any of a dozen or more animals. It could have been my imagination. It could have been a hallucination. I repeated this to myself over and over. It could have been anything *except* Bigfoot. My heart was pounding. I hadn't ever worried about anything like Bigfoot. It was silly that I was doing it now. Ludicrous, even. I could worry about any of a dozen other things, serious things that had a likely chance of happening, like a bear attack, but at that moment, the only thing that played through my head was pulling one of those curtains around the RV and seeing the roughly humanoid face of an ape-man staring back at me. I didn't want to ever have that happen. At that moment, I felt extremely vulnerable, extremely alone, and I wanted more guns, bigger guns. I wanted an assault rifle with a fully automatic setting. I wanted knives, machetes, swords. I wanted anything that would give me even a false sense of security. I wanted to be back in the safety of my little library back in Sun Prairie where Bigfoot would never, *ever* visit.

I could feel the paranoia creeping through my brain like a tarantula, light, hairy-footed steps just spread more and more fear. I pulled the fleece blanket from my bed in the back and covered myself with it. I lay down on the floor in the center of the RV, scared to go back to the bed area where windows were so close to the mattress. The floor felt safer. No one could see me on the floor. I held my shotgun in my hands, my right hand resting on the stock, fingers brushing the metal trigger-guard. Fear was making me tremble. My head started to ache from being on alert. A new fear pulsed down my spine at that moment, one that I had not considered before. I started to worry that fear could drive me insane. I couldn't be on alert at all times. I had to sleep. The thoughts of what might happen while I was sleeping began to claw at my mind with long, sharp talons. I tried to breathe. I tried to push all thoughts of anything scary out of my head. I tried to visualize pleasant things. Nothing was working. My heart was in my throat. I thought of how much people depended on each other for things other than simple companionship. I thought about how people depended on each other for protection, for safety. I might never have another person to watch my back. If I couldn't gather myself and get a grip on my fears, I might never sleep again. I didn't know much about sleep, but I knew that going without it for a long time would lead to further paranoia, and uncontrolled paranoia would lead to insanity.

The most terrifying picture of all forced itself into my brain at that second. I saw myself crouched in the corner of a filthy house. My skin was unwashed. My hair was wild and matted. I was holding guns and muttering to myself, eyes wide and darting. I saw myself going insane. Alone. In a wasteland devoid of human contact and protection.

I didn't want to live in that world.

I didn't sleep that night. I lay on the floor, every muscle tense, until dawn came. Even when the sun rose and banished any demons or monsters from outside the RV, I was scared to pull the curtains and look outside. In the end, my bladder forced my hand. I had to piss like a racehorse, and I'd never gotten around to rigging up the tiny little camper toilet in the Greyhawk. Why have an indoor toilet in a moving vehicle that you'd have to clean and empty when the world was your toilet?

Even with the sun providing ample light, I was terrified to open the side door to my RV. I unlocked it, took a deep breath, and then slammed it open, banging the door to the side of the RV's body, hoping any creatures within a half-mile would hear the noise and run. I stuck my head out just far enough to look to the right and left and see that Sasquatch wasn't hanging around. I stepped onto the road and circled the RV, shotgun at the ready. After one full revolution, I even dropped to my knees and looked under the vehicle just to make sure there wasn't some sort of monster circling around the Greyhawk. Only then did I venture to the edge of the road to relieve my straining bladder.

When I got back into the RV and opened all the curtains, I felt a flood of relief. A surge of dopamine and endorphins calmed me. I was able to laugh at myself a little. I had been stressing out over the highly improbable chance that I was going to meet a Bigfoot. In the safety of the light of day, it seemed ridiculous. However, I knew that night would come again soon. I knew that night would return, and with it the fear would return, as well. I didn't know how to alleviate that fear. It was so absurd that it made me angry while I performed my morning rituals. The more I thought about the fear, the angrier I got with myself. Part of it might have been lack of sleep. I hated the fact that I was getting angry, and that only made me angrier. I was so angry that I couldn't eat.

I put a Coke in the drink holder in the front of the Greyhawk for the road. I took a couple of bottles of water and some soap and gave myself a quick, chilly shower in the middle of the road. I dried off, dressed, and got ready to drive. Fester was on the passenger seat waiting for me. He sat and regarded me with his dark green eyes. I looked back at him. "Fester, am I losing my mind?"

Fester gave a meow and flopped on his side. He rolled to his back and looked at me expectantly. I reached over and gave his belly a couple of scratches. He immediately curled into a ball and bit my wrist gently, holding it in place to make sure I didn't stop rubbing his belly. His eyes closed and he started his husky purring. I turned the key to the RV with my left hand and the engine roared to life. It scared him, and he relinquished my arm.

We continued east on Highway 80. I had no desire to explore towns or homes out in the rural areas of Pennsylvania. The hills and vales that I had enjoyed so much the day before were now areas of suspicion and required frequent scans for roaming cryptid monsters.

I crossed most of Pennsylvania over the next five hours. I didn't stop. I didn't leave the highway. While I was moving, I felt safe, protected. It wasn't until the middle of the afternoon, when I ran low on gas, and I needed to pee again, that I consented to stop.

I pulled off the highway at a gas station near the exit for highway 380 north. There were signs for the Poconos everywhere. The sun was still high in the sky. It was only mid-summer. The sun wouldn't be setting until at least nine. I figured I had a good five hours of daylight, maybe a bit more. I wanted to see the Poconos. I wanted to check out the fabled mountain resorts. If nothing else, I thought that maybe forcing my way into a solid building for the night, being able to curtain the windows and bar the door, might make me feel safe enough to sleep. I wasn't certain I'd sleep in the RV that night. I knew I would have to get over the fear at some point, but for the moment, it felt like an impossibility.

After I'd done everything I needed to do at the gas station, I got back in the RV and headed north into the Poconos. My gut got tight. My skin got itchy. The fear was crawling back into me. Thinking about staying somewhere overnight made me remember that the dark was coming back. I didn't feel safe in large cities. I didn't feel safe in the woods. I didn't know how to get through the night, anymore. I didn't have much of a choice, though. *Time and tide wait for no man.* I think Chaucer said that. The sun was falling toward the western horizon. The light was beginning to wane, changing from the clear, white light of day to the hazy, yellowed afternoon light. Time certainly wasn't waiting for me.

CHAPTER SEVEN

The Pocono Resorts

There were resorts aplenty in the Poconos. The rolling mountains were dotted with unbelievable castle-like hotels filled with hundreds of luxury rooms. There were also amazing homes dotting the countryside, palatial mansions and cute little weekend cabins—places for which my mother would have cut off her right leg to own. The whole area reeked of money and prestige. I pulled off the road at the first massive mega-hotel I saw, a place called the Buckskill Lodge and Conference Center. In the light of day, it didn't look too intimidating. At night, with every window dark, I imagined the place would look like a haunted asylum, the kind a group of dumb teens would visit, and six of the seven of them would be dead by dawn. It did not feel, at first glance, like the type of place where I wanted to spend the night.

I drove up to the covered entry. At least if it stormed, the RV wouldn't suffer more hail damage. Gripping the shotgun, I left the Greyhawk and approached the front doors of the hotel. The lobby was lit through the side windows by the afternoon sun. When I cracked the door, the smell of old death was thick. People had died in this hotel. A lot of people. That struck me as strange. The world is ending, people are dying left and right, and some people decided to spend their last days in a luxury hotel. I suppose I couldn't fault them: If you're going to go anyway, you might as well go in style.

The lobby was expansive and done up in a faux-rustic style. It was supposed to look like a rugged mountain cabin, but the decoration didn't look anything like what I knew of mountain cabins. It looked like someone had some snooty New York designer remake a cabin in what they thought a rustic cabin should be. There were expensive pieces of art on the walls and a large marble sculpture near the expansive front desk. Where were the taxidermied animal heads and the mounted trophy fish? If a rustic cabin doesn't have a singing plastic fish on the wall, can we really call it a rustic cabin?

The lobby squelched all sound. The wood timbers along the walls swallowed any noise and the carpeting and acoustic ceiling tiles created a very quiet room. It was very strange to find a place that was even quieter than the hushed, ambient world. I'd grown used to the noise of nature and winds, but this room lacked either. It was the kind of quiet that pressed on my eardrums. I found myself coughing occasionally just to hear something, to break the silence.

There was an office behind the lobby desk, so I figured I'd start exploring there. The door was slightly ajar. The smell of decay increased slightly as I moved toward the door. I'd like to say that I was prepared for the corpse in the office, but in reality, even after encountering numerous corpses, even after living amongst the houses-turned-mausoleums, I was never prepared to see another body. I doubted I ever would be. I didn't get sick to my stomach when I saw them anymore, but I certainly didn't enjoy finding them. They were just an unpleasant part of life, like mold.

The corpse in the office was still dressed in an employee's uniform, white shirt with frilly lace at the neck and a maroon skirt. A gold-bar name tag on the shirt read "Kayla." She was curled up in a corner of the office on the floor, a jacket balled up under her head as a pillow. Why had she stayed at work to die? I would have gone home. *Sorry, boss—everyone in the world is dying. I quit.*

Kayla had mummified well. Insects had their way with her eyes, unfortunately. Her skin had shrunk and pulled back around her mouth, giving her a ghastly, leering grin. The skin on her fingers had dried, too. Her fingernails protruded like talons. It was pretty easy to see how vampire myths started. Her hair was around her face in stringy, matted locks. It was probably nice hair at one point in her life, but the last hours of her life had been spent on a hard floor in feverish misery. My heart went out to her. I hoped she'd at least called her family and said good-bye. She looked like she had been young, maybe early twenties. It was hard to judge age on dried corpses.

I found a set of master keys in the office, and then closed the door, letting it click shut behind me. Kayla deserved to rest undisturbed. It was a lousy place to die, but the whole situation was pretty lousy.

The rest of the hotel was largely dark. The long hallways had small windows at the far ends of them, but the light they gave was barely enough to see the shape of the hall. Long stretches of the corridors were left in complete darkness. I needed a flashlight, and if I was carrying a flashlight, I couldn't carry a shotgun, too. I had to ditch the comforting weight of the shotgun and rely on the pistol on my hip. I actually had to take a moment to tell myself that Bigfoot hadn't taken up residence in the lodge, and shotguns would not be effective against ghosts, either. I went back to the RV, ditched the shotgun, and got my police-style MagLite. The MagLite wasn't quite as comforting as a shotgun, but its long handle filled with six D batteries was heavy enough to knock a man unconscious with a single, well-placed swing. It definitely helped give me a fortitude boost. It also had 178 lumens. A normal flashlight runs around 20-80 lumens, depending on quality. This thing was basically a portable spotlight. The MagLite helped put my mind at ease. With its blinding beam splayed out ahead of me, there was no way Bigfoot could jump out and surprise me inside a several-hundred million dollar hotel.

I walked the first-floor hallway. It was a long corridor with rooms on either side. All the room locks were key-card locks, those new-fangled locks that required a plastic key like a credit card. You'd think that they wouldn't work, but I tried the master card in the first lock. The little red and green lights on the top of the lock glowed, and I was able to open it. Apparently, the locks were powered with a few AA batteries and if no one was using them, they had the ability to last a long time. They would eventually fizzle out, I was sure, but it was a testament to their quality that the doors still worked after a year and a half.

The first room I tried had a body in it, a single corpse, and it looked like a man's corpse. It was lying in the king-sized bed in the center of the room. The covers were pulled up to his chest, and his arms were lying on either side of his body. He looked peaceful, like he'd died in his sleep instead of gasping for air. I saw an empty bottle of painkillers and an empty vodka bottle next to the bed. I couldn't be sure, but I felt it was safe to assume he'd committed suicide. The writing was on the wall pretty quickly during the Flu, and a lot of people, upon coming down with symptoms, chose a fast, painless death instead of drowning in their own fluids. I backed out of his room and let his door close behind me. After that, I didn't bother with any more rooms. I was certain that I did not want to spend the night in that hotel.

I did explore a bit more of the hotel, going through some of the convention center and the restaurants therein. I found the pool, but the pool was unbelievably gross. There was still water in it, but that water had grown green and slimy. Despite the stagnant chemical smell in the air, black mold was sprouting on all the walls in the pool area. I didn't even waste time unlocking the door. I immediately felt dirty just being there, and I tucked my mouth and nose into my shirt to prevent inhaling any more of that mess than I already had. I backed out of the pool area, found my way to the nearest exit, and went back to the RV.

That hotel had probably cost at least $100 million to build. It was massive, five stories, with a convention center that could have hosted a regulation college basketball game. It was a monument to American excess, a beautiful structure in a beautiful area, and it had probably provided tens of thousands of people with a fun vacation over its lifetime. Now it was just a dark, multi-room tomb. The rot in the pool area would probably speed its decay. In another five years, storms and weather would take their toll and the siding would be coming off, some of the windows would be broken due to the building shifting and settling as it deteriorated, and animals might try to build homes in the areas they could access. The building would continue to fall to rack and ruin. Eventually, it would collapse in on itself, and the earth would send up weeds and trees to try to reclaim it. In fifty years, maybe a hundred, it would be a pile of rubble in the midst of a burgeoning wood—the same sort of wood someone had probably had to chop down just to build the damn thing. In the end, everything dies; nothing lasts forever. That is just the way it has to be. That's the way it will always be.

While I pulled away from the hotel, I told Fester about the bodies inside, and the black mold. He was curled up on the passenger seat with his paws tucked underneath him, a pose I liked to think of as "furry bread loaf with a head." He squeezed his eyes and looked unimpressed.

I pulled off the main highway onto a private road and saw large, expensive houses mostly hidden by trees and brick walls. Big money homes. Million-dollar places with million-dollar views of the mountains around them. Most of the driveways had large iron gates in front of them, the kind that were powered by keypads or remotes. My dad always hated solicitors, be they religious or commercial. He would have loved to have had a gate like these. I had to park the RV on the road in order to go into the homes. I needed to see inside these places. I needed to know what sort of secrets they held.

I picked the biggest one I could see, a sprawling, three-story job with a log-cabin look to the exterior. It had a few windows across the front of the main section that allowed me to see through the interior to the rooms at the rear where massive panes of glass provided a view of the expansive valley beyond.

I climbed the eight-foot stone wall in front of the house and landed on the other side. There, in the yard, was garbage. A staggering amount of garbage, actually. In one corner of the yard was a mountain of black 55-gallon garbage bags, each crammed with cans and bottles and other odds and ends. When whoever did this ran out of bags, he or she (or they, judging from the amount of debris) just started dumping trash in piles near the garbage bag mountain. The stench was powerful. Flies and hornets buzzed thickly around the waste piles. I had no doubt that vermin were about, as well. I could not see any, but I knew they were there. I hadn't expected to find this sort of thing behind the wall of a multi-million dollar home. However, this amount of garbage meant that someone, or several someones, had survived the Flu. There was enough garbage there to account for months of living, maybe even a year's worth.

When I realized I wasn't going to catch the Flu and die, I'd chosen to go live in a library. Plenty of reading material, and I was able to make a small annex of the library into my home. A small fire could heat the annex completely, and I was able to survive a Wisconsin winter there. The opposite sort of mentality for a survivor was to claim the biggest, best house they could find and make a go of it there, which is what these people had chosen to do. It was not efficient, but it was stylish.

Apprehension seized my gut and wound its way around my groin. Would these people be friendly? Scary? I didn't know. I did know that I had to take my chances on finding them, though. I rushed to the front door of the house and knocked hard. I listened. Nothing. I knocked again, this time using the stock of the shotgun to make heavy, ringing knocks. Still nothing. I tried the handle of the front door. Unlocked. The door swung open easily. I sniffed the air out of habit. There was a stale, warm smell, but no decay. No rot. Someone had at least given basic maintenance to that place over the past year.

The interior of the home had once been very nice. I could tell, just looking around, that it had been, at one time, like one of those *Better Homes & Gardens* houses, a showpiece worthy of being an interior design magazine centerfold. Ritzy. Extravagant. However, whoever had been living there had treated the place with less than kid gloves and where once had been a wonderful home, it now looked like a hoarder had been keeping residence. I'm not pointing fingers, though. I tried my best to keep my small annex living area somewhat neat and clean, but the rest of the library had taken a bit of a beating. I'd used the community center room to store wood for burning, and I'd used a lot of the main area for storing supplies. I had tried to keep my living area from succumbing to filth, though. I bagged my garbage and threw it into dumpsters around town in the winter. In the spring and summer, when the weather was nice, I drove sacks of trash to the Dane County landfill south of my hometown and dumped them there. Judging from the variety of clothes and assorted boxes of supplies, several people had lived in this house. It looked like at least two women and at least one man, maybe more. They had just stored whatever they found along the walls and piled it into spare rooms. There was a living area near the fireplace that was somewhat free of debris, but there were soot stains and wood bark all over the place.

I called out a greeting and listened, but no one responded. The ashes in the fireplace were ice cold. No fire had been built in that hearth for weeks, maybe months. Whoever had lived in this house had moved somewhere else. Maybe another house nearby. Maybe they had moved south like I was going to do. Maybe they went west to California. People had been in this house, though. They had survived the Flu. This discovery bolstered my hopes of finding more people. It was a needed breath of optimism. I would never know where the people who lived here had gone, but I at least knew they were out there somewhere.

I wasn't about to stay in the disaster the unknown people had left, though. I walked around until I found a very nice house that was relatively untouched. Supplies had been ransacked from the kitchen, but I didn't need supplies. I brought Fester, his food dish, and his necessary box from the RV and prepared to spend a night holed up on the third floor of a million-dollar home.

I started by hauling in all the supplies I'd need for the night from the Greyhawk: a change of clothes, towel, soap, two whole cases of water, some food for me and the cat, lanterns, and weapons. I made a survey of the house and locked all the doors I could find. I secured everything on the first floor, doors and windows, and made sure there was no easy access in the basement. There was an extensive deck with a sliding door on the second floor. I made sure that was locked. Sure, someone could smash the glass on either of the two sliding doors on the floors below, but I would hear that. I'd have time to wake up, get my bearings, and arm myself.

I stationed myself in the third story of the home. The master bedroom was clean and neat, albeit dusty from disuse. Dusty was just the way the world was now, though. I was used to dusty. There was a king-sized bed along the left wall, and a master bathroom to the right. Two matching oak bureaus were along the same wall as the bathroom door. To the left of the bedroom was a large walk-in closet. Men's and women's clothes hung on hangers in it, although most of the women's clothes had been picked over, probably by the two women in the hoarder house. To the right of the bed was another sliding glass door that led outside to a small observation deck, hardly big enough for two people. The view from the deck was stunning. A wide valley of green trees lay spread out before me like a carpet. I could see the glint of windows in other homes through the leaves of some of the trees, homes hidden from view otherwise. I watched the valley for some time, looking for telltale wisps of smoke. I inhaled the clean air, trying to taste the scent of a wood fire on my tongue. I only smelled the clean, tasteless scent of woods and winds.

I went through the house and collected several glass knick-knacks and some metal trinkets. Later that night, I would scatter them on the floor behind the closed bedroom door like caltrops, a final line of defense. It made me feel like the kid from *Home Alone*. Then, and only then, did I feel myself start to relax.

I went through the house thoroughly. The family photos on the walls made it look like it had been owned by a successful, middle-aged couple. No kids. From the pictures, I could see they'd been all over the world. Egypt, Tokyo, some island shots, maybe Hawaii, maybe the Bahamas; I couldn't tell. There were pictures of them at Penn State football games in one of the luxury suites. These people had been high rollers and big spenders, no paltry stadium seating for them. The basement was every bit as expansive as the rest of the house. It was a total man-cave, too. One room held a very nice study that looked more like it was for decoration than something that got used. There were bookshelves lined with those showpiece leather-bound tomes that you see in old movies, but not one of them had a single crack in the spine. I doubted that any of them had ever been opened. The rest of the basement was like a man-child's playroom. There was a gorgeous pool table, a full bar, a tiny theater room with an eighty-inch flat-screen and a fully loaded sound system. There was another room with some vintage video games, the kind in the upright cabinets like an old-style arcade. It made me want to go scavenge up a generator and play a few rounds of *Galaga*. Instead, I racked up the balls on the pool table and spent a couple of hours playing pool. It wasn't as much fun as it would have been with someone else, but it was still a good way to spend the night. It took my mind off Bigfoot, at least.

I went to bed in the third floor bedroom. I hauled up my cases of water and stood in the shower. I poured a couple bottles on myself. I soaped up, washed myself well, making sure to hit every crevice, even my toenails, and then I used about two dozen bottles to rinse. It wasn't the best use of good drinking water, but it felt good to be really clean instead of just using a washcloth and Wet Wipes to maintain a passable level of hygiene. I picked up a towel to dry myself, but stopped. Instead, I switched off the lantern in the bathroom and walked across the bedroom to the balcony. I stood naked in the night and let the warm, summer wind dry me.

The moon was full that night. It was perched high in the sky and illuminated the whole valley with dull yellow light. Far below me, insects chirped their symphony. I heard an owl in the distance. I leaned on the edge of the balcony three stories above the ground and felt safe. The door was barricaded. My cat was chilling on my bed. I was fed and clean. I had every right to feel good. I was planning to start reading a new book. I was looking forward to getting on to New York City. I was less than a day's journey away from the Big Apple; I could probably make it there before noon if the roads weren't too bad. I was confident that none of the boogiemen of my fear-wrought nightmares would scale the exterior of the house and get me while I slept. I had found more proof that others had survived the Flu, and I knew that they were still out there, probably on the road like I was. I had every reason to feel good, but I didn't. I looked at the moon, and my heart fell into my stomach. When I was a sophomore, I asked Jillian Wright to Homecoming. She looked me up and down and laughed. Then she walked away. At that moment on the balcony, I felt exactly the same way I did back then. I don't know why.

I went back into the room, dressed in a pair of shorts and a t-shirt, and climbed into bed. I looked at the book and the lantern by the bed and couldn't muster the energy to read them. I pulled the blankets of that fine, dusty king-sized bed over my head and cried myself to sleep.

CHAPTER EIGHT

The Big Rotten Apple

I left the Poconos just after dawn, the sun barely cresting the edge of the horizon. Any enchantment I had with life on the road was dwindling. It was three weeks since I had left my hometown. I was getting tired of being on the move. I was getting tired of sleeping in a cramped RV and eating canned tuna and endless bowls of salty ramen. I was just tired, period. I was processing too much information every day. Before the Flu, I had spent the majority of my life in a small town; I rarely traveled, and I had rarely slept anywhere but my own bed. I started the trip with the best of intentions, but now the travel was starting to grate on me. I have to think that it was because I was scared.

Fear is draining. It does things to the mind and body. During the day, I was not scared. I was a man in control of my own life and destiny. I was overcoming obstacles. I was blazing new ground in a brave new frontier. The second the sun went down, every noise demanded investigation. When I closed my eyes, thoughts of waking up to someone—or *something*—charging me down would play havoc with my mind. I wanted to find other people, people I could trust, just so I could stop feeling so alone against the world. I had to keep reminding myself that this whole situation was not something I could control. I had to keep reminding myself that when I settled in the south, that was it. I wouldn't be moving; I'd be working hard to eke out some sort of existence until I died, and if I was lucky, it would be a happy, fulfilling existence.

Searching for others started feeling as if I was looking for needles in a haystack. It began to feel pointless and tedious. I'd been stupidly lucky to stumble across Doug. If he'd been bedridden, I would not have found him. If I had decided not to go into the pharmacy that day, I never would have known someone in that town was still alive. If I arrived a week later, who knows if he would even still be alive? I knew people were out there—they *had to be* out there--but I had no reliable method of finding them. It was a near-impossible task. I felt like Sisyphus.

I crossed New Jersey quickly. I didn't bother searching any of the little towns along the way. If anyone in Jersey was still alive, I figured they would have gone to New York, or they would be out in the country. A large part of New Jersey felt like never-ending suburb. There was probably plenty to scavenge, but I just didn't feel like survivors would be hanging out in Toms River or Princeton with the big city and all its bounty so close. New York had a multitude of hospitals with medicine, stores rich with canned goods, and many, many apartments that could all be raided for whatever supplies they held. If nothing else, there would be tables and chairs that could be broken up and burned for heat. I didn't know where people would be in New York, though. Brooklyn? Manhattan? I had no idea.

I started in Manhattan because it was the first place I ran into when I crossed the Lincoln Tunnel from Jersey. Remember that I grew up near Madison, Wisconsin, a town of about 300,000. The county it was in had maybe 500,000 people. I had been to Milwaukee a handful of times and Chicago twice in my life. I was always impressed by their size compared to Madison. Even with the experiences of those "big cities," I wasn't prepared for New York. Even before I hit the tunnel, when New York was looming on the horizon, it felt like I was transporting to another world. Everywhere I looked were towering buildings. I was dwarfed. I was an ant. I'd been through cities on my way to New York, but New York was its own separate entity. Just in Manhattan alone, I felt like I could spend the next decade exploring and scavenging and still not breach all the apartments, grocery stores, restaurants, and every other place that might have held supplies. Throw in the rest of the boroughs, and all the surrounding suburbs in New Jersey and New York, and someone could live a good, long life just scavenging. The winters would still be cold, but there were trees to harvest and furniture to burn. Central Park alone could be turned into a tree farm and you could easily set aside a couple of acres for planting vegetables. New York overwhelmed me. I knew I should explore. I knew I should search for survivors or signs of life. I knew that there *had* to be someone, probably *many* people still alive in New York, but I didn't know where to start looking. I stopped the Greyhawk and tried to sort through the crisscross maze of streets. Everything was in a grid system and that helped, but for someone from Sun Prairie, Wisconsin, population 35,000, the maps I had might as well have been written with hieroglyphics.

I drove to the tallest building I saw and pulled the Greyhawk onto the sidewalk in front of it. I gathered weapons, my flashlight, and my ruck of tools and spare ammo. I closed the curtains on the RV and told Fester to hang loose. I'd be back as soon as I could. Fester yawned and sprawled on his side on the padded bench at the little table. Clearly, he was unimpressed by my big city daring.

The doors to the office building were locked. I used the butt of the shotgun to smash one of the doors. It took a couple of shots, but caved eventually. The glass was safety glass. It didn't shatter so much as it webbed and bowed until I could push it clear of the door and slip past.

I couldn't smell death in the building. I didn't know if that was because no one had died in there, or because the bodies were far above me and the smell wasn't carrying to the lower levels. The building smelled clean enough, but stale. There was a thick stillness that settled on the tongue like heavy cream. There was a faint scent of ammonia and institutional cleanser mixed with time and age. The air was warm and dry in the building, but given the sheer amount of windows and the excessive heat that day, that wasn't unexpected. The air was so dry that only a few seconds in the lobby made me thirsty and made my nose itch. I had to go back to the RV and get a bottle of water.

The elevators were obviously not going to take me to the top floor; I had to go by stairs. I climbed seventy stories in a darkened stairwell illuminated only by my MagLite. Each flight of stairs was nine steps to a landing, and then another nine steps to the next floor. Eighteen steps per floor. The first five or six flights were easy. No problem, even. I was giddy. It was exciting. Then, I started to lag. I was still moving quickly, but I lost any sort of bounce in my step. By the twentieth floor, my thighs were burning and I was trudging. By the thirtieth, I was dragging myself from step to step, and I still had thirty-nine flights to go! I could have bailed early. The fortieth floor was still a good view. I could have stopped, but I wanted to make it to the top. I wanted the reward of seeing the massive city spread out before me like a carpet. By the fiftieth floor, climbing the steps became a war of attrition. I would not let the stairs beat me. I was rationing my water because I had only brought one bottle, just a tiny sip every five floors to moisten my tongue. I was breathing hard. I started dreading the next day because I knew my legs would feel like I had gravel in all my leg muscles. The last ten flights, I was dragging myself with my arms on the railing as much as I was trying to lift my legs. For the first time in my life, I truly understood why StairMasters worked.

When I got to the door at the top floor, I was spent. I flopped on my back on the stairwell landing and gasped for air. I wiped a thick sheen of sweat off my forehead with my wrist. Rivulets of sweat were dripping down my body. The notion that I would have to go back *down* all the steps flitted through my mind. It would be easier, but it was still going to be a chore.

The door to the top floor was locked, of course. It was one of those big, solid steel fire doors, with a narrow window enmeshed with wire. I dropped my ruck and shotgun. I propped the flashlight on its end so it pointed straight up and lit the area. I tried the lock-pick kit but learned quickly the lock was outside of my range of talent. I had a small sledgehammer in the bag, a little 12-pounder with a short handle. I picked that up and began to lay into the door handle with gusto. The noise of each shot exploded down the stairwell and echoed. It was loud, sacrilegiously loud. The world felt like a church funeral service, and any loud noises felt like someone belching in the middle of Mass. I hammered and hacked at the door handle. It bent, but did not break. I decided to work on the narrow window in the door. These things were made to be difficult to break. You can shatter the glass pretty easily, but the wire in the middle was surprisingly tough. I had to get out a pair of tin-snips and cut through the wire. Once I did that, it was easy enough to reach my arm through the door and open it from the inside simply by pulling the handle. Interior doors leading to stairwells can never lock on the inside. Fire codes, and all.

The top story of the office building was a collection of cubicles and small offices enclosed with glass panels. On the far end of the office were three executive offices. You could tell the executive offices because they had Venetian blinds covering their windows for privacy and big wooden doors instead of swinging glass doors. It looked like nothing special. If anything, it reminded me of the set of *The Office*, but it was ten times as large. All around the office were windows overlooking the city. The view was breathtaking and astonishing for a kid from Wisconsin; it was everything I hoped it would be. I wondered how anyone in that office got anything done. I was always the kind of kid who could not sit next to the windows in class because something outdoors would always distract me and I would have to spend ten minutes watching it. Here, seventy stories above Manhattan, I could see down into a myriad of streets and alleys, each more interesting than the last. They were interesting in an empty city seemingly devoid of life. When everyone was alive, it must have been a hypnotic swirl of things to see. I did a slow lap around the office looking at the city. I was supposed to be looking for signs of life, but I was entranced by the different buildings. I pulled binoculars out of my ruck and started to look into windows of other buildings. If I'd ever been able to have a job in a tall office building, I would have been fired--I just know it. I would have spent every moment that I could spying on other people.

The roof access door was just above that floor. Another eighteen steps. I had to do it. I gathered my gear and marched up the last eighteen steps. This door didn't have a window like all the rest of the fire doors, but this door also wasn't locked for some reason. I was able to push it open. Wind caught the door and slammed it open. The chain at the top of the door kept it from slamming back against the wall of the rooftop portal behind it, but the wind held the door with force. I dropped my ruck at the corner of the door so if the wind died, it couldn't close on me. That would be all I needed—to survive a year and change over a Wisconsin winter, and then stupidly lock myself on the roof of a seventy-story office tower to die.

There was a massive stack of air conditioning blocks on the roof. They were their own engineering marvel. They extended at least an additional twenty feet on top of the roof. For a split-second, I considered climbing them and doing a Leo DiCaprio "I'm-the-king-of-the-world" moment, but an image of a gust of wind catching me and chucking me over the edge of the building ran that idea out of my head.

I walked to the nearest edge. There was a safety wall about four feet high around the edge of the roof. I put my hands on the little wall and glanced over the edge. That tickling sensation of vertigo whipped through my body. I liked heights, I liked that sensation, but it was a big difference to look down from this building than it was a five or six-story parking garage like I knew in Madison. Looking over the edge of this building made me think about throwing up and it filled me with an urge to pee.

I walked to the edge of the roof to my left to look down at the ground from there, but caught something out of the corner of my eye that froze me in place: Huddled in the far corner of that edge was a skeleton in a ragged, sun-bleached coat and fading jeans. Someone had chosen to die on the roof of this building.

The body wasn't mummified like most of the graying, dry skin-covered corpses I'd found. This person had spent a year exposed to the elements, to insects and birds. It was an actual, honest-to-goodness skeleton bleached white by the sun and rain. At least, it was bleached white at the spots that were exposed. Beneath the clothes, there was still a few piles of tissue, organs, and skin. The odor of death was present, but it was not thick, not heavy. It was still enough to make me wrinkle my nose and breathe through clenched teeth, but it was far better than many of the bodies I'd seen. The body was on its side, slumped back against one edge of the roof safety wall. The skull was tilted downward slightly, the neck curving so the top of the skull was resting on the tar and scattered pea gravel on the roof. There were a couple of empty bottles of booze next to the body, along with a pulpy wad of dried cardboard that was once a pizza box. I could see the corner of a plastic Ziploc bag jutting out of the corpse's fraying jacket. It seemed an odd thing for a dead body to have, so I knelt down and removed it as carefully as I could without disturbing the body. Inside the sealed bag was a note handwritten in blue ink on yellow legal paper.

My name was Charles Spangler. I was the last person to come into work at Morris, Heifetz, and Weiss Law Offices. Everyone else is dead or dying. They stayed home. I thought maybe being at the office would keep me healthier than staying home. I was wrong. When I started coughing, I knew I was dying, too. I came up to the roof to jump, but chickened out. The disease will get me soon enough, I guess. The disease is killing everyone. We all wondered how the end would come, and when it would come. It looks like we all know the answer to that, now.

I don't have any last words or a will. Doesn't look like it matters, anyhow. I just want it known that the skies over New York are beautiful without all the lights from the city to spoil them, but the city was better with all the street noise than it is with all the quiet.

I regret that I never took the chance to ask Jennifer to go to dinner. I will regret that I harbored that desire for her for so long and never acted on it. I don't think there is a kinder, gentler soul on the Earth than she.

I will miss Central Park in the fall. Wherever I'm going, I hope there is something similar. If there is, look for me there.

If there is a God, maybe Jennifer will be there, too.

The note was signed with a flourish. It was neatly folded into eighths. A dying man's last chance to say something to the world, and in the end that's all he had to say. I would not have done any better.

Seeing Mr. Spangler's remains made me lose my taste for being on the roof. It tainted the thrill. I could only think about that poor guy lying huddled in that corner, hacking and coughing, gasping for air, and eventually dying. It made me wonder again why I was still alive. Why had Doug lived an extra year only to die by cancer? I know that this sort of feeling is called *existential dread*. It is a realization that life lacks meaning or purpose. I was battling existential dread heavily now. I had no reason for living, no reason why the Flu didn't take me when it erased everyone else. I had no purpose on the planet other than pure survival; it wasn't like I was going to have a career or something. As far as I could process, I was only living to spite the Universe's attempt at wiping out the human race. That didn't feel like much of a life. It certainly wasn't a good reason to keep living.

I let the RV roll on impulse through the streets of New York. I wanted to honk the horn as I had in the smaller towns and cities, but I refrained. I tried it once and it felt profane. The blare of the horn echoed around the buildings, and it sounded tinny and harsh. It didn't sound right, which is funny considering how many horn blasts the city had endured since the creation of cars. I drove in silence, instead.

When I looked at New York City on a map, it looked tiny. Even including areas around it like Newark, it was still smaller than southern Wisconsin. It was literally a fourth or a fifth of the size of Wisconsin as a whole. I spent weeks combing Wisconsin roads, towns, and cities during the past summer. I'd found nothing. The population density of New York City would suggest that there had to be people alive inside the city somewhere, but where? I was not a local. Half of my knowledge of New York came from either watching the ball drop on television on New Year's Eve or an embarrassing amount of repeated viewings of *"Crocodile" Dundee*. My late girlfriend, Emily, used to watch *Sex & the City* over and over like I watched *Scrubs*. I kicked myself for not joining her now. Maybe I would have known more.

I found Central Park on the map and drove there, winding my way through the streets until the green expanse spilled out before me. I pulled my mountain bike off the back of the Greyhawk and took it for a spin through the park. I found only overgrown weeds and fallen trees, no signs of human life. It felt good to ride again, though.

I drove to Times Square. It was hauntingly empty. There were leaves and papers blown in from who-knows-where in the gutters. The myriad neon signs were dark and dusty. The Square felt melancholy, as though it missed the constant hustle and bustle.

I drove to the Empire State Building. I had no desire to see the observation deck, though; I was worried about what I might find up there. Maybe someday I would regret that, but I did not want to find another Charles Spangler.

The city streets were in bad shape. Many of them were lined haphazardly with cars. People had parked cars on the sidewalk, in the outer lanes of four-lane streets. I had to K-turn my RV a couple of times to get out of a street that was blocked by abandoned cars. I got lost a few times. One road was blocked, I took another, that road didn't let me get where I thought I would get. I was getting frustrated and angry. I missed the open, empty highways. I missed the peaceful country roads. If I was this pissed with zero traffic, I fully understood why New Yorkers were considered angry people.

I pulled off the road underneath an overpass bridge to stop for the night. The area underneath the overpass was congested with abandoned cars. The RV would not stand out there. It was camouflaged from potential passing eyes. I pulled the RV into a tight spot next to a rusty school bus that had a bad homemade paint job, sky blue with the words "NY SuperTaxi" on the side in white. The sky was getting dark. Ensconced inside the maze of monolithic darkened towers, I couldn't see the sun to tell the time of day. I killed the engine and quickly pulled all my curtains. In the twilight, I left the RV to perform my nightly ablutions and returned to eat dinner. I ate prepackaged, simple food that didn't need cooking and drank a couple of bottles of water. Fester ate his cat food crouching on the floor near me, and then he joined me at the table, flopping on his side and stretching his paws toward me playfully. I rubbed his head and he purred. Fester was a loud purring cat. When he really wanted to purr, he sounded like someone trying to crank-start a Model A. While he was purring, I realized something else was blending into his purr, something outside the confines of the RV. I cocked my head and listened. It was an engine. I could hear a car engine.

I froze. I had to assess the situation. What was I hearing? Friend or foe? Where was it coming from? I shut off the lantern on the table and the RV plunged into darkness. Fester protested the end of head rubs with an annoyed meow, but he wasn't one to hold a grudge. He rolled to his feet and retreated to the upper bunk. I like to believe he sensed something was up.

I grabbed my handgun from the holster hanging near the door and crept out into the darkness. I held my breath. I stepped lightly, moving toward the street by slipping behind positions of cover. In the distance, I could hear the distinctive, unmistakable sound of a car engine.

I crouched down behind a dusty, rusty car, one of those big, boat-like 70's-style ragtop sedans. Headlights were illuminating the buildings a few blocks down. I waited, and eventually a large Jeep came around the corner. The engine sounded a little ragged, but it was still moving. The top was off the Jeep and I could see four people riding in it. Four! My first instinct was to jump out and flag them down, but I didn't. Something felt wrong. The hair on the back of my neck raised. I got goosebumps. Something in the lizard-brain survival-at-all-costs section of my head said, *Don't. Stay down.*

I trusted my gut, and stayed very low. The Jeep passed. There were four men of various ages. They each carried a large gun. They looked rough, tough, hardened. The three men who weren't driving were looking up, scanning the windows of buildings, probably looking for the tell-tale signs of flashlights or lanterns. They didn't see me. I didn't know what they were doing or why they were doing it, but everything in my body told me to hide, to get away from them. Everything about them told me nothing good would happen if they found me. The Jeep rolled down the street. I tasted exhaust. It rolled around a corner and out of view. I stayed crouched and hidden until the noise of the engine faded to silence.

Now I was given an interesting quandary: I knew for certain people still lived in the city, but did I really want to go to those people? How could I be certain they were good people? Could I be sure they wouldn't kill me and take my supplies? Worse, what if they beat me and enslaved me? What if they just locked me in a cell and left me to starve to death? I had no idea what rules would apply to existing communities in this post-Flu world. I had so desperately wanted to find people, but now that I had, it was time to question whether or not that was what I really wanted. The four men in the Jeep were all alpha-male looking dudes. They held their guns easily, like they'd known weapons well before the Flu wiped out society. I was the opposite of that. I was an awkward boy, barely eighteen, and a pacifist at heart. Even when I wrestled, my favorite part was the end of the match. Hug the guy you just fought and congratulate him if he beat you. No hard feelings, my friend. Well done, you. These guys were different. They were not my type of people.

All this only served to enhance the fear I battled constantly. Why was I so scared of everything? In all the books I'd ever read, the heroes were always the type who were able to rise above their fears. They would stare a dragon in the eye or make the suicide charge into the swords of the oncoming army. They would stand on the deck of a wind-sheared, madly tilting ship and scream curses at Poseidon himself. I wasn't one of those guys. It made me mad. All the hours I spent reading those books, I always wanted to be the hero of the story. I wanted to be the one who pulled the enchanted sword from the stone and ruled a nation. Now, cowering beneath the quarter-panel of an Impala, I realized that I wasn't even in the hero's entourage. I wasn't the plucky comic relief or the strong, silent best friend who had the hero's back. I was a minor character, at best. A two-chapter character, long forgotten by story's end. I was an armorer's apprentice who stayed back in town, married a horrible woman, and hated myself forever. I wanted to rage at my own weakness. I hated myself for it. I was a coward, and I couldn't even bullshit myself into believing otherwise.

I resolved to go back to the RV, get as much of a night's sleep as I could, and then get on the road heading south again before the men in the Jeep discovered that I was in their territory. Being alone forever wouldn't be too bad, I told myself. I could learn to enjoy it.

Because I didn't hear any noise in the vicinity, I didn't crouch and move from cover-to-cover like I had when I'd heard the Jeep. I just strolled relying on the darkness and the abandoned cars under the overpass to hide me, sidearm held lazily in my right hand. This was a mistake, I quickly learned. Never assume you're alone in the city, even after the viral apocalypse.

"Get on your face!"

I had not been prepared to hear another person's voice, and certainly not one shouting commands at me from somewhere nearby. I froze, raising my arms. The voice reverberated off the cars and the concrete of the overpass. I couldn't tell from what direction it was coming.

"Get down! Put your face to the pavement. Now!"

The voice was female. Had to be. She was trying to sound gruff and male, but I could tell it was a woman. I knelt on the ground, and then lay flat.

"Get rid of the gun."

I had no choice, at that point. I could not start wildly shooting. I didn't know where the voice was coming from, for starters, and I certainly did not want to alert the guys in the Jeep by firing a gun. I slid the handgun away from me. I heard footsteps off to my left. I craned my neck around to see who was approaching. I could make out the shape of someone in the darkness. Definitely female. Short, curvy hips, and long hair in a ponytail.

She walked over and picked up my gun, slipping it into the back of her cut-off jeans shorts. She had a shotgun cradled in her right arm. "You got anything else on you? And I swear, if you make a stupid joke about your penis, I will end you right here and right now."

I shook my head. "Not a thing. Honest."

"You sure?"

I was wearing a sleeveless, heather gray t-shirt and a pair of black basketball shorts. What else would I be carrying? "Positive."

She leaned back against a car. "You're real lucky those guys didn't see you."

"Why?"

"You're not from New York, are you? Outsider? You sound like you're from Chicago." She leaned back against a nearby SUV, shotgun held in front of her. She wasn't pointing it at me, but she could have spun it and gunned me down before I could have gotten to my knees. I stayed on the ground.

"I'm from near Madison, Wisconsin."

"Close enough," she said. "To me, that's Chicago."

I was not about to argue with her over a matter of two hundred miles. "How many people are still alive here?"

"Too many for my tastes." She spat on the ground. "The Big Apple has survivors. I've been able to count at least twenty since television went dark. There are more, though. I don't know how many more. Those guys in the Jeep call themselves 'Patriots.' They say they're trying to rebuild America, but they're really just ransacking peoples' private supply stashes and trying to find people they can enslave to do scut work for them. Bad dudes. I've had a couple of run-ins with them. Barely escaped both times. I just try to stay out of their way, stay hidden. You should do likewise."

I risked pushing myself up a little so I could better see her. Her face was obscured in shadow, but I could see she was wearing hiking boots that showed the creases and shiny leather that came with a lot of use. She held the shotgun in the crook of her arm. It wasn't pointed at me. Her fingers were nowhere near the trigger guard. That let me relax a little. It meant she did not intend to shoot me. I feel that not shooting each other is always a good basis on which to begin a friendship.

"What's your name?" she said.

"Twist."

"That's a stupid name."

"Nickname. My real name is Barnabas."

"That's even worse."

"Yeah. My mom really loved that old *Dark Shadows* soap when she was younger. It's not the most practical of names."

"Got a last name?"

"I do, but does it matter anymore? Just Twist is fine, isn't it? Are you going to confuse me with all the other Twists you know?" There was a silence after that. I feared she took my response as being too sarcastic. I had to change my tone. "What's your name?" I asked. When she hesitated, I said, "It's just a name. Make it hard to be friends if we don't exchange names."

"You think we're gonna be friends?"

"I'm hopeful. I could use some friends."

There was another long hesitation. Finally she said, "Ren. Renata, actually, but people call me Ren." She moved back a few feet and gestured with the barrel of her shotgun. "Stand up. Don't try anything, though. If you even think about moving toward me, I'll cut you down."

"Fair enough." I stood. I was not scared at that moment, though. I was staring down the night-black barrel of a police-style Remington 870, but I didn't think for a second she'd use it on me. I think it was the tone of her voice. She sounded rational. She wasn't scared of me. She wasn't showing any fear, herself.

She started to circle me. "How old are you?"

"Eighteen." I didn't like her being behind me, but I didn't have much control of the situation at that moment.

"You came here from Wisconsin? How'd you get here?"

"Drove."

"You got a working car?"

"I did." I lied. I didn't need her stealing the RV out from under me. "Broke down in Newark. I walked here."

Ren whistled through her teeth. "That's a helluva walk."

"Didn't have much choice, did I?"

"I would have found a bike somewhere."

"Wise."

"Anyone else with you?"

On this, I told the truth: "Until today, I'd found three living people. All of them are now dead. One was killed by someone else. That someone else died from injuries he'd given her. One died from cancer shortly after I found him."

Renata stopped circling. "Is it that bad out there? I mean, how many people are still alive, you think?"

"Not many, sadly." I told her about exploring most of Wisconsin, Minneapolis, Chicago, and northeast Iowa. I told her about driving across Indiana, Ohio, and Pennsylvania and coming up snake-eyes. I heard her lean on a car behind me.

"Damn." That was all she said.

We were both quiet for a long time. I broke the silence. "How about you? Have you been in New York the whole time?"

She cleared her throat. "Yeah. Brooklyn born and raised. When the Flu really got bad, I was sort of conscripted into the hospital where my sister was a nurse. I watched a lot of people die. I just kept hoping it was better in other states, though. I thought New York was just bad because everyone is so close together, you know?"

"Yeah. I thought the countryside would have been better because people were so spread out. Flu took them out just as fast as it killed people in the city. It was hyper-contagious." I heard her sniff behind me, the sort of sniff of someone trying not to cry.

"So that's it, then. The Flu was global. If it was the same overseas as here, then the world is dead."

"Looks that way." I lowered my hands. My shoulders had started to ache.

A low droning rose in the distance. The Jeep was returning. I spun around to face Renata. She was looking toward the sound of the engine. "We need to hide," she said. "C'mon."

Ren started to run. I followed. She led me to a hole in a wire fence beneath the overpass. We slipped through it and ran across a street to the remnants of an old bar, the kind of neighborhood place that would have been ignored by tourists. The door was unlocked and Renata slipped inside. The bar still clung to that stale beer smell for which old bars were famous. The bottle racks inside the bar were picked clean, not even a dusty jar of pickled pearl onions remained. "The Patriots hit this place months ago. I moved in after they left it. I knew it was safe because they probably wouldn't be back."

Ren led me to a back room. The back room had a door that led to a narrow stairway. The stairway led to a tiny apartment above the bar. The flat was stark, but it had an actual fireplace. There were two windows facing the street. They were both blocked off with thick blankets to prevent anyone on the street from seeing any sort of light from behind them. There was a queen-sized mattress on the floor in one corner, a plush leather chair in another. Near the hearth was a rather eclectic pile of things to burn, mostly broken furniture and old pallet slats, none of it cordwood. There was a supply of canned food, bottled water, toilet paper, and other necessities. Clothes were scattered around the apartment. There was a small, square balcony outside of a narrow door next to the bathroom. On that balcony, Ren had a bunch of five-gallon plastic paint buckets grouped in a square. "My water collection system," she said. "It was easier in the winter when it snowed a lot. This summer has been pretty dry. Water is starting to get sparse. I could drink water out of the East River, but I'm not *that* desperate, yet."

I looked around at her place. It was small and spartan. My digs at the library had been pretty cushy in comparison. "It's nice." It was a lie, but a tactical lie. She knew it wasn't great. She didn't need me reminding her.

"Can I trust you?" she said. "You seem like a nice guy and all, but I need to know you're not going to try anything stupid." She still had the shotgun in her hands and my handgun in her pants.

"Can I trust you?" I countered. "You're the one with the guns, right now. I honestly mean you no harm. I'm just making my way south to start to build a new life."

We stood in the dark looking at each other. Eventually she sighed and put the shotgun in a corner of the little apartment. "Damned thing wasn't even loaded, anyhow." She pulled the revolver out of her pants and set it on the mantel over the fireplace. "Mind if we just keep it there for a while?"

"If it makes you feel better."

The sound of the Jeep was coming closer. Renata crept to the window and pulled back a corner of blanket. I crept to the other window and pulled the other blanket, peering out through just a crack of space. The Jeep was rolling down the street where I'd first seen it. I couldn't see the Jeep itself, but I could see the illumination of the headlights and hear the engine. When the Jeep rolled out of sight and out of range of hearing the engine, Ren relaxed visibly. Her shoulders slumped with relief.

She knelt next to the fire and lit a few scraps of newsprint for tinder. In a moment, she'd coaxed the flames to light into some old chunks of wood that looked like they'd once been part of a hardwood bureau. It was warm and stuffy in the apartment, but the fire was needed to cook a can of soup. "It's not much," she said.

"It's how we live now." I sat in the leather chair. The fire lit her face, and I could see what she looked like for the first time. She was pretty. Her hair was brown, naturally wavy; it was thick, too. She looked Latina. She had dark eyes and high cheekbones. Her face was smeared with grime, but it only served to make her look rugged and alive.

When the soup was ready, she split the contents of the pot, ladling them into Styrofoam bowls. She jabbed a plastic spoon into one and held it out for me. "Chili," she said. "Before the Flu, I was one of those annoying-ass college student vegan types for a couple of years, the kind that lectured everyone about how good it was to be vegan. Took me exactly four days to abandon that lifestyle after the final week of the Flu."

"What caused you to do it?"

"You know we have coyotes in New York?"

I shook my head; I hadn't known that, but I did not doubt it. I knew they were hardy little critters. I'd seen them on rare occasions out in the countryside in Wisconsin, and I knew they had started to move into the outer edges of Madison, even well before the Flu. They were like canine cockroaches. They would survive, no matter what it took to do so.

"Well, we did. We do," she corrected. "I was out picking apart a head of wilting lettuce to eat, and I saw one of the little buggers at the end of the street. He was munching on a discarded crust of pizza, happy as a lark. I realized that stupid coyote was the perfect symbol of my future. I decided that my future was going to be as a scavenger. Scavengers don't get to be choosy. They certainly don't need to stand on a moral high ground."

"That's true," I said. "I've done more than my own fair share of scavenging."

Ren arched an eyebrow. "A fellow master of the canned goods, I see. What's your favorite thing to eat?"

"Chef Boyardee lasagna. Love it."

Ren smiled. "Those are good. I like pumpkin pie Pop Tarts. Hard to find them, especially since the Flu hit in May, but when I do—watch out. I will eat the entire box in a single sitting."

We lapsed into silence again. I was finding Renata a lot harder to talk to than Doug had been. There was a lot of quiet in the room. Doug's house had been silent, but out on his patio, we'd talked easily. I ate the can of chili she'd cooked for me. "You know what I miss most?" She looked at me expectantly. I said, "Pizza and garlic cheese bread."

Her eyes lit up, and she laughed. "Oh, man. You are not kidding. Even when I was in my most hardcore vegan phase, I would still sneak garlic cheese bread. I used to take a bus halfway across town to go to this little Italian place just to have garlic cheese bread where none of my vegan friends might see me. I used to get so embarrassed about having it, too. Stupid, I know. It was my own private Ortolan."

I didn't know what an Ortolan was, but I didn't want her to think I was dumb, so I just nodded. I made a mental note to look it up next time I found a library. (*Turns out, it is a little bird that French chefs force-feed and roast whole, and then the diner would eat it whole—feet, beak, and all. It was said that it was such a despicable and extravagant act, one should shield their face from God with a napkin while one does it. So…Renata has brains. I was a little intimidated. Scratch that—a lot intimidated.*)

Renata kicked off her boots and sat cross-legged on her bed, her back against the wall. "Did you think it'd be like this?"

"No." I had never even thought about how life would be *after* the Flu. I'd fully expected to die during the Flu, and then when I realized I wasn't going to die, I'd spent every waking moment just surviving. I had no expectations of life after the Flu in the least. I lived day-to-day, while trying to plan for an uncertain future as best I could.

Ren said, "Ever watch any of those apocalypse shows on TV?"

"Not really, no. I liked comedies and video games."

Renata yawned and stretched. "I used to watch a couple. I liked how the survivors all banded together and helped each other survive. When I knew I wasn't going to die, that's what I tried to do. My sister, Elena, and I both survived. So did my little brother, Carlos. He had pretty bad cystic fibrosis, though. Without the ability to get him on his treatments, he didn't last."

"I'm sorry."

She shrugged. "Ain't that a bitch? He survives the Flu just fine, but a stupid lung disease kills him two months later. Elena and I dug a grave for him and our parents in the cemetery near our house. Took us almost a week to dig out three graves. Blisters for days." Ren laughed at the memory. "My hands hurt so bad, man. I didn't think they'd ever be normal again."

"Where's your sister now?"

Ren didn't reply. I had an inkling of what happened. Ren took a deep breath. "Patriots got her. Found her scavenging and tried to take her back to their little fortress. I was up on a roof looking for an entrance to an apartment. I heard her screaming, and then she somehow pulled her gun and shot and killed one of them. The other two responded in kind to her. I saw her die on the sidewalk."

"I'm sorry." Condolences for something like that felt hollow, but it was the only thing I could think to say.

Ren shrugged. "Thanks, but it is better that way. I'd hate to think about what those misogynist assholes might have done to her if she was still alive. I know that other women survived the Flu, but I have never, ever seen them out with Patriot patrols. A few months ago, I run into this dude while I was combing through an office building, right? I got the drop on him, but he turns out to be an okay dude. He tells me he's been spying on the Patriot encampment for weeks. Says he's seen women in the encampment. Some are washing clothes. Some are cooking. Some are cleaning. The guy tells me that the Patriots want to 'breed a new America.' Sounds like a code word for rape to me. There are men with guns guarding the encampment at all times, and if one of the women stops doing whatever they're told or tries to rebel, they die." Ren was quiet for a moment, and then she said, "Some of them figure it's better to die, and they take that bus, you know?" Renata stopped talking. She looked down at her hands. In the firelight, I could see scars and callouses. She was a fighter. A survivor.

I didn't know how to respond.

"Why do men think they can just do that?"

I didn't know how to respond to that, either. "I don't know." I was a weak representative for my gender.

"Elena was smart. She was an ER nurse. She was tough. It sounds sick, but I'm glad they killed her. She didn't deserve to be a slave. She would have hated it." After a moment, she shook off thoughts of her sister. "What about you? Brothers? Sisters?"

"Only child," I said. "Buried my parents and my girlfriend after they died."

"You said you were going south. Why?"

"Because I spent a winter in Wisconsin and decided I did not want to do that again. Too cold. Too brutal."

"But why the South?" Ren turned to face me. "It's so far away. And hot."

"You never thought about leaving New York?"

"No. Not once. It's my home, you know? It's where I was born." Ren got up from her bed and went to the window. She pulled back the curtain and what little moonlight there was outside helped illuminate the apartment. "It ain't great, but I understand it. It makes sense to me."

"You could probably survive here for years. Plenty of food, plenty for places to scavenge. Plenty of things to burn for heat. Just stay away from the Patriots."

"Yeah. That's what I figured." Ren dropped the blanket. The light from the fire became our sole source of light again, rich, yellow-and-orange tones. "That's what I was planning to do, anyhow."

"But then what?"

Ren squinted at me. "Then what? What do you mean?"

I shrugged. I gestured at the canned food. "You're going to get tired of canned food, aren't you? In the south, there will be fresh food. Fruit trees. Fresh game animals. Ocean fish. River fish."

"I got river and ocean fish here," Ren said defensively.

"You actually want to eat what you pull out of the rivers around here?"

Ren shrugged, then shook her head. "Nah. The East River is really gross. I found a couple of bodies floating in it last year. Figured that people probably were dying of the Flu and chose to bail off the Brooklyn Bridge."

"The South will be warm," I said. "That's my main reason for going. It took a lot of wood to get through a single Wisconsin winter. Down south, I won't have to fear freezing to death. There will be plenty of food in the South, too. All kinds of animals and farmland. Orchards. It just seemed to me that if I was going to live someplace for the rest of my life, I should live someplace where it was warm and food would be plentiful, and then I could figure the rest out as I went along."

There was a silence, and then Ren walked toward me. She looked at me with serious eyes. "Can I go with you?"

CHAPTER NINE

The President of the United States of America

I wasn't about to tell someone who did not shoot me or club me to death when she had the chance that I wouldn't let her come with me. I needed friends. I needed friends badly. I did not know for certain if I could trust Renata; after all, she did hold a gun on me. An empty gun, sure, but a gun nonetheless. I would have done the same thing in her position, though.

I held back the knowledge of my RV. I didn't want her to decide to clobber me in the middle of the night and steal it. I had no desire to face off with the so-called 'Patriots.' I wanted to get free and clear of New York as fast as possible. I told her she could come with me. When I said it aloud, I realized I wasn't just being nice. I really wanted her to come with me.

Turns out, Renata was not sure she could trust me, either. After we talked about the South for a while, she said, "I'm going to bed. If we're going to leave New York, we need to go early. The Patriots tend to sleep late. The first couple hours after dawn are pretty safe for moving around the city. Meet me under the overpass tomorrow morning where we found each other, okay? Be there early."

I didn't blame her for being cautious. I asked for my gun back. She hesitated. "If I give you this back, do you promise not to shoot me?"

I promised. It was a major moment of trust-building between us. She held it out, I took it back, and then I ejected the magazine and popped the single bullet out of the chamber, just to show her that I wasn't going to use it against her. "Friends?" I said. I held out my hand.

"Friends." She shook my hand. I'd like to say something like *her touch sent electric shocks up my arm, and our eyes met*. If there's something that my journals lack, it's love scenes. Unfortunately, if I'm completely honest with you, at that moment there was no love, only a tentative friendship, a sincere bond between two people who each desperately needed a friend and someone to trust.

She walked me to the door of the bar and locked it behind me. There were three large deadbolts in the door. No one was getting through that door without hitting it with a truck. Once outside, I reloaded my gun. I decided to play it safe and took a roundabout path back to the RV. I went north for six blocks, ducked down an alley, and climbed a fire escape just to make sure she wasn't trailing me with a group of armed goons waiting to take whatever supplies I had. I even considered just sleeping on a roof. It was a nice, warm night. It was the sort of judgment call that I hated to make. If she was in cahoots with others, I could be foiling their plans. If she was alone, I was just making myself miserable for nothing. I waited on the roof for maybe an hour. I had no idea what time it was. Easily after midnight, probably closer to dawn than midnight. I listened for engines, voices, footsteps, for anything. I heard nothing but wind, crickets, and the occasional distant bark or howl of stray dogs. Eventually, I decided to trust that Ren was as alone as I was, and I went back to the RV.

I slipped in the side door of the Greyhawk. I retreated to the back bedroom with my shotgun and semi-auto pistol, and I lay down on the bed, shotgun barrel pointed toward the narrow door. I didn't sleep, though. I laid awake and listened to the night, my heart in my throat, until dawn.

Was I doing the right thing? I couldn't know. I wouldn't know. Renata had given me no reason to doubt her, but I didn't know her. I had no way of seeing down the road, as it were. Was she using me? Would she steal my RV later on? Could I trust her? In everything, there comes a time in every relationship where both parties have to make a leap of faith. Sometimes, it comes back to bite one of the parties in the ass, and sometimes it pays off for both parties. I had to hope this was one of those times where it was the latter.

Minutes after dawn broke, I was crouched low behind an old delivery truck. All four tires on the thing were flat as crepes. I positioned myself so that I could see clearly in the direction of Ren's bar. I wanted to be able to see her approaching. I had a foil-wrapped breakfast bar in my hand, but no desire to eat it. I only brought it in case Renata was late, and I got bored. I also had my shotgun on my shoulder on a sling. I wasn't going to draw it unless necessary, and I wanted to trust in Renata, but I couldn't risk losing my RV now. If she tried to rob me of it, I'd be stuck in New York. I didn't think I would be able to get another vehicle running, so that left trying to walk or bicycle all the way to the South.

I didn't have to wait long. Ren showed up a few minutes later. She was carrying a large duffel, something like a hockey bag, and the police-issue shotgun. She had her head on a swivel, scanning the cars for trouble. When she ducked under the chain-fence at the edge of the overpass, she paused and squinted into the shadows. She looked cleaner than she did the night before, like she'd bathed herself since then. She was wearing different clothes, a pair of green cargo-style Capri pants and an Iron Maiden concert t-shirt. She was wearing the hiking boots she'd worn the previous night.

Leap of faith. Ignore the fear. Point of no return. I took a deep breath and made a conscious choice to trust Renata. I stood up and walked around the corner of the delivery truck. "Over here!" I called. The sound of my voice echoed off the concrete overhead. It was very loud against the stillness of a summer morning.

Ren jumped when she heard my voice, but when she spotted me, I saw her visibly relax. She hustled through the maze of cars. "I was worried you might have left without me."

"Nope. I waited." I tried to give a genuine smile. I don't know if it worked. I was never good at smiling. Every photograph I've ever taken where I had to force a smile ends up with me looking slightly constipated. "Are you ready to go?"

Ren held up the bag and the shotgun. "This is all I need, I guess. Anything else, we can pick up on our way south. Do you want to stop and try to find some food? I know plenty of buildings that no one has gotten into, yet."

"I've got food. C'mon." I started to walk toward the RV.

"Wait." Ren didn't follow. "Can we talk for just a minute?"

"Sure," I said. I turned to face her.

Ren bit her lip. She looked me up and down. "You're not a psycho or anything, are you?"

"What do you mean?" I knew what she meant. I was thinking the same things about her.

"Like, you're not a rapist or a murderer, are you?"

I shook my head. "No, not in the least. I'm just a guy from Wisconsin who didn't get to die when the rest of the world did."

"Wisconsin doesn't have the best reputation when it comes to serial killers, you know."

"That's true, but I'm not one. Honest." I held up my right hand in a Cub Scout salute.

Ren bit her lower lip. "We're going to be together for a long time, aren't we?"

I nodded. "If neither of us ends up being a psycho, I guess. I need a friend. *We*," I corrected myself, "need friends."

"I'm putting a lot of trust in you. You seem like an okay guy. Just...don't disappoint me, right?"

"I'll try not to," I said.

"Just be honest with me, okay?" She smiled and rolled her eyes. "Christ, this sounds like we're starting to date or something."

"In a way, we are," I said. "It's a partnership, right? We don't know what else is out there, or who else is out there. We have to look out for each other. I get your back, you get mine."

"Trust is earned, though." She adjusted the hockey bag and slung it over her shoulder.

She had a point. I said, "I will try to earn your trust. You try to earn mine."

She looked me up and down again. "Deal. Now, let's go, eh? We got a long way to walk. Maybe we can find some bikes?"

"I can do you one better than that." We walked to the RV. I held out an arm toward it. "We travel in style."

Ren's mouth dropped open. "Oh, my god. That's amazing. It runs? I thought you said it broke down?"

"I didn't know you last night. I was protecting myself."

Ren approached the RV and pulled the side door. "Oh, you have a kitty!"

In that moment, she sounded like a teenage girl, her voice lost any grit or edge. She clambered into the Greyhawk, dropped her bag and gun, and scooped Fester into her arms. Attention hog that he is, he let her hold him, instantly going into super-purr mode. She buried her face into the fur of his neck. "Oh, what a sweetie."

"His name is Fester." I pulled the curtains in the cab and climbed into the driver's seat.

"Like, Fester Addams?"

"Exactly like."

"I love him." Ren cradled the cat in her arms belly-up like a baby. When I did that to him, he would flip himself around and climb up my chest to perch his front paws on my shoulder. When she did it, he purred louder, the furry traitor.

I started the RV, pulled back to the street, and slapped it in drive. I had no desire to stay in New York any longer. I took the Brooklyn Bridge back to New Jersey as fast as I could. The tunnels would have been better, less chance of being seen, but the bridge was faster. I was operating on what Ren had said about the Patriots sleeping late.

Ren slipped through the gap between the seats and plopped into the passenger seat. She was still holding her weapon. "Look! I'm riding shotgun! Literally!" She seemed different than she had the night before, more alive, more vibrant. I hoped it was because she was feeling good about finding someone alive, someone whom she might learn to trust. That's what I was feeling, too. After a year of near isolation, it was surreal to turn my head and see an actual, living, breathing person in the RV next to me.

After a few moments of riding shotgun, she hopped up and went into the back of the RV. She started poking through the drawers and cupboards. "I hope you don't mind. I just wanted to see what sort of supplies you have."

"I don't mind," I said. "When I stop for gas, I usually hit up any stores or shops in the area and scavenge."

"Smart thinking." Ren found a box of Rice Krispies Treats. "Mind if I have one?"

"Ren, this is your home now, too. Just help yourself. Don't even ask." I glanced over my shoulder. She was smiling.

"You mean that?"

"Partners, right? We ride together. What's mine is yours."

Ren came back to the passenger seat with her snack. She put her bare feet on the dash. "What's the plan, boss?" She unwrapped the treat and took a bite. Her eyes rolled upward with joy. "I love these things."

I shrugged. "I guess I was just going to continue doing what I was going to do, even if I hadn't found anyone else. I was going to head down to Washington D.C. If anyone is still alive, I have a feeling they would go there. New York and D.C. were my two likeliest scenarios for finding people. Oh, and Disney World. On the way, I find small towns and look for signs of life."

"Wouldn't major cities give better odds?"

"Yes, and no. Statistically speaking, I think they would. But I was in a small town, and I went through all the major cities in Wisconsin and didn't find a single person. I've been through Chicago and Minneapolis, and I didn't find anyone. I might have missed them. In a small town, it's easier to find someone if they're still alive, I guess. Fewer places to hide, more chances to cross paths."

Ren considered that and bobbed her head. "Makes sense, I suppose."

We lapsed into silence and I found the highway heading south through New Jersey. When Ren was able to get out of her microcosm of New York City, she was able to see the desolation and entropy of the rest of the country. She gave a low whistle as we hit an elevated section of the highway and she was able to look down and see some of the suburbs with their overgrown lawns, fallen tree branches, and houses with siding coming off them in sheets. "Looks rough out there."

"It is." I wanted to hold back, but I figured she knew already. "Almost all of those houses have decaying bodies in them."

"Just like the apartments in Brooklyn," Ren said. "I was in the hospital, sort of being a CNA to help out my sister. I cleaned up a lot of puke, changed a lot of bed sheets. Then, there were just too many people. People lying on beds, slumped in chairs, sitting on the floors, lying on the floors. People everywhere. And they started dying, right? I couldn't….we, my sister and me, we couldn't do nothing, man. They just died. All the doctors, all the nurses, everyone. Toward the end, we just went home. We'd been working for days. There wasn't nothing else could be done. We just went home because Carlos came in and said our parents were gone. We had to abandon people. We just left them to die. I still feel horrible about it, but there wasn't any other choice."

"I can't imagine," I told her. I'd been sequestered in my family's house watching my parents die.

"In the first couple days, Elena, Carlos, and I, we had to break into our neighbors' places to find food, water, and wood to burn. We found them lying in their beds, on the couches. It was tragic. Some of them, their pets were dead. Some, the pets were still alive and we released them to the wild. What else could we do, you know?"

"I did the same thing. Well, as much as I could."

Ren looked out the window at garbage on the side of the road. She heaved a heavy sigh. "I'm tired of death, man."

Washington D.C. looked like a war zone. I don't know what happened after television went dark midway through the third week of the Flu, but it was apparently not good. Many buildings were destroyed around the outskirts of town. In the distance, I could see a chunk of the Washington Monument was missing, like someone had hacked at it with a gigantic ax. The obelisk was still standing, but it didn't look structurally safe. Tanks, honest-to-god Army tanks littered the streets. The cold, charred wreckage of a fighter jet was scattered around the soot-black, crumbled remains of the apartment building it hit when it crashed. There were remnants of bodies in the streets, skulls with spines still attached, pelvic bones with femurs lying nearby. The capitol city looked cold and dark, even with a sky full of sunshine.

"What the hell went down here?" Ren was leaning forward in the cab, her face almost pressed to the front windshield. "Last I saw, everything in the capitol was copacetic, you know?"

The last time I'd seen Washington on TV, the president had been telling us that everything in the country was being taken offline. He was admitting that the Flu was unstoppable. He'd called it the "end of Mankind." His face was stern and stoic. Presidential. He'd wished any who might survive good luck, and God bless. He asked any who might survive to rebuild the country and remember the principles for which America has always stood. Then, he got into *Marine 1* and helicoptered away from the White House, probably to the secret base in Virginia to see if he could survive the Flu with the most advanced medical treatment that could be found.

"What do you think happened?" Ren pointed toward a toppled apartment building. "Looks like a war happened."

"Might have. Probably once the president abandoned the White House, anyone still alive got mad that he was abandoning us. Maybe a mob mobilized against the White House. Maybe some foreign enemy attacked us?" That seemed unlikely. All the tanks were US Army. I didn't know, though. Riots or attacks were the only likely possibilities.

Ren had my book of maps spread out on her lap. She directed me through the streets of the capitol to the White House. There, we saw more evidence that there had been some sort of disturbance. A tank had been driven through the tall iron fence in front of the White House and was now a permanent monument on the lawn. There were more skeletal bodies on the roads and the sidewalks. Neither Ren nor I could speak. Everywhere we looked were the remnants of chaos.

Ren sniffed. "Some of the neighborhoods where I lived in Brooklyn, some of the survivors went crazy with the looting during the second and third week. There were a lot of fights, gunshots. Pure panic. Think this is something like that?"

I couldn't tell her, so I just shrugged. I knew some looting had gone down around Madison. I think it was just a natural response to impending death. Mostly, it'd been pharmacies and gun stores that had taken the brunt of the looting. People had been desperate for any sort of cure, and should they survive, they were desperate for weapons to protect themselves from any possible roving bands of marauders.

"Pull over here." Ren pointed to a clear spot on the sidewalk in front of the south face of the White House. I did as she asked. We got ready to explore. I showed her my ruck with tools. I told her how I equipped to scavenge. She raised her eyebrows. "You were way more prepared for this crap than I was."

"I had more time to prepare. I also didn't have to contend with the Patriots."

"True enough." She held up her shotgun. "You got anything that will go in here?"

"Probably," I said. I had no idea if I did or not. I'm not a gun guy. I figured out most of what worked and what didn't by reading guides. I figured most shotgun ammo was similar, though. I handed her a box of the same stuff I was putting in my shotgun, and she loaded it. The shells look like they fit. I looked like I knew what I was doing. I did not know for certain if they would work, but we would only have to worry about that if we needed to shoot the thing.

We walked through the fallen gate toward the White House. We started out a few feet apart, but Ren drifted to her right, away from me. "Stay far away," she said. "If there's someone with a gun, give him two targets, not one." I figured that was sound advice. We parted, each of us taking one side of the expansive, overgrown lawn.

The White House was impressive, even in entropy. According to history, it had been built to intimidate visiting dignitaries and instill confidence in the American people. Even with the lack of upkeep, it still held true to those ideas. It loomed like a beacon of brilliant white. It was, perhaps, a little more *worn* than any pictures I'd seen of it, but time hadn't started to beat it down yet. The windows, all bullet-proof glass, were lasting a little better than the standard plate-glass in most homes.

I kept scanning the roof. I know that before the Flu, Secret Service snipers would sit on the roof, ready to take down any encroaching threat. If we were going to be in danger, I assumed it would be from that. After a year, I doubted that anyone was still in the White House, though. There wasn't anywhere to get supplies nearby. There were better homes with more practical access to wood and food. The White House was too big to maintain, too. Smaller homes were more practical, more viable. I thought about the log cabins of the pioneers; most were the size of a master bedroom in a really nice house. Easier to heat and weatherproof. The White House, the great American icon, was impractical and it was going to rot just like everything else.

We approached the front door. It was open. Ren had her shotgun in her hands. She held a finger to her lips and motioned for me to halt. She slipped in the door like we were sneaking into a building to arrest a serial killer. After a second, I heard her hiss. I peeked in the gap in the door. She was motioning for me to enter. I shoved the door and walked in, shotgun still hanging on my shoulder.

"Really, dude?" Ren shouldered her own weapon. She gave me a look of disgust. "We could have gone all Serpico on this place, secret agent-style."

"Just listen for a second." I craned my neck to listen to the stillness in the house. "You hear anything that would suggest anyone is here?"

Ren listened and shook her head. "Quiet."

"Do you smell death?" I inhaled. There was a slight funk. Someone had died in the Whitehouse, maybe a couple of people. Not many, though.

"I think so."

I was pretty confident the White House was empty. "Anyone here?" I shouted just enough for my voice to carry to adjacent rooms. I didn't want to scream out my presence, but a small announcement felt safe. No one responded. I shrugged at Ren. "Empty."

We walked through the initial foyer to the reception room, a large, round room where visitors would have been greeted. That led to the Center Hall, a wide corridor that ran the length of the house. I tilted my head toward the left hallway. "Let's see what we can see."

In moments, it was clear that what we could see wasn't great. The White House had been ransacked. Plates were smashed, portraits were torn from the walls, holes had been kicked in the walls. It looked like someone had a major rager and the old building couldn't keep up with the party. It was more damage than one person could have done. It had to have been a mob of some sort. We meandered to the East Wing where the President and his family would have lived. It was trashed out, as well. There were three stories above ground, a basement, and a subbasement. As we walked through the house, it became more and more evident that no one was there. People had lived there for a time, though. We found evidence of food wrappers, clothes, and dried human waste, as gross as that sounds. People had been content to turn the corners of rooms into private latrines.

"I don't think anyone has been here for at least a year," Ren said. "I would have thought people would have come here to live. Resettle the country."

"I guess they did at first." I opened a drawer and poked through a desk in one of the bedrooms.

"Maybe thirty or forty people still alive in New York. About half of them, maybe more came to New York after the Flu was over, though. The first weeks after everyone died, there were only a handful of us roaming New York from what I saw. You said you found at least three others, though they're dead now. Judging from the damage around here, maybe five or six more people. That sound about right?" Ren closed her eyes to do the math. "That's what, let's say fifty people we can be sure are still alive."

"Okay. Let's go with that. If that figure holds true, and we project it throughout the rest of the US, maybe we hit what—two hundred? Two-fifty?"

"Safe estimate," said Ren. She poked through a different drawer, found a solar calculator, and hacked in some numbers. "If that's true, that's like a tiny fraction of the population. If it held true throughout the world, we're looking at something like maybe only six-thousand people still alive in the world, give or take. Six thousand out of what was almost eight billion. That's like what, one ten-millionth of the population or something?"

I knew towns back in Wisconsin that were six thousand people. It was hard to picture one of those little places being the entire world.

Ren fell back into a desk chair. She looked defeated. Her face was slack. The melancholy etched into her expression was unmistakable. "There's no coming back from that, is there? The world is really done, isn't it?"

I didn't know how to answer her. I had the same sentiment. Humanity was over.

We walked through the second story to the West Wing of the White House. The West Wing had survived the anger of an unknown crowd no better than the East Wing. We went to the Oval Office. The door was hanging wide open. At some point, someone had battered it from the frame, probably with a sledgehammer. The door was heavy reinforced steel. The person or people who'd breached the room had to knock the door from its hinges. The wall around the doorframe was wrecked.

The Oval Office looked like pictures I'd seen, except the office had been entirely trashed. The couches in the center of the room had been slashed with knives. Stuffing was everywhere. The pictures on the walls had been ripped down and spray-painted or slashed. The sculptures were shattered on the floor. The chair where the President normally would have sat behind his desk was slashed to ribbons. The desk drawers were all dumped. And, as a crowning glory, someone had left a healthy defecation on the desk, dead center.

"Lovely," Ren said eying the dried pile. "Looks like he had a lot of fiber in his diet."

"I can't believe this place got destroyed like this. I would have wanted to live here or something. Maybe declare myself President of the United States of America. I don't understand the mindset of someone who sees this place and thinks that it needs to be wrecked." I moved to the desk. On the side of the wood, someone had carved *Good-bye America. Good-bye World.*

"Anarchy. True anarchy." Ren flopped on one of the couches. "The country fell. The world fell. Everyone died. No more governments. No more world rulers. It was all done. Why not destroy the symbols of it?"

I crossed to the couch opposite Ren. I sat carefully on the shredded cushions. "I guess I hadn't expected anyone to still be alive here in D.C. If anyone is still alive, they're in that bunker in Virginia."

"Probably. I know the Vice-President was showing signs of the Flu before TV went off. He's dead now; I guarantee it."

"The President looked okay," I said. "That speech before television signed off was pretty good."

"The First Lady didn't. Did you see her nose? It was all red. She had the start of it. If she had it, the Prez was infected, too. That bunker in Virginia is probably a mausoleum now. The only way you and me got through this was dumb luck."

I leaned back on the couch. The cushions did not feel right. It was uncomfortable. "You ever think about why you're still alive? It doesn't seem right, you know? Out of eight billion people, the Flu didn't affect you. You ever remember being sick in your life?"

Renata's eyes looked up and off to the left. "No. I remember being angry at my brother because of his CF. He got to stay home from school a lot, and I never did. Neither did Elena."

"Me too. I used to have to fake sick just to stay home. I'd hold a heating pad to my forehead to fake a fever just so I could stay home and play a new video game or something. I was never sick."

Renata glanced around the Oval Office. "Ever just stop and think, *Why me?*"

"Every second of every day."

"Would have been easier to pull a trigger on myself after my sister died, you know? Less heartache. Less struggle. Less worry."

"Less fear." I said. My voice came out as a whisper.

"Yeah!" Renata said. She leaned forward. "Less fear! I spent too many nights scared to death, scared I might get taken by the Patriots, scared I might starve or freeze. Why are we here, man?"

I couldn't answer her. I was searching for that meaning, myself. I told her about the Indiana preppers, Jim and Nancy. I told her about their supply store and how they left the world with a gun in their garage.

Renata shook her head and gave a weak laugh. "I never watched those prepper TV shows, you know? I figured anything that came down, it was gonna kill me, too. I was expecting nuclear war or maybe zombies. I figured being prepared for an apocalypse was a waste of time, because no one sane would want to keep living after the power grids and sanitation stopped working."

"So why did you keep living?" This is a question I came to terms with in the first days after the end of the Flu. The only answer I could come up with was that I was still living just to spite Nature.

"At first, it was for Carlos. He needed help. After he died, I still had Elena. We had each other. It was almost fun sometimes. We broke into people's places and took what we needed. We stole batteries and played CDs and danced. We broke into stores and took haute couture, you know? We dressed up like fashion models and swam in rich people's pools. It was fun, for a while. But, after she died...I guess I don't know why I'm still alive. Maybe it's because I'm too much of a coward to end it."

"Did you ever...try?"

Renata licked her lips. She looked at her hands. "Once. Had the gun in my mouth, finger on the trigger, but I couldn't find the strength to pull it. I just started crying."

That sounded familiar. "Me too."

"Do you believe we're here for a greater purpose? Like, maybe there is a God and this is His test for us?"

I shrugged. I had no real answers. And even if I did, it felt sort of moot at this point. "I don't know. Maybe. Seems like a pretty extreme test, though. Like, I would have been fine if God would have just let me find a wallet with a thousand dollars in it to see if I would have kept it, or if I would have turned it in. That's probably all the testing I really needed."

Renata laughed. "Yeah. This is like when you went to school expecting a pop quiz and instead the teacher throws a research paper at you."

"I don't miss those," I said.

"Me neither. I'm kind of mad that the Flu didn't hold off for another month, though." Renata held out her thumb and forefinger almost touching. "I was *this* close to getting my B.A. I almost had a degree."

"In what?"

"Nursing. Like my sister." Renata stood up from the couch. "It would have been nice to take that walk and get the paper. I was really looking forward to seeing my dad cry. I was really looking forward to seeing my dad cry. He cried when Elena got hers. Bawled his eyes out during the ceremony. He came to this country from Venezuela when he was sixteen. He never went to school or anything. He just got a job and worked his ass off as a garbage man to provide for us." Ren moved toward the door. She swiped a tear from her eye with her fingers. "I just wanted him to be proud of me, too."

"I'm sure he was proud of you," I said. It was a hollow condolence, but I had to say something.

"Oh, I know he was." Renata's voice steadied. "He told me so before he died. I just really wanted to give him that gift of seeing me in that cap and gown. I wanted him to see me be successful."

There was a Bible on the floor of the Oval Office, a thick, leather-bound version near the desk. I leapt off the couch and grabbed it. "We can give him another gift, how about that?" I held out the Bible. "Renata, how would you like to be sworn in as the President of the United States of America?"

She rolled her eyes. "Stupid. I'm not thirty-five."

"Speaking as the only other human being in Washington D.C., which makes me the senior lawmaker in America, I'm waiving that stipulation. Desperate times call for desperate measures. I just held an emergency election and you won unanimously."

Her eyes narrowed for a second. "What if I become a tyrant dictator?"

"There will be a general election to remove you from office."

"And how will you accomplish that?"

I raised an eyebrow. "Are you ticklish?"

She raised her own eyebrow. "If you try to find out, I'm gonna kick you in the balls."

"That's a yes, then. If you become a tyrant dictator, the people shall tickle you until you relinquish your office."

Ren hesitated. She jutted out her hand. "Deal. Swear me in, man."

I held out the Bible. She put her hand on it. "Repeat after me: I, Renata…"

"I, Renata…"

"Uh…I don't know your last name," I whispered.

She whispered back, "Lameda."

I cleared my throat. "I, Renata Lameda, do solemnly swear to uphold the Constitution of the United States of America."

She repeated my words. "Wasn't there supposed to be something about 'executing the Office of the President of the United States?'"

I looked around at the debris around us. "I think the office has already been executed."

"Good point. I accept your appointment of me as President, so help me God. I look forward to leading this nation into a bleak, unknown future free from corruption and big corporations. I shall hereby be known as the 'Back to Pioneer Times' President."

I tossed the Bible aside and clapped. "I guess we're starting to rebuild America, aren't we?"

She bowed. "Thank you. I agree. I bet one of those Patriot assholes has already thought to declare himself President, though."

"Did he get sworn-in in the Oval Office? I think not. We shall refuse to accept his declaration."

"I agree," said Renata. She picked up her shotgun. "I declare the Patriots enemies of the State, and refuse to acknowledge their sovereignty. As my first official act of office, I declare that Washington D.C. is no longer the capitol of America." She started heading for the door.

"Really? Where's the new capitol?"

She shrugged. "I don't know, yet. Somewhere in the South." She looked over her shoulder at me. "C'mon, Twist. Let's go find a home."

CHAPTER TEN
Long Empty Roads

We left Washington and went south toward Richmond, Virginia. The sun fell low in the sky near Fredericksburg. I pulled off the highway and found a gas station near some woods where we could set up a decent campsite well away from the gas pumps. I started to erect camp, and it quickly became apparent that Renata's camp skills were almost nil. She'd been purely scavenging, living day to day since the Flu. She knew how to light a fire off of newspaper, and only had wood because she'd used an axe to hack up furniture. I had to show her how to hunt down firewood and simple comfort items like camp chairs, which were always available from someone's front porch nearby. I had to show her how to unload the necessary gear from the RV. She was a quick learner, though. She watched me with fascination as I moved around setting up wood in a pyramid shape and starting the fire with dry pine needles as tinder. Instead of a match, I used a magnifying lens that I found in the gas station. It only took a few seconds of concentrating the sun through the lens and angling it to the needles before a few embers sparked and quickly caught flame. I was showing off, I admit.

"That's some real Boy Scout shit right there," she said. "Amazing."

"How'd you survive the past year if you didn't know how to do this?"

She shrugged. "I don't know. I made it somehow. Sheer force of will. You look like you really know what you're doing, though."

"I'm no outdoorsman by nature. I learned over the past year. Real trial by fire. It's not too difficult once you get the hang of it, but to maintain, it's really time consuming. I don't know how people used to do it. Like the pioneers, the pilgrims—how did they survive? We might have been thrown for a bit of a loop here, but at least we still have a lot of modern advancements." The fire bit into the wood and climbed to a nice little flame in moments. White smoke streamed upward.

Ren inhaled the wood smoke deeply. "This is like real camping." She sat back in the lawn chair I unfolded for her and put her feet toward the fire. After a few seconds, she kicked off her shoes and peeled her socks. She wriggled her toes gleefully in the heat of the flames. "I could get used to this."

"I don't think you have much of a choice in the matter," I told her. "This is how it is now whether we like it or not."

I showed Ren how to pump gas for the RV. She watched me pump for ten minutes, and then I gave her a chance to help out. After five minutes, she was looking at me like I was insane. "And this is how you have to do it every time? My shoulders already hurt."

"Every single time. Takes about a half hour of solid pumping to fill the tank."

"No wonder you look so ripped."

I never once in my life had been told I looked ripped. I was a little doughy until the Flu struck (*thanks, job at McDonald's…*), and then I had to start working harder for my daily existence. I guess not eating a Big Mac a day and being forced to work constantly just to continue to live had made positive changes in at least one aspect of my life. I know I blushed when she said it. I wanted to issue a smart comeback, but I was tongue-tied at that moment. I didn't say anything. I guess I was a lot more "ripped" than I used to be. Figures, though: best shape of my life and only one person to see it. If society ever magically rebuilds itself, I will write a book and call it *The Post-Apocalypse Pioneer Diet Plan: One Year of Starvation and Daily Struggle to a New You.*

For dinner, I made ramen with canned chicken. I found some green onions in the window box planter of a house near the gas station so I cut them and threw them in for color and flavor. After dinner, I showed Ren how I washed dishes and silverware. I showed her how I repacked the gear for the next day's travel. Then, that was it. We each sat in a canvas-covered and steel-framed lawn chair staring at the fire and sipping on warm root beer.

These journals I am writing are for the future, a hopeful future where the American people have rebuilt society and my little stories provide a record of how we lived in the early days of the Flu until rebuilding was possible. If you're reading this far in the future, let me recommend the activity of staring at a campfire to you if you've never tried it. Flames are hypnotic. If you have never spent time seriously watching them, you should. Don't become an arsonist or something, but sit back and learn to appreciate the beauty of flames. There is something supernatural about them. They dance and weave, they swell and dive. One moment it shivers like a dancer, and the next a tongue of flame can crack like a whip. Fire can be destructive, but when it's controlled and contained, it soothes. Flames have always made me feel myriad emotions. It feels like they tap into something ancient, something primal. I can be swelled by comfort, and then destroyed by melancholy in a matter of seconds. When I sit before flames and clear my mind, I feel at peace with the Universe, like I'm where I'm supposed to be in the grand scheme of the cosmos. Maybe I'm not. Maybe I never was. But, those flames erased doubts and fears. I was able to take a vacation from the world every night for a few minutes. Looking back on those many, many nights of sitting in front of the hearth in the library, or sitting in front of small bonfires outside, those nights might have been the only thing that truly kept me from losing it out there.

Or maybe I'm just full of myself.

"What do you miss most?" Ren's voice roused me from my flame hypnosis.

"What?"

Ren sat up in her chair and leaned forward to poke the ashes on the edge of the fire with a long, thin stick. "What do you miss most?"

I thought for a second. "My parents, I guess."

Ren rolled her eyes. "Not who. What. What thing or things?"

"I don't really know." I thought for a bit. A year ago, I would have said TV, the Internet, movies, football games, taking everything for granted. I closed my eyes and sorted through everything I'd done without for the past year. I finally came up with something. "Pizza."

"Hell, yeah." Ren held out a hand for a high-five. I slapped it. "New York had great pizza. I could go for a big floppy slice right now in the worst way. What was your favorite kind?"

"Brand, or toppings?"

"Toppings, man. Of course."

"I'd eat anything you put in front of me, but I really loved any sort of bacon cheeseburger pizza. Extra cheese, of course."

"Wisconsin and cheese, right? What's up with that?" The tip of Ren's branch caught on fire and she held it up in the air. The little flame held its own in the still night, but eventually snuffed to ember and smoke.

"Cheese is religion in Wisconsin. Honestly, I'm surprised churches don't top the Communion wafers with a little disk of Monterrey Jack."

Ren smiled. "You know what I miss most?"

"Tell me."

"Subway."

"The sandwich place or the method of mass transit?"

Ren smacked me in the shoulder playfully. "The sandwich place, doofus. A thousand cool, unique little sandwich shops in my neck of Brooklyn, each with their pretentious *artisanal* bread and locally-sourced ingredients, and for some reason, I just loved Subway. I could go there, get my Cold Cut Combo with lettuce, pickles, extra onions, mustard and mayo and it was always the same, always wonderful. I used to eat at least one of those a week. If I got the same stuff to make one at home, it never tasted the same. How did restaurants do that, by the way? I could make anything at home that I could get in a restaurant, but it never tastes the same. That's some sorcery right there."

"Weren't you a vegetarian or a vegan or whatever?"

Ren laughed. She shook her head. "I wasn't a very good vegan, truth be told. And that was really only during college. I don't think my mother would have let me live at home if I'd tried to be a vegetarian during high school. I always tried to mentally justify Cold Cut Combos by telling myself that bologna wasn't really meat."

"I miss going to the movies, too."

"I never went to a lot of movies. We weren't poor, really. We just were your average lower-middle class family. We weren't starving, but we weren't rolling in extra income, you know? Movies in New York are hella expensive. It's like a ticket, a small popcorn, and a small drink run you thirty bucks! At that price, my parents just waited until the movie came out on DVD and bought the DVD for seventeen or eighteen bucks. Then, my brother and sister and I could watch it as many times as we wanted. We had a good DVD collection."

"I never went to night shows," I said, "only matinees, because I was cheap. In Wisco, a matinee would only be five or six bucks. Popcorn and a drink would usually cost about ten or twelve. Plus, it gave me a reason to not be home for two or three hours."

"That's not too bad. I should have told my dad to move to the Midwest. What's your favorite movie?"

Before I could respond, an animal roar broke the stillness. Not a howl or a scream, but an honest-to-goodness *roar*, a deep, throaty declaration of presence and territorial acquisition from a large, male lion. I froze in my chair, but Ren leapt to her feet so hard and so far, I thought she was going to stumble forward into the fire. Her chair shot backward and clattered to the ground on its side. "What the hell was that?" She ran to the RV and grabbed her shotgun from where it stood leaning against the passenger door.

"A lion, I think," I said. I stood and peered into the darkness toward where the roar came from, for whatever good staring into darkness will do.

"Is there a zoo near here?"

"Any zoo animals still caged would likely be dead now. Starvation. Lack of care." I told her about seeing the elephants in Ohio. "Other zoos must have released their animals, too. It was the only humane thing to do. Either let them go or put them down. I guess if they let them go, it at least gave the poor things a fighting chance to survive."

Ren backed into the RV. She stood in the doorway, ready to slam it shut in an instant, should the need arise. "I spent a year in New York and didn't ever see no damn lions. Are you kidding me?"

The lion roared again. A lion's roar is impressive. It can be heard for miles under the right conditions. It is an unmistakable sound, one of those things where there's no wondering what it was—you know instantly that it's a lion, even if you have never heard a lion roar. It sends chills up your spine.

I'd read fiction novels about African safaris where the heroes built a big fire because it would keep the lions and other predators at bay. I have no idea if that was true or not, and I didn't feel like experimenting to find out.

"I guess we turn in, then. If it comes around here, it won't get into the RV. We'll be safe enough," I said.

"Are you sure?" Ren's eyes were wide and scared.

"I'm positive. A lion isn't going to open the door to the RV. A Bigfoot might, though." Ren gave a little laugh. She thought I was kidding. I wasn't. I think. Bigfoot has fingers and an opposable thumb.

I poured water over the fire until it was doused. Steam rose from the ashes. "We'd better go to the bathroom quickly."

"Bathroom? What about—" Ren pointed at the little lavatory closet in the RV.

"It's not hooked up. It's just easier to pee outside."

Ren's eyes were still wide. "What if…you want to do other things?"

"Like…" I held up two fingers. She nodded. I said, "Well, what did you do in New York?"

"I carted a couple of gallons of river water to my toilet every day. As long as I filled it up, it flushed. If the sewer had stopped working, I never noticed, and it never bothered me."

I looked toward the gas station a hundred yards to the left. "There are bathrooms in there. You can just go—"

Ren shook her head. "With a lion out there? You're nuts. You have to come with me."

"The lion is at least a mile that way, maybe more." I pointed to the right. "The bathrooms are a hundred yards that way." I pointed to the left. "Unless that lion has super powers, he isn't going to be a problem. It's not like he's going to sprint here and be waiting for you."

"Regardless. Just…come with me." Ren was starting to shift uncomfortably. She picked up my MagLite.

"Fine. Let's go." I started to walk away, but rethought it. I went back and picked up my shotgun. It never hurts to be safe. Just in case.

When we'd first gotten to the gas station that afternoon, we'd found the doors unlocked. The little station was ransacked, like so many gas stations. Most of the cigarettes and booze were gone. The aisle with the chips and candy was picked over, as well. A few odds and ends were scattered about, but that's all. The two cash registers were emptied, too. The world was dying, and still some people thought about money. I guess that is human nature. However, at the moment, a million dollars cash was worth zilch unless you were desperate for toilet paper.

"Stay by the doors," said Ren. "I'll be as fast as I can." She ran to the women's room in the rear of the store, lighting the way with the flashlight.

I stood by the doors listening to the night. The lion didn't roar again, but the night still felt different than usual, charged somehow. And stupid me, I started to wonder what it would be like to watch a Bigfoot fight a lion. I bet it would be awesome. If TV still existed, I would put that fight on pay-per-view. It would put the UFC or heavyweight boxing to shame. And screw watching the Superbowl—if you're trying to tell me you wouldn't pay all the money in your bank account this second to watch a Sasquatch get loose on a fully-grown lion, you are either a liar or you're deluding yourself.

While I waited for Ren, I stared out into the night. The gas station sat on the side of a main road, four lanes. The road led to a small commerce district. Fast food restaurants and a Walmart lay just down the road. I stared at the McDonald's. I'd worked at a McDonald's for almost a year before the Flu. I didn't miss working there. My brain drifted back to those days. The McDonald's wasn't an overly busy one, and there was a lot of goofing off after the dinner rush. My buddy, the late, great Hunter Winslow, and I used to waste time making monster sandwiches. The Chicken McFishNugget Mac was my favorite. Enough carbs in that thing to choke a camel. I was so deep in the haze of remembering my McDonald's stupidity, that I almost didn't notice the light in the distance. When I did notice it, all my thoughts about screwing around at work instantly shut down. I slipped into a vigilant, hyper-aware mode of being. There *might* be someone alive. There was an actual light of some kind down the road. It was a small dot of light only slightly bigger than pinpoint, not very bright, and unmoving.

I waited until Ren emerged from the bathroom, and then I pointed out the light to her. "What is it?" she asked.

"Let's drive down there and find out."

"What if it's another person?"

"Then, we hope they're nice."

Ren's fingers tightened around her shotgun. "What if they're not?"

I shrugged. "Then we put out that fire when we have to."

The light got bigger as we neared. It was a glowing plastic or glass orb hanging in the window of a flower shop. I pulled the RV to the side of the road. Through the window, I couldn't tell what was glowing, but it was definitely a light.

"Solar." Ren cracked the door and slipped out into the night. "It's a solar 'Closed' sign, I think."

I killed the engine to the RV and followed her. The light was a small globe, smaller than a volleyball. It did look like there was once the word "Closed" on it, however sun and age had bleached the word to almost nothing. The solar panel that powered it was still pointed at the window, though. Every day, it gathered power. Every night, it glowed.

"That's the future, right there," said Ren. "Solar. You know anything about solar panels?"

"Not a thing," I said. "However, I imagine we will have to learn, won't we? Libraries have books. We can figure it out."

"You handy with tools and science like that? You think you can make solar panels work to generate power?"

I had no idea. My first thought was to tell her the truth, that I was absolutely winging everything every step of the way, but that did not really impart any sense of confidence. "I guess we'll find out, won't we?"

Ren pressed her face to the glass of the shop, shielding her eyes with her hand. "Jesus!" she leapt backward. "Something moved in there."

"What? Where?" I pressed my face to the glass.

"In the back."

I squinted into the darkness. The solar globe helped illuminate the shop, but it gave the dim interior a shadowy look. The shop had a counter in the center, and several display tables filled with wilted, dried flowers in vases. Refrigerator cases lined the store on either side of the shop. The main area had a door to the rear marked "Employees Only." There was a gap between the central counter to the work area at the rear of the store. I stared into the back and saw a shadow dart past the gap. Something big. Not human big, but big enough. "Animal," I said.

"A lion?"

I chuckled. I couldn't help it. "No. I'm fairly certain if it was a lion, there would be no question about it. Maybe a cat."

"Never seen a cat that big."

"Maine Coons are that big," I said. I walked to the clear glass door of the shop, but it was locked. I used the butt of my shotgun to smash the glass and clear it out of the frame. I heard something scrabble in the back of the shop. Sounded like something with four legs. I slipped under the push bar and stepped into the shop. The air smelled musty and wet. "Pass me a flashlight, please."

Ren ran back to the RV and grabbed the MagLite from its spot by the door. She slapped the handle into my palm. I clicked the power button and the shop was flooded with light. Ren slipped under the push bar of the door and stood next to me, shotgun in hand. "Smells in here," she said. The darkened coolers on either side of the room were black with mold.

I stepped to the counter gap and shone a light to where the shadow had been. I shined it straight on a fat, angry raccoon. The fuzzy bandit hissed at me and scattered, clambering to a table with a single jump off a short file cabinet, and then jumped from the table to the counter.

Ren shrieked and pulled the trigger on the shotgun out of panic. She hip-fired, off-balance and unready. The blast roared, the recoil sent her spinning. The raccoon, unharmed and scared, immediately crapped itself and pissed all over the counter and floor while sprinting out the broken door and into the night. If you've never smelled raccoon urine, it is a far cry from Chanel

No. 5. I started to gag. Ren and I retreated back to the clean air outside the shop.

"How did a raccoon get in there?" Ren said. She jammed her pinky into her ear and tried to clear the ringing.

"Probably a hole somewhere. It was too fat to have been trapped in there for a year. I started walking around the building.

Ren inspected a welt on her arm where the shotgun had smacked her. "This hurts. I never fired a shotgun before."

"Never?"

"I never really had a reason. The movies make it look easy. It's not. It's scary. You know how to shoot?"

"Not really," I admitted. I'd fired my shotgun before, but I was not skilled with the thing. I had read manuals, though. I had read books on guns. Shooting a gun is one of those things where book-learning is a far cry from practice, though.

Ren waved her arm in the night air to cool the burning. "One of us had better learn to shoot, then. If we plan on hunting fresh food ever, we might need to."

"It's been on my list of things to do." I found the rear door to the flower shop. The door's deadbolt had been extended so the door couldn't really close. The winds probably battered it open and closed at their leisure. A creature with clever paws like a raccoon could easily swing open the door. "Mystery solved."

"Disappointing," said Ren. She was looking at her shotgun. She looked like she didn't want to hold it anymore. She looked around at the quiet, desolate city. "It would have been cool to find another person."

"What would another person have been doing in an abandoned flower shop in the middle of the night?"

Ren rolled her eyes. "I know. I just..." She tilted her head toward the vacant road. "There's nothing out there, you know?"

"There are lots of things out there. Just not people."

"That's not what I meant..."

"I know what you meant." It was the same question I battled daily.

Ren sighed. "I'm ready to go to bed."

"Me, too."

We climbed back into the RV. Renata said, "You want to go back to the gas station?"

"Not really. We don't need to. We can just sleep here."

"That feels weird. We're parked on a street in a strange town."

"You'll get used to it. This is life now." I started pulling down cases of water from the bunk over the cab and stacking them on the little table. "Do you want the bunk up here or the bunk in the back?"

"What?" She looked confused.

"I figured you didn't want to sleep together," I said.

Realization crossed her face. She flicked her eyes to the two bunks. "Oh. Yeah. Of course. I just...I guess I hadn't thought about sleeping arrangements until now. I don't want to kick you out of your bed."

"Then you can have the bunk up here. I've got a sleeping bag for tonight. We can get your sheets and real blankets tomorrow, if you'd like." I cleared the last case of water, stacking them up on the benches next to the table and the table itself.

Ren looked around the cab and scratched at her arm. "It feels kind of...open out here, doesn't it?"

"You can have the back bed. I don't mind." And I really didn't. Both bunks were comfortable. "You might have to sleep with Fester, though. He usually sleeps in the rear bunk at night."

She looked to the door of the back bedroom, and then the cab bunk. "No. It will be fine. I'll take the bed out here. I don't want to take your bed."

"It honestly doesn't matter to me," I said. It didn't really.

"No," she said firmly. "I'll take this bed up here. It looks cool."

I dug the sleeping bag out of the storage compartment where I'd stashed it and handed it to her. I pulled one of the spare pillows from my own bed. "We'll get you your own bedding and pillows tomorrow."

"Sounds good."

I unrolled the sleeping bag and tossed it to the top bunk, smoothing it out flat for her. I looked to Ren, and she looked back at me. She looked to her hockey bag of supplies and then down at her clothes. I took the hint. "Right, sorry. I just—I'll go to bed."

"Thanks, Twist." Ren smiled warmly at me. "Really."

I went into my bedroom and shut the door. I stripped out of my cargo shorts and t-shirt. It was hot and humid, of course. Virginia in the summer. I had taken to sleeping naked just for comfort's sake, but with a new traveling companion, I decided that probably was not a wise thing to do anymore. I left my boxer-briefs on. I started arranging my unmade bed. There was a knock at the door. It was such an unfamiliar sound that my heart jumped. I cracked the door.

Ren was standing there in an over-sized green New York Jets jersey. "Hey, I just wanted to say thank you, you know? I don't know why we met, but I'm glad you took me with you. There was nothing left for me in New York. I am really glad we are making a new start."

I wanted to say five or six witty lines. I wanted to be charming or dismissive. Instead, I just took the sincerity she gave me and returned it. "You're welcome. I'm glad you're here, too. I needed a friend."

Ren smiled. I smiled back. She shrugged a shoulder. "I guess I'll see you in the morning."

"Sure. Good night."

"Good night." Ren turned and went back to her bunk. I closed my door. Fester was impatiently waiting for me to lie down so he could get his nightly dose of attention.

Sleeping in the RV with another human was a new experience. I could feel Ren's movements. If she rolled over, the whole vehicle swayed slightly, waking me. It was reassuring, though. It was a reminder that I was no longer alone. It actually helped me sleep better.

My alarm went off at its usual time, and I shut it off. I dressed in my shorts and a Wisconsin Badgers t-shirt. I opened the door to the rear bunk and saw Ren's sleeping form huddled under the sleeping bag in the front. I wanted to let her sleep, but when I stepped forward, I crunched down on a dozen empty plastic water bottles. They made a cacophonous sound. Ren was instantly sitting up in bed, shotgun in hand. Her head whipped toward me, and then to the window in the front bunk. She saw it was morning. She fell back to her pillow.

"What's this?" I asked. I picked up one of the bottles.

"Ghetto door alarm," she said. "Sorry. It's just…"

"You were taking extra precautions in case I tried to attack you in the night?"

"I put them in front of the side door, too, man. I was just trying to be cautious. I mean, I really like you and all, but we still don't really know each other."

I couldn't fault her for being cautious, I guess. She was five-three and maybe a hundred-ten pounds. I was six-feet and change, a buck-seventy, maybe buck-eighty. I was a big guy compared to her. I shrugged off the bottles. "No problem. Honest. It's all good." I smiled sheepishly. "I locked the door to the back bunk last night for the first time since I started sleeping in the RV."

Ren smiled. She shoved the heels of her hands into her eyes and rubbed. "Yeah, I guess it's like getting a new roommate. You hope they're nice, but you still need to know if they're going to be psycho, you know?"

"I get you."

Ren rolled out of the sleeping bag. "What's the plan for the day, boss?"

"Get some breakfast. Get on the road. First department store we see, we'll stop and get you some sheets and stuff."

"Sounds good."

I stepped out to take a leak behind the flower shop. When I returned, Ren was dressed in shorts and halter-top. "Is there a bathroom in the flower shop?"

"Probably." I had spaced-off the fact that basic urination was pretty simple for a man, unzip and go. For a woman, there were a few more logistics involved.

"If it's gross, we're going to have to find another one." She started out the door to the RV.

"You can just go outside, too."

Ren stopped and held up a finger. "I accept the fact that I will probably have to do that one day…but that day has not yet come. I will use a toilet for as long as I absolutely can."

When she returned, we drove to Richmond and, as promised, looted some high-thread count sheets, a comforter, and several pillows from a Target. We made up Ren's bunk together, and then she climbed up to give it a test run. "This is doable," she said. "I like it." Fester leapt up next to her and curled into a ball at her side. He approved, as well.

"It's only until we get to Madisonville, Louisiana," I said. "Then we can live in a house."

Ren climbed down and dropped into the passenger seat. Fester ran over and climbed into her lap. "Not much between here and there, though. Is there?"

I didn't know for sure. I answered her honestly. "I don't think so. Just long, empty roads."

Ren inhaled sharply through her nose and blew out a long, slow exhale. "I guess so. Onward, Jeeves. The world awaits."

I climbed into the driver's seat and fired the engine. There was a whole lot of no one to see and nothing to do that day.

Ennui is one of the biggest problems with the apocalypse. I say ennui because I'm not "bored." I'm rarely bored. There is always something to do; survival is a full-time occupation. However, there exists a general *blah* feeling that settles over you on a daily basis. It's hard to ignore. I didn't fully appreciate how distracted I was before the Flu until I lost everything that distracted me. TV, laptop, tablet, phones, friends, family, job, school— so many things kept me from stopping and appreciating silence. At first, I didn't mind it. Over the winter in Wisconsin, the silence almost drove me insane. Now, the static noise of wind in the windows of the RV drowned out the desire to converse for both of us, and the malaise of the road set in heavily. I had been dealing with it for weeks before Ren came along. It was a new experience for her. The first day, everything was still new and interesting. Early in the second day of being stuck in a twenty-five foot vehicle, the shine was quickly wearing.

We continued south from Richmond. The sun rose and baked the day. The humidity felt like a velvet cloak. Speaking as a Wisconsin boy, I thought I knew humidity; Wisconsin got quite humid in the summers. However, Midwest humidity was *nothing* compared to the southern coastal states. Even Ren, with her Venezuelan heritage, cursed the humidity every time we stopped and got out of the RV. Even though it probably cost us some gas, we cranked that A/C hard on the main roads. When we slowed to creep through towns, though—the A/C had to be shut down. It was just too hard on the engine when we weren't cruising at highway speeds. The humidity was so uncomfortable I ended up stripping off my t-shirt and going shirtless. Ren held out a little longer than I did, but eventually she took her hockey bag into the back bunk and emerged in a black sports bra.

Highway 95 out of Richmond was the route we were following, but I continued to veer from the highway to smaller towns and side roads hoping to find signs of life. We only found continued evidence of the Earth reclaiming homes and roads. I saw herds of cattle wandering freely through towns. Herds of free-roaming Holsteins were a new sight. Cattle are not wild animals. They never were. When you look at the history of the domestic cows, they were created to be work animals, bred to be smaller and more docile. They were bred down selectively from the large and powerful Auroch. Now, this domestic species was starting to have to learn to be wild, again. One time, where we were passing a large group of them outside of a small town, I saw a large bull standing apart from the larger congregation of females. A couple of small, gangly calves milling about, playing amongst the cows. The herd was perpetuating. They were adapting. I pointed this out to Ren. "We can adapt, too."

"We're going to have to," she said. There was a silence. She added, "I worry about stuff, though."

"Like what?"

"Like when we run out of stuff. Like, what happens if we run out of toilet paper?"

"I think we'll be able to scavenge enough paper to cover us for the rest of our lives." I pointed at the homes we could see to the left. "All those homes there have paper in them right now, I guarantee it. If we ever can't find any in stores, every house in this country has a supply, and a lot of them are in plastic."

"Think long term, though." Ren wiped sweat from her forehead. "A lot of these houses are going to go to hell in the next five years. A lot of these homes will be compromised over time. Who knows for certain what we'll be able to scavenge in ten years, in twenty years? What about things like tampons and pads, even? I know you don't need them, but back in the day women had to pin folded up cotton towels into their underthings and then wash that shit every day. I don't want to have to do that." She shuddered. "Gross."

I had a lot of those same worries, albeit not about tampons. I wondered how long canned food would hold out and not spoil, especially in warm, humid conditions. That stuff would start to rust and rot. I wondered how much longer I would be able to keep the RV running. I wondered if the ammunition for the guns would go bad. Could I make more? Could I make gun powder? Would I have to get really good at archery? Could I make my own arrows? The future held a lot more questions than answers, none of which could be answered at that moment. "I guess that's part of adapting. We'll have to figure it out as we go."

"I hope I don't run out of feminine products until well after I hit menopause."

"I think there will be a lot of bridges we won't have to cross until we get to them. It's natural to worry, but I think for a lot of things Necessity will have to be the Mother of Invention. At least we have blueprints. Could you imagine being the pioneers or explorers? They had to figure stuff out on their own. We have a head start on all of them."

"When I was a kid, I loved the Laura Ingalls Wilder books," said Ren. "As a city girl, they made the empty prairies sound almost romantic. I wanted to live there."

I whipped my head around to look at her. "Those are my favorite books!" I told her about how my mom read them all to me when I was little, and how I spent an inordinate amount of time reading *The Long Winter* during my snowbound days in the library in Sun Prairie.

"Get out!" Ren said. Her eyes looked alive for the first time that day. "I used to sit in the library down the street from our apartment and read those things over and over again. I adore Laura so much, I even ignore all the racist bullshit about Indians." She leaned toward me. "Did we just become best friends?"

"If you just referenced *Stepbrothers*, we sure as hell did!"

"We can make bunk beds so we'll have more room for activities!" Ren held out her hand, and I slapped it. After that flurry of excitement, neither of us said anything more. It was like a firecracker had just gone off, and then we realized we didn't have any more fireworks. Ren leaned her head against the passenger window. "Be nicer if we didn't have to do any of that, though. I hate not *knowing*. I just want the future to be planned and laid out for me. Go here. Do that. Everything will work out."

We passed a sign pointing to the Petersburg National Civil War Battlefield, site of the longest battle of the Civil War. For nine months, Union troops under Ulysses S. Grant conducted a long and brutal trench warfare campaign against Confederate soldiers. Taking Petersburg would have been a deathblow to General Lee's troops because it would have severed supply lines, but eventually Grant gave up the battle and retreated north to intercept Lee's troops at Appomattox, leading to the end of the Civil War. I veered to the exit.

Ren looked at me with narrowed eyes. "What is it with boys and war?"

I shrugged. "Couldn't tell you. I do not care for war. I do enjoy history, though."

Ren protested. "Why? What's the point? History is over. We're writing our own history now. Isn't that why you spent so much time writing in your little journals every night?"

"What's that line about people doomed to repeat history?" I retorted.

"The Civil War doesn't have to exist anymore. We are at the dawn of a new era of history. We decide what's worth including. We can wipe out that era of history, start a new world where there is no inequality, no Confederacy, no more stupidity!"

"Doesn't sound logical to me," I said. "We are human. There will always be stupidity. The Civil War was a volatile time in the history of this land. Even if America no longer exists, it seems folly to ignore the fact that it existed, it happened. Hundreds of thousands of Americans gave their lives to it, right or wrong. We would dishonor their existences if we just tried to forget what happened."

"Maybe," she acquiesced. "What will people remember about the Flu? Hypothetically, say we somehow recover from this as a species. Will people remember you and me? Will they remember how good we had it before everything went to hell?"

I couldn't answer her. I doubted it. "Maybe they will remember us. I started my journals for that purpose. There will be a written record of what we did, and how we survived, just in case someone cares someday. Maybe that's good enough for now. Maybe someday we'll build a monument to ourselves."

"I like the idea of a statue of me. Could I be doing some dramatic pose like a conquering Valkyrie, with wings and a spear?"

"I don't see why not."

The corner of Ren's mouth turned up in a cat-who-ate-the-canary smile. "Hell, yeah."

The battlefield was overgrown like everything else. The monuments stood above a sea of long grass and new tree and shrub growth. Cicadas droned everywhere. I parked the RV and we got out to walk around and see what we could see. Turns out, there wasn't a ton to see. I'd been to other historical sites before. I remember seeing Indian/Cavalry battle sites on trips west with my parents. Usually, I got a spooky feeling from them, like I was looking at a holy place or something like that. It felt overwhelming. I still felt that at Petersburg, but it had lessened considerably. I don't know if that's because I was older, more jaded, or if it had something to do with the fact that almost every building I passed was basically a mausoleum now. If the dead needed to be venerated, I spent all day, every day in near-constant veneration.

The heat and humidity of the day was like a choking fog. Walking became a miserable activity. We poured water over our heads and tried to ignore it, but it was sometime in the middle of August at this point. The temperature was easily over a hundred, and the humidity felt like 100 percent. Heat waves rose from pavement and made the distance hazy.

"This is miserable." Ren said. She slugged some water and grimaced. "Scratch what I said about Subway. I really miss ice. I miss refrigeration."

"Ever think about how 'fridge' has a D in it and refrigeration doesn't?" I said.

Ren squinted at me. "No. Never once. What's your point?"

I shrugged. I felt a flash of embarrassment and stupidity. "No point. Just pointing something out." It was an awkward cover, and thankfully Ren let it slide.

We stopped on a concrete sidewalk to read a plaque about the battlefield we were overlooking. The plaque informed us about what the Civil War-era cannons were pointed at during the battle, and how the charge on the field went down. It also mentioned that almost eight hundred men died on the field on which we stood.

"Ever think about ghosts?" Ren said. She brought it up out of nowhere.

"Ghosts?"

"Yeah. Like, eight hundred people died here. Right. Here." Ren pointed to the field. "They died in tragic circumstances. Do you think their spirits still wander this field looking to right wrongs or something?"

"If ghosts are real, then we're surrounded by them right now. Everyone who died in the Flu would be watching us at all times."

"What if they are?" said Ren. "What if your parents are watching over you right now."

"I'd feel bad that the afterlife is so dull that they feel a need to do that. But, I like the sentiment. I sort of feel like my parents have been around me. The only problem is that I can't decide if they are really there, or if I'm just hallucinating because I want them to be around me."

Ren leaned on a walkway railing. "If my sister was a ghost, I'd know if she was near me; I'd feel her. I haven't felt her presence, though." She looked at the clear sky. "I kind of wish she was, though. It would make me feel better."

Ren pushed off the railing and turned back toward the RV. "This sucks. It's hot. There's no one here, and I'm not going to camp on a Civil War battlefield…just in case there are ghosts."

I followed her. I didn't want to sleep around ghosts, either. Bigfoots were bad enough.

We drove south another couple of hours. It was still hot and humid when we stopped for gas and set up camp. We were just past the Virginia/North Carolina border in a little town called Gaston. As we left the battlefield, I explained to Ren that I picked towns to investigate based on names that were corny or fun to pronounce. She immediately dove on the map book and started scanning. Upon finding Gaston, North Carolina, she immediately burst into song, going through an exaggerated version of "Gaston" from Disney's *Beauty & the Beast*. A destination had been duly selected.

We filled up with gas at a Citgo station. We explored the town. Before the Flu, it had only had a population around 1,150, and it appeared that none of them had survived. Gaston was a northern suburb to the much larger Roanoke Rapids, a town formerly of about 15,000. It was nice. Homey. Simple. We parked on the road next to a city park that had bathrooms. There was a lot of open area around us. In a way, that was comforting. I was glad that there were not any trees where escaped lions could hide from us.

It took a couple of hours to scavenge enough wood for the night's fire and to gather bottles of water and other supplies from the stores and restaurants in town. When we reconvened at the campsite, we were both sweaty and cranky. We tried to bathe by pouring water over our heads, emptying a couple of gallons of the lukewarm bottled water. It helped a little. Instead of sitting near the fire that night, we did our cooking on a small fire, a simple meal of canned soup and crackers, and then let the flames die out. It was too hot for a bonfire. We sat in chairs and looked up at the night sky. We took turns pointing out the constellations we knew, and inventing fake stories for ones we didn't. It was fun.

"I can't get over how many stars there are," Ren said. "You never see this many in the city. The sky is so big out here."

"In Wisconsin, some nights we were lucky enough to see glimpses of the Northern Lights. Those are amazing."

"What are those like?"

"Like…dancing ribbons of light in the sky, usually green. A vibrant green."

"That sounds cool. I heard people in New York talk about going upstate to see them, but I never did. Going upstate was for rich people." Ren shifted in her seat. We were quiet for a long time. Ren squeaked. "What the hell is that?" She pointed into the sky. I tried to triangulate where she was pointing. High above us, she could see a small light that looked like it was moving. It was barely a pinpoint and it was hustling.

"Satellite, probably," I said. "You can see them sometimes."

"Satellites are still working?"

"Most of them were solar-powered," I said. Then another thought hit me, and I blanched. "Oh, god…the astronauts on the ISS. What happened to them?"

Ren sat up in her chair. "Are they still up there? Could they live that long without supplies?"

I didn't know. I remembered reading something about escape pods, Soyuz rocket capsules the crew could use in an emergency situation, but what if the situation on Earth was dangerous? Would they just sit up there until they died? Would they just depressurize the ISS and let space do them in quick and easy? Did they wait until the Flu was over and then try to return to Earth? If so, did they land in Russia, like normal? How did they land without help from Mission Control? This was something that would keep me up at night for a few days. I couldn't *not* think about it, and at the same time, I had no answers for it. The only way I eventually put it out of my head was the realization that there were going to be a lot of things to which I'd never have solid answers. I closed my eyes and wished those astronauts well, no matter where they were and whether or not they were alive.

We eventually went to bed. The heat in the RV was stifling. I considered hanging a hammock between two trees and sleeping outside, but despite the open terrain around us, I just couldn't bring myself to trust the night. It was silly, I know. My brain just kept telling me Bigfoot was coming. I felt better inside the Greyhawk. I slept in the back bunk; Ren slept in her bunk. She still slept next to her shotgun. She fashioned a spot to hang it from while she slept so that she wasn't in danger of accidentally hitting it, but it was still within easy grasp. The next morning when I left my bunk at dawn, I didn't step on empty bottles. The floor was clear. I smiled. That was progress on the Trust front.

CHAPTER ELEVEN

Guidestones

Renata and I spent weeks on the road repeating the same endless pattern. Up, breakfast, drive. Explore towns. A snack for lunch. Drive. Explore more towns. Stop. Scavenge. Camp. Sleep. We explored as much as we could, crisscrossing through North Carolina and South Carolina, hitting a lot of towns. At first, Ren's enthusiasm for finding others kept us going. Her optimism was renewed each morning. "Today we're gonna find someone, I just know it!" By the end of the day, she was a little dejected, but at each night's fire, she'd shake off the disappointment and tell me, "Tomorrow. Tomorrow's the day. People are out there waiting for us."

In the meantime, as we rolled through the countryside, we learned to trust each other more and more. By the end of the first week, I felt comfortable around her. By the end of the second week, she was the best friend I'd ever had. We were different people. She was street smart and city-wise, almost a college graduate. I was four years younger than she, and something of a bumpkin from the sticks, comparatively. However, I'd somehow acquired skills in my suburban upbringing that she lacked, and she had thoughts and ideas that I lacked. We had similar senses of humor, though. We liked a lot of the same movies and books. We complemented each other well. In short order, we had become family tight because we had no other choice in the matter. We bonded.

I taught the city girl to drive, something she'd never thought she'd have the need for in New York. I tried to explain that every town in Wisconsin was a ten-to-twenty minute drive from the next-nearest town, and our public transportation system was almost non-existent. That fact alone blew her mind. The first couple of days when she took a turn behind the wheel, it was a little rough. It is tough enough learning to drive in a small family car, but to learn at the wheel of a long, bulky RV—well, let's just say it made me very glad there were no other cars on the road.

Ren taught me some things about First Aid and medicines. She was invaluable in sorting out my medicine stash, and she took the point on our pharmacy raids. She taught me how to do stitches correctly. A year ago, I'd sliced my palm open on some sheet metal, and when she saw the lumpy scar tissue across my palm, it made her cringe. Although, she was impressed that I had been able to stitch it one-handed.

We had fun along the way, too. Occasionally, we went swimming when we found a nice lake or river that was not overgrown with algae. Some nights, we played catch with an Aerobie we'd found, one of those orange, plastic, Frisbee-like rings. We played around in a climbing gym one night, scaling walls and swinging from ropes into a foam pit. We played ping-pong and basketball another night in a school gym. We played table tennis so long, the next day both of us had sore shoulders. We broke into a mall in Charlotte, North Carolina. The mall, surprisingly, was mostly intact. A few of the stores had been looted, but not many. I guess there aren't a ton of survival necessities at Hot Topic and Spencer's Gifts. We set up a bunch of battery-powered LED lanterns along the corridors to make the mall seem less scary. In the mall, we broke the lock on a gate to a skateboard shop and spent a night roller-blading and skateboarding the long, smooth floors. We had races. I wasn't very good on a skateboard, but I was better than average on the roller-blades, thanks to growing up in a hockey town. Ren could roller-skate well. She could skateboard, too. She could ollie and do kickflips. To me, skateboards were the work of the devil. I didn't understand how people could jump off the board and make the board come with them. It looked like it was defying physics. The mall had one of those little places where you could put on a harness attached to some bungie cords and bounce on a trampoline. We spent at least an hour on that thing, bouncing, laughing. My stomach hurt from laughing. My cheeks hurt from smiling. It was the most fun I'd had since before the Flu.

Maybe the most fun ever.

I thought a lot about Doug Fisk when we were in the mall. Being in the mall, laughing and goofing off with my only friend in the world, it was the first time I felt like I was *living* and not just surviving. It wasn't part of the daily grind. It wasn't slavish devotion to making sure the next day, the next week, and the next month would happen. It was a happy deviation in which I let myself be immature and stupid. It was fleeting moments where, for little windows of time, I could have just been my stupid teenage-self screwing around with friends, and my parents were still alive at home, probably watching *NCIS* reruns or complaining about how there was nothing on Netflix they wanted to watch. For those little windows, I had no pressures, no responsibilities. I wasn't worried about a storm destroying my home. I wasn't worried about running out of gasoline. I wasn't worried about how I'd make clothes in the future, if I had to. I wasn't worried about anything. And it was glorious. I just hoped Renata felt the same way.

Ren was something of a mystery, despite how much we'd shared and done. She was cryptic, hard to read at times. I trusted her with my life on a daily basis. I like to believe that she trusted me, too. We got along well. We made a good team. If it hadn't been for the Flu, neither of us would have ever met. I would have spent my life in Wisconsin. She would have spent hers in New York. There were some cultural differences between us, too. She grew up first generation American, while my parents' families had been here for at least 150 years. One of my great-great-great-great grandfathers fought in the Civil War. She was city. I wasn't exactly country, but Sun Prairie, Wisconsin is as good as country to someone from Brooklyn.

I know that the more astute readers of these journals (if there ever will be any) would be wondering about romantic relations. As of the night I wrote this passage, there was none. Nothing. We were as asexual as amoebas. We were friendly—no, beyond friendly. We were bonded together through extreme trials. We'd both survived a year alone in a wasteland. We'd both faced loneliness and isolation. We'd both walked a fine line between sanity and raving madness during that year. We'd both faced the unanswerable questions about why we continued to live in a world that so clearly wanted human beings gone from its surface. We both faced questions about why we were such aberrations to the natural order of things. We'd done all that, and yet we kept kicking. We kept fighting. We were tight because we understood each other; we each knew how the other had lived. But, there was never any outward signs from Ren that she was interested in me beyond friendship and reliance. She wasn't overly touchy. She didn't laugh at my bad jokes. She didn't lean toward me when we talked. I'm not any sort of player. I was on the cusp of nineteen—women were still very much a mystery, and maybe they always would be. I just felt that any sort of romantic instigation was not for me to do. I didn't want to weird her out or make her reconsider coming with me. I needed her. I think she needed me. That was a bond more important than sex or romance. I did not want to try anything and then have to spend the next fifty years in an awkward place with her, always measuring every action, every gesture. Maybe she didn't want to risk it, either. I couldn't know.

The heat and humidity continued to be a daily factor, and I started to reconsider my desire to live in Louisiana. I couldn't imagine ever being used to heat and humidity like this. A friend of my dad's was a librarian at the UW. He'd been a librarian for a school in southern Florida for a few years before taking the job in Wisconsin. He said the first six months of being Down South were miserable. Then, he got used to the heat. Then, after a year or so, he said he didn't even notice the heat. When he moved to Wisconsin, seventy degrees—a temperature at which almost all Wisconsinites go t-shirts and shorts—was sweatshirt weather for him until he adapted to the cold. In Wisconsin, I wore a sweatshirt until the temps fell below freezing, and then I'd break out my light winter coat. I didn't break out my heavy winter coat until the temps were below 10 degrees or worse. Wisconsin: Where you need two different winter coats.

We crossed the South Carolina/Georgia border, near Greenville, late in the summer. I was driving. We passed a sign for a town called Elberton. Ren's face lit up, and she grabbed my arm. "Here! Turn here!" After some map consulting, she directed me to Highway 77 South, and then told me to turn left onto Guidestones Road. A hundred yards in, there was a small parking lot to the side of the road, and beyond that lay a granite sculpture of a quartet of monoliths. "We *need* to see this." Ren's voice was solemn and insistent. I didn't question her.

"These are the Georgia Guidestones," she said as we walked up to them. "I saw them on one of those weird unsolved mystery shows, the ones that talk about ghosts and aliens. There was a little feature on YouTube about them, too. These are important." The stones were tall, almost twenty feet. There was a central slab flanked by three other slabs. They were topped with a smaller capstone, almost like Stonehenge.

"I told myself that I would see these someday." Ren ran up to the nearest one and placed her hands on it. "You know what these are?"

"Sculptures?"

Ren's eyes were wide and full of reverence. "No. They're a guide for rebuilding society after an apocalypse."

In 1979, a man calling himself "R.C. Christian" went to a local granite finishing company to commission the statue on behalf of a "loyal group of Americans." The granite company thought he was cuckoo, and perhaps he was. They overbid the job in an attempt to discourage Christian, but he accepted their bid and paid what they asked. He told the company that the design of the stones had been planned for more than twenty years.

R.C. Christian was a pseudonym. Some believe the name was an adaptation of the word "Rosicrucian," tying the guidestones to the Rosicrucian movement, an old semi-secretive mystic order that sought a bridge between religion and metaphysics and looked to unlock the secrets of the universe. The Rosicrucians sought a reformation of mankind. No one knows who really commissioned the guidestones. They were put in place to function as "compass, calendar, and clock" in case of a cataclysm. The stones were astronomically aligned, and each stone bore a series of instructions for maintaining the world following a massive societal collapse. At the site, there was a square engraved on an explanatory tablet. It read, *Let these be guidestones to an Age of Reason.*

When Renata explained the stones' significance to me, I felt chills rush up and down my spine. She said, "The stones feel charged. Touch them." I reached out my hand and placed it on the warm, gray granite. They did feel different, but I don't know if it was my own imagination doing it, or if they really were special.

The inscriptions on the guidestones said the same thing in multiple languages:

1. Maintain humanity under 500,000,000 in perpetual balance with nature.
2. Guide reproduction wisely — improving fitness and diversity.
3. Unite humanity with a living new language.
4. Rule passion—faith—tradition—and all things with tempered reason.
5. Protect people and nations with fair laws and just courts.
6. Let all nations rule internally resolving external disputes in a world court.
7. Avoid petty laws and useless officials.
8. Balance personal rights with social duties.
9. Prize truth—beauty—love—seeking harmony with the infinite.
10. Be not a cancer on the earth—Leave room for nature— Leave room for nature.

Ren ran her fingers over the inscription in English. "Number one, check. Number two, check; nobody's reproducing around here, anyhow. Number three—who knows? You and I both speak English, I speak some Spanish. It's all good. Number four, check. Number five, no people or nations anymore, so…check. Number six, no nations: check! You know, an apocalypse did a really nice job of ending petty laws and useless officials."

I laughed. "Yeah. No more census takers or city aldermen knocking on your door, that's for sure. I guess there really is no great loss without some small gain."

"I think we're doing pretty well. Ol' R.C. Christian set a low bar for a societal rebuild after everyone died." Ren walked around the monoliths touching the stones. "Spooky, though. This group forty-some years ago said, *Hey! Shit's getting out of hand. Let's figure out rules for after everything falls apart.*"

"How smart were they, though? If they put up the stones in 1980, you'd think they might have expected the collapse to happen sooner than it did, I don't think they anticipated a virus wiping out everyone, either. I think they were thinking about an economic collapse." I walked to the spot where a slab said there was a time capsule beneath it.

"An economic collapse would have been brutal. The virus was a mercy." Ren saw the time capsule slab and raised her eyebrows. "Want to dig it up?"

"Not in the least." I said. "I bet it's buried beneath concrete. It looks like it would be a bear of thing to get to without heavy equipment."

"What if there's like some sort of Genesis pod in it that would spread humanity all over Earth again?"

I looked at the quiet, peaceful countryside surrounding the stones. I listened to the meadowlarks' song and the cicadas and frogs chirping along. "Maybe it's for the best that it stays put. As much as I'd like the world to go back to how it was before the Flu, I don't know if that sort of recovery is possible. Or if the Earth really even wants it."

"You think that maybe we're a mistake? Maybe we should have died, then?" Ren's eyebrows knitted together when she frowned at me. "That there is no point to us still being alive?"

I shrugged. I felt stupid when I did it. "I don't know. Maybe."

Ren shook her head and fell backward in the tall grass, splaying out like she was going to make a snow angel in the weeds. "Maybe," she agreed. "But at least we're having fun, right?"

I flopped into the weeds next to her. "Yes, we are."

"Out of everyone who didn't die, I'm glad I found you, Twist. You're making being alive feel like a good thing again."

Ren didn't move after she said it. I almost thought that sounded like an invitation, like maybe I should have tried to kiss her. I did not try, though. I looked up at the blue Georgia sky and kept my mouth shut. I should have said something.

I'm such a coward.

CHAPTER TWELVE

The Kingdom of New America

I always hated it when people called the city of Atlanta, "Hotlanta." I had a friend in Wisconsin who did that. He was one of those guys who thought he was going to be a rapper, always talking about some non-existent mixtape he was going to cut. Good kid, but it was always a little weird to hear a chubby suburbanite teenager talk about how the rap scene in "Hotlanta" was the place to be. When I got to Atlanta, I understood why the name originated, though. It was hot as hell. Ren said, "It feels like I'm breathing sauna air." That's probably the best analogy for it. It was hot, thick, messy air magnified by the concrete and asphalt to another level of magnitude. The tar on the roads was sticky from heat. It was too hot for this Northerner.

"The Atlanta metro area, plus the suburbs, had a population of four million people. We're going to find someone here," Ren said the morning after our first camp in Atlanta. As usual, her optimism percolated.

"You said that in Charlotte, too. Same sort of size," I reminded her.

"But this time, I feel it, Twist. I feel it in my bones." She sounded so definite, so sure of it, that I didn't bother to contradict her. Her hope was helpful. It gave me hope.

We went downtown. The downtown part of Atlanta didn't feel especially big. The suburbs that sprawled around the city made the area feel bigger, but to me, the downtown felt like going into Milwaukee. There were some tall buildings, but nothing like New York. There were some park areas, and a lot of commerce and restaurants and apartment buildings. It was a lovely city, but looking at the roads around it, I just knew there were probably some heavy traffic issues that would have made commuting a miserable endeavor back when people still existed. We parked somewhere near the center of town in the shade of a tall office building. It was at least ten degrees cooler in the shade. It was a noticeable and welcome change. I popped all the windows to vent the RV for Fester.

"Why are there peaches everywhere?" Ren asked. She had abandoned her shotgun for one of the pistols from my small collection. After the misfire at the raccoon, her taste for long guns evaporated. I gave her a snub-nosed

Smith & Wesson .357 that she said felt comfortable in her hand and we found a holster and a nylon tactical belt for it at a gun shop along the way. It made her look cool, I have to say. As much as I'm not a fan of guns, the way the belt hung on her hip gave her a roguish appearance. She reminded me of Han Solo the way she stood with her palm resting on the knurled hand grip, her curvy hips cocked to the side. As a kid, when I played Star Wars, I always wanted to be Han Solo. I think everyone did, male or female. Han was the man, easily a thousand times cooler than Luke, even though he didn't get his own lightsaber. Unfortunately, as I got older, I found myself to be much more C-3PO than Han Solo, stiff, awkward, and spouting facts and data no one asked for or wanted.

"Georgia is all about peaches. State fruit. They produce a ton of them here." I pointed to a license plate with a big peach on it. I slung my ruck over my shoulder, fastened a gun belt with the semi-auto at my hip, and picked up my shotgun and a MagLite. Ren had her own Maglite now, too. She was an old hand at camping and scavenging now. It had become second nature to us. We walked to the office building in front of us. The doors were locked. None of the glass was smashed. All good signs. We walked around the building trying other doors. A freight entrance was unlocked on the backside of the building. We walked in, flashlights illuminating our way.

The office building was plain and boring. Much like the tower I climbed in New York, the place was full of different companies using different floors as office space. The offices were pretty standard in that they usually had a reception desk, a cubicle farm, and a couple of executive offices on the corners. There were restrooms on every floor, and every office had a break room with vending machines. On the first floor, at the first vending machine, Ren used her flashlight handle to shatter the glass. She pulled out a bag of Cheetos and read the expiration date printed on the crimped foil edge. "Sell by twelve-sixteen." She frowned, opened the bag, and sniffed them. "Hell with it, I'm eating them anyway." Office buildings were goldmines for expired junk food and packs of ramen.

We walked up the darkened stairwell to the twentieth floor. We could have gone higher, but neither of us had a desire to keep going. Twenty stories gave us plenty of view over the area. We moved through the offices looking out the windows. I took the offices that faced north and east. Ren took the south and west corners. I saw nothing. I hadn't expected to see anything. Ren called for me, though, her voice betraying excitement and nerves. "Twist. Get over here!" From her vantage point, she was able to look down into a cluster of buildings. Nothing was immediately visible. I raised an eyebrow, but she pointed at a dark brownstone building. Against the dark of the stonework, I noticed something ghosting past it. Smoke. White smoke from a cooking fire. Someone was alive.

Ren and I sped down the stairs in near darkness. We hit the front entry of the office building near the Greyhawk. There were emergency exit push-bars on the doors so we could get out easily. "Should we take the RV?" Ren said.

"It's not too far away. Probably be better to go over there and see what we're dealing with first," I said. "Could be someone harmless. Could be a bunch of ass-hats like the Patriots. We can't risk losing the RV."

We made a beeline toward the area where we saw the smoke. It quickly became evident that there was definitely a person, or people, still alive there. Garbage was piled neatly in the alleys toward the block of brownstones. Wood was stacked in the alley, mostly from old shipping pallets, and there were open plastic barrels under downspouts to catch rain water. As we got closer, I could hear singing. "The Great Pretender" by the Platters was being belted out by someone with a mellow bass voice. He sounded really good, too.

I grabbed Ren's wrist. "Stay back. Stay hidden. If it's safe, I'll come get you."

Ren nodded and fell back behind me. "What if it's not safe?"

"I'll need you to come rescue me."

"Like a damsel in distress?" Ren winked at me. She started to creep back to hide behind a pile of trash bags. "Should we have a code word or something so I'll know to come rescue you?"

Code word? I think she needed to stop reading my spy novels. I said, "How about if I just scream, *Help*?"

Ren blew her hair off her forehead with a puff of air. "Good plan, genius."

I pressed myself against the wall of the alley and moved toward the street. At the corner, I steeled myself and peeked at the row of tenements. I wasn't exactly prepared for what I'd see; it's hard to be prepared for something like this. A large, black Weber kettle grill was standing in the middle of the street. A fire raging in its cauldron shot flames a foot or two into the air. A large steel pot was sitting precariously in the midst of the flames. It was black from heavy use and lack of cleaning, as camping supplies tend to get over time. A full dining room of expensive patio furniture was arranged in the street including comfortable chairs, a metal table with large umbrella in the center, and plastic tableware set for four. The master of the feast was a rather large, elderly black man. He had a large, scraggly beard that was almost purely white. He wore a pair of thick, black-rimmed spectacles straight out of 1955. He also wore a full suit of plate armor complete with a lancer's helm, the face-guard flipped upward so his face was unblocked. He had a medieval longsword buckled to his side with an elaborate, jeweled belt. He was rocking back and forth next to the grill while singing Oldies. He had a wooden spoon in his hand and a cooking mitt on the other. He poked at some sort of animal carcass that was bubbling away in the stew pot. Judging from what I could see, it may have been a cat or a small dog. I couldn't be certain. Over his suit of armor, like a tabard, he wore an apron that proclaimed in bold font:

> *This Ain't Burger King--*
> *You Don't Get It Your Way;*
> *You Get It My Way*
> *Or You Don't Get the Son of a Bitch.*

I set my shotgun down at the corner where it would be out of sight, but close enough for me to dive back and grab it, if I needed. Fear started to clench my guts again. I had no idea how this man would react, especially since I caught him wearing a full suit of armor on a one hundred degree day. I stepped around the corner, my hands in the air. I cleared my throat and said a very respectful, "Hello."

The man's head snapped up and his eyes grew large. He drew the sword. "What, ho! What demonry is this? Be you a minion of Hell sent to claim me? You'll not take me without a fight! Prepare your greasy talons, demon!" He advanced, sword-tip making slow circles in the air.

"Easy, sir." I held my hands up higher so he wouldn't think I was going to go for the gun at my hip. "I'm not a demon. My name is Twist. I'm from Wisconsin."

The sword stopped twirling. The tip lowered a bit. The man squinted. "Wisconsin? Is that in my northern realms? Have you come to swear fealty to my realm and pay your taxes?"

I looked at his eyes. I saw not one hint of jest in them. I think he was dead serious. I went with it, playing into his game. "Yes...uh...sir." Thankfully, I'd read more than my fair share of fantasy novels over the years. I knew what swearing fealty meant. I dropped to a knee and bowed my head. "I am...Twist, of the Northern, uh, Prairie Lands. I have come to swear fealty to...uh, you."

The sword-tip flipped up and rested on his shoulder. The eyes went wide and he smiled a filmy, yellow-teeth smile. "Good, good! I have been awaiting messengers from the Northlands for many moons. Tell me, Northman. How goes the battles? Have we a full army in the north yet, or have they succumbed?"

I don't think it was a game; I think he was mentally ill. Maybe he was sick before the Flu, maybe isolation made him snap. I couldn't be sure. I decided to continue to play along. I bowed my head to my chest. "I'm sorry, m'lord. The Northlands have fallen. I am the final emissary from the Central Northlands, the only one left. I met up with an emissary from the Eastern Northlands, and have brought her with me. We are sad to bring you news that the dreaded pox riddled the armies of the Northlands, much as it did in the Southlands. I fear the kingdom is lost, your majesty."

The man—the king?—sat heavily in one of his patio chairs, his armor clanking in protest. "Then it is as I feared. The realms have fallen. I was named knight-protector of the realms, but if they have truly fallen, then the Archangel Gabriel sent unto me the proclamation to become king." He tore off the lancer's helm and chucked it aside. It bounced into the street. He ran to a box of stuff on the steps of the brownstone. He thrust his hand into the box and withdrew an actual gold crown studded with jewels. He placed it on his head slowly, with great reverence. It reminded me of Napoleon crowning himself Emperor. "As the Archangel decreed unto me, I proclaim myself King Francis Delacroix, First King of New America, Ruler of the Divine Province of Atlanta, Protector of the Southlands, the Georgian Realm, and Defender of the Remnant of the Living World." He pulled his hands away from the crown and stood in glory on the first step of the tenement, staring into the sky with wide, wild eyes. Then, he turned those eyes to me. I sensed he was waiting for something.

"Oh…uh, long live the king!" I shouted.

"Long live the king," King Francis repeated. "Long live the king."

Ren came out of the alley after me. "What the hell is going on?"

"I'm not certain. Kneel."

Ren, without questioning it, dropped to a knee next to me. "Who's the geezer?"

"Our new king."

King Francis strode over, sword in hand. He stood before us. "And who is this brave young woman? Is she my emissary from the Eastern Northlands?"

"She is, uh…your Majesty. I present, uh, Renata of Brooklyn."

King Francis stared at her. "Speak truth, Renata of Brooklyn—is it as my emissary from Wisconsin spoke? Have the Northlands succumbed to the pox? Is my kingdom fallen?"

Ren looked to me, and I nodded slightly. She cleared her throat. "Uh, Twist *speaketh* truly, your Highness. We have traveled many days and found very few have survived the pox. There is an enclave of…uh, orcs in the Eastern Northlands. They have seized control of…" She looked to me for help.

"The orcs have seized York and Jersey, sire. Those provinces are a lost cause."

King Francis' face fell into a stern mask. "This is grave news indeed. Grave, grave news."

The pot on the grill behind him began to bubble over and the water and fat in the stew made the fire wildly hiss and spit. Steam rose in great clouds. King Francis spun and pushed the pot away from the center of the grill with his cooking mitt.

He turned back to us. "There shall be a feast this eve. We shall celebrate your safe arrival in the Southlands, and we shall celebrate my coronation."

"What's cooking?" Ren stood and eyed the fatty gray-brown stew in the pot.

"Nothing you want to put in your mouth," I whispered. At that second, a skull with bits of meat clinging to it and a melting jellied eye rose above the lip of the pot. It was a raccoon. Definitely a raccoon. The stew had a thick, gamy smell. It smelled like manure and copper pennies. It was enough to gag me.

King Francis strode toward us removing his cooking mitt. "But first, we must reward my subjects for their bravery. Kneel, and be recognized."

Ren gave me a look that clearly said, *He has a sword, should we run?* I shook my head. I dropped back to a kneel and hoped for the best. The old man seemed harmless. Delusional, but harmless. Ren took a knee beside me, reluctance etched on her face.

King Francis lowered his sword to my left shoulder, lifted it over my head to the right, and then back to the left. "I knight thee Sir Twist, of the Northlands, Defender of New America." He repeated the sword motions on Renata. "I knight thee, Sir Renata of Brooklyn, Defender of New America. I shall now hear your oaths."

Ren's eyes went wide and she whipped her head around to look at me. *"Oaths?"* she mouthed.

I stammered for a second. "I, Sir Twist, do hereby swear fealty to the Kingdom of New America, and to its rightful sovereign. I shall defend my King and his shores from all enemies foreign and domestic. So say we all."

King Francis smiled. He seemed pleased with my oath. He repeated, "So say we all."

Ren's mouth worked like a guppy for a second. "Uh…I, Sir Renata of Brooklyn, do hereby swear fealty to King Francis and his country. None shall harm my king while I hold breath in my chest. So say we all."

"So say we all," King Francis repeated. "Rise now, my knights, and we shall feast!" He turned and walked back to the bubbling stew pot on the grill. He put on a pair of heavy leather gloves and carried the pot to the table. When the pot moved, the smell seemed to fill the entire street. It was awful.

Ren grabbed me before I could move toward the table. "Is he mentally ill?" She said it low enough so that King Francis couldn't hear.

I nodded. "I think so. I'm pretty sure he is."

"He is definitely crazy if he thinks I'm going to eat that stew." Ren leaned closer. "Did you really quote *Battlestar Galactica*?"

I felt a sheepish smile play on my lips. "I did."

"Nerd."

"Hey, you knew where it came from," I said. "Takes one to know one."

We sat at King Francis' round table. He ladled big servings of fatty, nasty stew onto the plastic plates at the table. "Wait! This shall be a grand feast!" He ran inside the tenement, plate armor clanking, and returned moments later with a large wooden bowl full of fresh, beautiful peaches, and a bottle of wine. I don't know anything about wine, but judging from the bottle's design and how it was corked, it looked expensive. My parents usually drank wine out of a box they bought on sale at the local grocery store. I'm hardly a connoisseur.

King Francis used his sword to smash the neck off the wine bottle. He poured wine into yellow plastic wine glasses on the table, slopping excess liberally over the edges and onto the metal table. "Eat! Drink! This is a celebration!"

Ren practically face-planted the peaches. She bit into one and her eyes rolled backward into her head. "Oh, sweet heaven…these are *ah-maz-ing*."

I grabbed one and bit into it. Ren wasn't exaggerating. I'm from the Midwest. My experience with peaches was that I usually only saw them canned in a thick syrup. Those are pretty good. I liked those. I did not know how much I was missing with fresh peaches, less than a day from being on a tree. The smell, the texture, the taste—the only word for it is amazing. I understood why the little things were on the license plates. Over the past year, I'd eaten very little fresh food. The difference in quality made me realize that I was missing something important. I made a mental note to eat more fresh food. That meant I was going to have to learn to farm, to grow my own fresh food. Prior to the Flu, the only gardening I'd ever done was helping my mother plant a few herbs in a window box. And they mostly died.

"Eat up! Eat up!" Francis insisted. He wiggled out of the apron and breastplate of his armor and cast them aside. Underneath his armor, he was wearing an Atlanta Hawks basketball jersey. It looked like a real one, like he'd taken it directly from the locker room. I was willing to bet that was where he had found it, even. King Francis sat and picked up a fork. He used his sword to cut his meat, awkward as it was. He didn't hack at it, either. He used it daintily, sawing back and forth like someone would with a standard table knife. It did not work too well, but I was not going to argue with him about it.

I stuck my finger in the sauce of the stew and brought it to my tongue experimentally. When I tried to wipe the sauce on the tip of my tongue, my body rebelled, and I gagged. The stew went untasted. I wiped my finger on my napkin. I devoured the peach I had and picked up another one. "So, King Francis…" I didn't know how to breach the subject of the past year. I wasn't certain how far gone his mental state was. "Do you have…a queen, to whom we could pledge ourselves?"

King Francis' eyes narrowed, and he smacked his lips. He chewed some of the filthy meat and swallowed. "Ah, you speak of Good Queen Denise."

He set down his fork and touched his fingers to his forehead. "The pox, I'm afraid. She has been gone from us a year, at least."

"I'm sorry to hear that," I said. "That is a tremendous loss for the kingdom."

King Francis didn't seem to hear me. He was looking off into the sky. "A year, at least," he repeated. "And then Prince Francis, the second, fell…and then Princess Janelle, and Princess Michelle…and the grand-princes…and grand-princesses." Francis' lower lip trembled for a second, but he inhaled sharply through his nose and snapped back to whatever his reality was. He squared his shoulders. "A great loss for the kingdom, indeed."

Francis stood. "Come, come." He beckoned me toward the tenement. I followed and so did Ren. We stepped into his home. The living room was a disaster, cluttered with all manner of odds and ends scavenged from all sorts of places, scraps from museum exhibits, hospital supplies, and expensive cookware from a restaurant supply shop. There was a single recliner, well-used, that could be accessed from the entry, but that was it. All the other furniture was buried in junk. The bathroom in the home was filthy. King Francis used a five-gallon bucket for his business, and then took it out into the alley behind the home to dispose of it when full. The smell of urine and feces was thick in the hall.

Francis led us to the second story. He took us down the hall to a bedroom, paused, and whispered, "The queen rests waiting for the day that the goodness of my service inspires the angels to resurrect her." He opened the door. Inside, the dried corpse of Good Queen Denise was lying in the center of a queen-sized bed. Her decomposed body was melding with the sheets. Her face was dried and stretched tight to the skull. Her hair was scraggly and limp around the skull. The room was immaculate, though. It had been dusted frequently. Everything was in its place. There was no clutter.

"Jesus," Ren whispered. She backed down the hallway to the stairs.

"The pox claimed her," Francis said. "But in my wickedness, I was not claimed. I was not allowed to join her. So now, I must repent for that wickedness and hope that my efforts please the Archangel. They will bring her back to me. This was promised." Francis knelt by the foot of the bed and pressed his hands together in prayer. "Each day, I beg forgiveness and pledge my service to the kingdom. Soon, the angels will return to resurrect her. Very soon."

I wanted to say something, but nothing was coming to me. What do you say in a situation like this? This was far beyond my paygrade.

King Francis turned his head to the side. He spoke to the empty air. "I know, children. I know. Mother will come back to us; I promise you this." He turned to me. "The children—they miss their mother." He turned back to the emptiness. "Settle down, all of you. The day is coming. The horns will blow, and Archangel Gabriel will bring her back to us just as he promised!"

I backed away from the room. King Francis began telling his "children" to clean the living room, like he asked them to do yesterday. I walked down the steps to the street where Ren waited.

"What do we do?" Ren was chewing on the corner of her lower lip. It was her nervous tic. "This guy needs help, but…there's no help."

"I know." I said. "We should bring him with us."

"We should—but we're not going to." Ren was adamant. "Listen--I did an internship in a hospital, right? We had to go to all the wards and spend time. In the psych ward, they had this old guy—Mr. Blue, everyone called him. Mr. Blue was a jolly fat guy, kind of reminded me of a Currier and Ives Santa Claus. He wore old-fashioned pajamas, one of those Hugh Hefner robes, and leather slippers every day. Sometimes he had a paisley ascot. He was really smart, could talk about anything. Someone told me that he used to be a professor of physics at NYU. I don't know if that was true or not. He was kind. He was sweet. You'd think he was the sort that wouldn't hurt a fly. Turns out, he wasn't taking his medication at night and the night nurses weren't doing their job checking on him. One night, he had a break with reality, and he picked up a steel bedpan and beat a nurse almost to death with it, raging that she was trying to kill his wife. She had to quit nursing. She had severe brain damage."

"I get it. I know." I put my hands on my hips. "Moral questions like this were never brought up in my philosophy class in high school."

"They weren't in philosophy classes in college, either," said Ren. Through one of the upstairs windows, we could hear King Francis raging at invisible children and their misdeeds. His royal inflection and syntax were still intact. "We should just leave."

"Leave?" I didn't like the sound of that. It felt cruel.

Ren nodded. She was already drifting toward the alleyway. "We run. If he's as far gone as I think he is, he will probably think we're still here, just in hallucination form. Maybe he'll think he dreamed us up."

"But, he's old, and he's probably suffering." The idea of abandoning him made guilt churn in my stomach. It made me queasy. I thought about Doug. Doug was probably the same age as King Francis. Maybe King Francis was a little older than Doug. He looked like he was in good health, still getting around well, able to wear a full suit of armor. Those things aren't light. Upstairs, King Francis was screaming at the world, demanding to speak to the Archangel Gabriel or one of his messengers.

"I don't like it, either," said Ren. "But this ain't the world we knew anymore. We have to make tough decisions like this now. Can we take care of him? No. I don't even know what sort of anti-psychotics he needs to be on, nor do I know if we'll be able to find them. It is hard enough making sure we're okay every day. We can't do it for him. Fish or cut bait, right? We *have* to cut bait, Twist."

"But, to just leave him?"

Ren grabbed my arm at the elbow and started to pull me toward the RV. "It's not like we were taking care of him to begin with. He's gotten along on his own over the past year. He's eating. He's drinking. He's definitely taking care of his excretory needs. What more could we do for him? Do you want to stay here in this alley with him?"

"No."

"He's not going to leave his wife without a fight. Mark my words on that." That was a big trump card. Ren was right. There was no way a man who believed his wife was going to be resurrected by an angel was going to abandon her, and there was no way I was going to haul a dried corpse around in the RV. Ren stopped pulling at me and put her hands on my shoulders. She looked at me with her dark eyes. "We have to go."

She was right. I hated that she was right, but she was right. There was still enough daylight left that we could get into the countryside beyond Atlanta before stopping for the night. If a year had gone by and no one else had found King Francis, I was willing to bet that Atlanta was empty. There was nothing there for us. We had to leave. It didn't feel like it at the time, but later, after reflection, I realized it was our only logical choice.

"Come! Eat up! The feast recommences!" King Francis was standing at the door to his home.

I looked at Ren. I couldn't even hide the pained look from my face. "What do we say?"

Ren stepped forward and curtsied. "My king! A herald has just delivered a message. He says there may be an army to the east!"

"My word." King Francis loped down the steps and grabbed his longsword from where he'd left it on the patio table. "We shall be ready for them! Man the parapets, men. They'll not take us unaware. Send word to their herald that I am willing to meet with their leader to parley. If he will swear fealty, there need not be bloodshed. If he does it quickly, there may be a province in it for him to lord over in my stead, provided he pays his taxes!"

Ren saluted by closing her right fist and tapping it over her heart twice. "My king, it will be done. Sir Twist and I shall deliver the message immediately."

"Good, good! Go forth! Bring back any other survivors of the pox. We shall rebuild my kingdom together. I shall await your return." I copied Ren's salute, and we backed away. King Francis turned to the hallucinations of his children. "Did you hear that, children? Another army! The angels will be pleased. Your mother's resurrection is nigh!"

Ren and I backed around the corner. I grabbed the shotgun from where I'd left it propped up against the wall. Then, we ran. We ran like scared rabbits back to the RV, jumped in, and started it up. I slammed the gear-shift to drive and tromped the gas pedal. The rear wheels squealed as the RV lurched forward. We got the hell out of Atlanta as fast as we could.

Neither of us said anything. We didn't even look at each other; we just stared straight ahead through the windshield. The guilt we both felt filled the RV like a heavy, wet fog. It hung on our shoulders and pressed us into our seats. It made breathing a chore. I felt like crying, but I didn't. I swallowed those emotions and tried to convince myself that this was for the best.

We set up camp outside of Atlanta in Fairburn, a good-sized suburban town along Highway 85. We stopped at a Shell station across a wide, four-lane main thoroughfare opposite one of the South's finest institutions, a Waffle House.

While I dredged the ditches and the trees around the gas station for firewood, Ren walked off by herself, crossing the highway. She had no weapons. She took no supplies. She just walked away and hid somewhere nearby. I saw her shoulders shaking slightly as she walked away. I knew she was crying. *It was for the best*, I had to remind myself. *It was for the best*. I wonder how much absolutely horrible stuff has happened throughout history because someone convinced himself that it was for the best. No—scratch that. I never want to know the answer to that question. It would just depress me.

We could not have taken King Francis. As much as I wanted to, we just couldn't. He wouldn't have left his wife's corpse. He needed more help than either Ren or I could give. I had to repeat it like a mantra, *It was for the best. It was for the best. It was for the best. It was for the best.* If you lie to yourself enough, maybe after a few decades you might believe it. That was my hope, at least. I did not know if I would ever forgive myself for abandoning the old man. I knew I would remember the moment we lied to him and scampered away for as long as I lived. It was burned into my brain with crystal clarity. If it was one of those character-defining tests we get every so often, I'm pretty sure we just failed it.

Every good moment in my life is ephemeral, nothing more than vague passing thoughts. A first kiss. Dancing with my old girlfriend at a friend's house. My first football game at Camp Randall. All just snapshots, fading afterimages. Every bad moment, every blunder, every stupid mistake and dumb thing I've done lives in a part of my brain that replays them constantly, without being asked, in brilliant 4K HD and stereo surround. This moment leapfrogged all other previous stupid moments to take the lead. As I gathered wood, my brain played the old man's face on a loop. I saw his wagging beard and warm smile. My brain didn't play the images of the decaying woman in his bed or his diatribes at his invisible children. It only played the parts that would make me feel guilty.

I crawled down a small slope behind the gas station and walked through the trees and came upon a farm field. The field had been a cornfield at one point, but now it was choked with weeds. Thistles grew as tall as the new corn plants. I dropped the wood I was carrying, walked into the middle of the field, and just sat. I hated myself at that moment. I hated everything about the world. I hated the fact that I had to make a judgment call like that. I should be a freshman in college. My biggest decision should be between going to a house party or a campus-sponsored alcohol-free event. My biggest decision should be whether or not I was going to try to chat up a blond or a brunette at the party. Instead, I had just condemned a mentally ill man to die alone, trapped in his own delusions. I hated myself. If there was a god, I hated him. If there wasn't a god, I hated the universe.

I eventually went back to the campsite and made up the fire. I strung up my nylon Bear Butt hammock between the RV's rear ladder and a tree. I lay in it with a book on my chest, Steinbeck's *East of Eden*. It was a book I'd been meaning to read for months, but just never felt like starting it. On that day, the book would continue to go unread. I lay in the shade of the tree idly swaying, staring at the leaves in the tree above me and the sky beyond them. Fester came out of the RV to explore the surrounding area. He disappeared into the weeds for a while, but eventually emerged and leapt into the hammock with me. I picked a couple of burrs from his fur and cast them aside. I rubbed his ears and scratched his chin. He purred happily.

It was almost dark before Ren came back. Her eyes were puffy, her nose red, but she put on a brave face. She walked to the fire and sat in one of the canvas folding chairs. Neither of us spoke for a long time. I hadn't made any food because I didn't feel like eating. Ren didn't ask about food. I think she felt the same way.

"We did the right thing, right?" she asked. "We could still go back for him."

"We did the right thing," I said. "It feels like the wrong thing, but you were right. We couldn't have helped him. He wouldn't have left his wife."

She was silent for a long time. She put her face in her hands and rubbed her fingers against her forehead. "It doesn't feel like the right thing. It feels like we just murdered an old man."

"Maybe he was already dead. Maybe we're already dead. I don't know if there is a right answer."

"I hated philosophy class. Did I tell you that? I hated it. Medicine was a science. Cause, effect. Philosophy was all gray areas. I hated that. I want a clear answer. I want a defined path to follow." Ren stood up and grabbed a stick to stab into the low flames of the campfire. She stoked the embers and added another chunk of wood. "We did the right thing, right? It was my idea. You were going to help him. You were going to stay with him, weren't you? Like you did for the guy in Indiana."

"Maybe. Maybe not. I don't know. The old rules of humanity don't necessarily apply to us anymore. We have to make our decisions based on the needs of self-preservation, now. That guy—he was pretty far gone."

"How long until we break with reality like that? Is that our destiny?" Ren circled the fire to get out of the smoke. She ended up on the opposite side of it from me. In the light of the flames, she looked demonic. The shadows flitted across her face giving her low key-lighting like a horror movie villain.

"I don't think so," I said. "I think we'll be okay."

"Because we have each other?"

"And Fester." The cat was still on my chest.

"What happens if I die? What happens if you die? What then? Twist, there's a hell of a lot less people out here than I thought there would be. New York was a city of more than eight million people. Almost all of them died. Do you know what that was like?"

"It was like you've been hearing a rock concert your whole life, and suddenly that concert ended. Now, there is only deafening silence."

Ren folded her arms across her chest. "Yes. Exactly. I was worried about myself last winter. It got so lonely that I was sleeping sometimes twenty hours a day. I'd wake up, eat a cracker, put more wood on the fire, and go back to sleep. At one point, I figured that I was dead and just didn't know it, a full Cotard delusion. I started losing touch with reality. Is that going to be us someday?"

I got out of the hammock, much to the displeasure of the cat. I walked to the edge of the fire opposite Ren. "Yes. It might be." I wasn't going to lie to her. "I don't know what tomorrow holds. I don't know what five years from now holds. I certainly can't look ahead to twenty years from now, or forty, or sixty. Who knows anything? All I know is that we're still alive and relatively sane."

"And that has to be good enough for now, doesn't it?" she said.

"Yes."

Ren wiped the kernel of a tear from her eye with her fingers. "I hate this, man. I hate this whole situation. It's bullshit."

"Me, too. But, what other choice do we have? As long as we stay alive, we have the chance to make something of our lives. If we stop living, then that's it. Game over."

We were silent again. We stared at the flames, smelled the burning wood. Eventually, Ren spoke. "We did the right thing, right?"

"We did."

"Even if the right thing was the wrong thing?"

"Even if."

Ren sat down in the folding chair. "I hate this world."

We did not eat that night. Fester did. But, he was just a cat and understood little of the gravity of what Ren and I had just done to King Francis.

Eventually, we retired to the RV. We went through our ablutions and nightly rituals. We pulled the curtains, just in case. I went to the back bunk. Ren went to her bunk. I lay in the queen-sized bed and stared at the sky through the screen of the roof vent, my hands folded behind my head. I felt small and insignificant. The entire scene with the King of New America replayed over and over in my brain. If there were any positives about meeting King Francis, it was only that any thoughts of Bigfoot had been pushed out of my brain. I had other, more important things to fear at the moment, insanity being foremost among them.

An hour or so after we'd retired, I felt the Greyhawk shift and rock slightly. Ren was climbing down from her bunk. I heard a knock on the narrow door to the rear bunk. "Yeah?"

Ren opened the door. Her eyes were puffy again. She was clutching one of her pillows to her chest. "Can I—I mean...do you mind if I sleep with you tonight? In your bed?" She buried her face in her hands. "Christ, I sound like a child."

"No. Yes. I mean, yes you can sleep in here, and no you don't sound like a child." I moved over and made room in the bed for her.

Ren slipped into the sheets with me and lay on her back. She pulled the sheets to her chin. "I was just out there thinking about being alone again. I don't think I could do it, you know. If I was alone again—like, if you died or disappeared or something--I think I'd probably just swallow a bullet. The more I thought about it, the more I didn't want to be alone ever again, even in that bed, if just for tonight."

"I understand," I said.

Ren reached over and patted my hand. Her hand was so small compared to mine. Her fingers closed around my fingers. "Be here when we wake up, please. I don't think I can keep living in this world without you."

"I'm not going anywhere," I said.

She rolled over to face away from me. I lay on my side looking at her for a long time, at least an hour. Her breathing shifted into the slow, rhythmic breaths of sleep. Her body relaxed. I eventually laid my head down on my own pillows and stared at the vent in the ceiling.

I felt strange, though. Different. Was I falling in love with Renata?

Was I already in love with her and just hadn't realized it?

Eventually sleep claimed me, but I thought about that question until it did.

CHAPTER THIRTEEN

The Wedge

The next day, Ren wanted to drive the RV. She guided us south to Columbus, Georgia. We explored that city. Neither of us said anything about the previous day. It just hung in the air between us, a massive elephant in the room, but neither of us dared verbalize any thoughts. It was as if we both just decided to let the day be forgotten.

In Columbus, we raided a bookstore because Ren didn't like my taste in reading material. She got some books that I considered "too girly" or "too popular" for my tastes, mainly mass-market paperbacks like Nicholas Sparks, John Grisham, and Jodi Picoult, but she also picked up some things that I recommended that she hadn't read, yet. Stuff like L.M. Montgomery's *Anne of Green Gables* series and Robert Jordan's *Wheel of Time* series. We left with four canvas sacks of books loaded to the hilt. "This will keep me busy for at least a couple of years," Ren said as she stored them in the corner of her bunk.

We scavenged through a Sam's Club, through a few odd shops, and through the remnants of two grocery stores, both picked nearly clean before the Flu ended. Judging from the settled dust, I could tell that no one had been in the stores in well over a year.

Ren scooped canned goods into bags. "It's a good thing I really like corned beef hash."

"You say that now. See if you can continue to say it as it becomes a daily food source."

"I want more peaches." Ren blew the dust from some cans of beans. "We should find an orchard."

"We should," I said.

"We should also find a place to live near an orchard. Walking distance. And then we should plant our own peach trees."

"Probably a smart plan." I carried some boxes of plastic-sealed Wet-wipes to the RV. Even if they were dry, they could be revived with a little water. Wet-wipes were always good to have around.

"Twist, what time of year do you think it is? September?"

I shrugged. "Probably early-to-mid September, sure." I glanced over my shoulder at Ren. "Why?"

"I'm getting tired of being on the road."

I was, too. "We're in the South. We could stop anytime. I had planned on going to Madisonville, Louisiana, but I guess it doesn't matter too much where we stop. Where do you want to go?"

Ren raised her eyebrows. A mischievous smile lit on her lips. "I got a place to go. Not to settle, mind you. But, I've got a place to go."

The place ended up being Panama City Beach, Florida. As we cruised into town, Ren at the wheel, she said, "I came here on Spring Break during my sophomore year. Busted my ass working two jobs for most of the year to save up for it. It was a lot of fun, but afterward I wished I'd just kept the money and stayed home."

I'd only ever seen Spring Break beach parties on MTV. "Was it everything television said it would be?"

"Worse. Much, much worse. Everybody was bombed out of their gourds for a solid week. Vomit everywhere. Used condoms on the streets. Drunkards pissing in alleys. It was just gross. So much drama, too! I went down with a couple of girlfriends, and by the end of the week we were barely speaking to each other."

"Sounds like fun."

"It had its moments," said Ren. She guided the RV carefully through town while I rode shotgun. The town was battered. In the past year, at least one, but more likely multiple hurricanes had rolled through the area, maybe not direct hits, but damage had been done. Windows smashed, trees downed, and debris scattered everywhere.

"Looks like someone fought a war here." Ren gave a low whistle.

"It did. Mother Nature's side won."

The roads were choked with debris and damage. We had to park the RV in the shade of a tall building, and then hike to the shore. The clean sea breeze coming off the ocean helped to chase the musty mold smells coming from the windows of the apartments and office buildings and homes in the vicinity. It chased away the lingering sewage and death smell, too. Stray dogs scampered around the city, most had returned to at least a semi-feral state where they wouldn't approach us, but they respected us enough to stay away from us.

The Gulf of Mexico loomed at the end of the street. At first, it looked like nothing. The sun reflected hard from its surface and made the water look like it was full of floating gemstones. The closer we got, the more the blue-green colors surfaced in the distance. Up close, the water was spectacular, a hazy crystal blue and so clear! Being from Wisconsin, I was used to the dark, black-blue colored water of the lakes. This water was worthy of romance novel descriptions. The size of it was impressive. Gentle waves were coasting in from the gulf in two-foot swells, breaking into foamy whitecaps near the shore. The beach was clean and empty. Everything that usually pollutes beaches (specifically, other people) was absent. If there had been lifeguard stands, they were gone, stripped clean by storms. If there had been tacky beach furniture, it was also gone, blown to god-knows-where. Once we cleared the final edge of buildings, there was nothing but the water, the sand, and the sea air, a heady mixture of salt and clean breezes from far off the shore. It filled my senses, and I let it.

We walked to the beach, stopping at the edge to peel off shoes and socks. The sand was hot, almost too hot. I curled it in my toes and raked the top layer off to find the cooler, damp sand beneath. The texture of the sand was incredible, light and powdery. It was not the coarse sand I knew from the beaches on Lake Michigan or Lake Mendota back in Wisconsin. This stuff was sand from a fairy tale. If Ren had told me that she was done traveling, and she wanted to stay on that beach, I would have agreed wholeheartedly.

"We should have brought chairs," I said. "Or a blanket. The sand is too hot to sit on."

"We should have brought towels," said Ren. She strode toward the water. At the tidal edge, she set down her backpack and her gun belt. I watched as she slipped out of her t-shirt and shorts, and then peeled her sports bra over her head. She ran to the water in only a pair of black cotton shorts, splashing for the first few steps and then diving into the first wave that rose to meet her. She disappeared under water for several seconds, but then popped up shaking her head, water spraying everywhere. She called to me. "You coming or what?"

I followed her lead. I tossed my shirt, guns, and ruck at the spot where she ditched her gear. I emptied the pockets of my cargo shorts, tossing the odds and ends onto my shirt. Then, I ran to the water, splashing into the surf and letting the incoming swells swallow me. I closed my eyes and listened to the rush and surge of the waves crashing over me. It was a new sound, and I reveled in the freshness of it. I tasted the saltwater on my tongue and felt light and clean.

When I surfaced, Ren was standing waist-deep ten yards to my right. She was laughing and turning her back to the waves, letting them crash over her. I sputtered and tried not to stare at her breasts. Believe me, though, I wanted to.

Hers were not the first breasts I'd ever seen. I'd seen Emily's, of course. Em and I never had sex, but we weren't exactly prudes, either. I'd seen my fair share of illicit websites, *National Geographic* magazines, and Health class textbooks, which obviously aren't the same thing, but all had breasts. I had seen random flashes of breasts when I was near the UW campus during Freakfest. I was no stranger to female bodies, but it had also been a year and a half and change since I'd last seen boobs, and I was still an eighteen year old, red-blooded, American male. I couldn't *not* look, but I also tried hard not to look. I think I made it too obvious. I'm sure I made it creepy and awkward, like I tend to make every social situation. I was scanning the sky with Ren standing right in front of me.

She rolled her eyes. "It's okay, fool. You can look. We've come this far together; I think I can trust you with getting an eyeful of the ladies." I knew I was blushing furiously, but I looked anyhow. Ren continued, "I mean, we're probably going to have to get used to each other, y'know. We're not Amish. This is the South. It's going to be hot."

"I suppose you're right."

"Besides, it's not like it's a big deal, right? Especially since…" She trailed off and shrugged a shoulder at me in a manner that suggested I was supposed to know what she meant."

"Since what?"

"Since you're…you know." One side of her mouth smiled. She made a shrugging motion.

"Since I'm what?"

Her eyebrows knitted together. "You know."

"I know what?"

She looked exasperated. "Since you're…gay."

"I'm *what?*"

Ren's eyes went wide. There was the most painful and awkward silence between us. Then Ren clamped her hand over her mouth. "Oh, jeez. I'm sorry. Were you not *Out* yet? I don't know what you're waiting for, in that case. It's okay. Most, if not all, of the anti-LBGT people are dead. Be who you want to be, be who you are. It's okay. I don't care."

"But, I'm not gay." I meant to say it in a normal tone, but I think it came out slightly panicked and whiny.

Ren's mouth fell open. "What?"

"I'm not gay. At all. Why would you think I was? I mean, I've told you stories about my girlfriend, Emily."

"I know, but I…" She cringed. "I thought she was like a beard or something. I thought that she was one of those fabled 'high school girlfriends' a guy used to keep the bullies at bay until he graduated and could come out in college."

"I'm not gay!" I sounded too defensive, but I did not care at that point. "Never have been. I mean, it's not as if I'd be ashamed to admit it if I was, but I'm not. One hundred percent not gay. Totally into the ladies over here."

"Oh…geez." Ren half-covered her breasts, and then dropped her hands. "I just…thought--"

"What did you think?"

"Well, you're really well read for a Midwestern guy."

What kind of regional racism was that? What did that even mean? I sputtered, "We do read in Wisconsin, you know."

"I don't mean it like that. Just—you're kind and thoughtful. You haven't tried to make a pass at me the whole time we've been together. I mean, I slept in your bed and you didn't even try to cop a feel or something. You didn't even put a hand on my hip. I'm used to guys who..." She bit her lip. "I just...assumed..." She cringed again. "Twist, I am really sorry. I guess I shouldn't have assumed. I...didn't mean anything by it."

I was hurt, really. But, I buried my feelings and waved off her apology. "It's okay. I'm not, though."

"Oh." Ren's mouth twisted into a half-smile. "I guess I feel slightly more self-conscious now about being topless."

"What's done is done," I said. "I won't complain." I tried to smile, but I don't smile well, and I'm sure it came across like some sort of creeper pervert.

There was a long pause. Ren sank deeper into the water so it rose to her neck. The clarity of the water did not do a good job of hiding her. She licked her lips and looked at me. "Twist?"

"Yeah."

"I don't want to have sex with you."

My eyebrows arched. "What? Where did that come from? Who even brought that up?"

Ren crossed her arms over her chest. She gave me an awkward smile through gritted teeth. "Let's not talk about it now. Let's just have fun."

I was confused and a little perturbed. I'm sure it showed on my face. "Oh-kay." I fell backward into an approaching wave, but it wasn't fun anymore. I felt like she just dropped a bomb on me, like there was suddenly a massive wall between us. I stayed underwater for probably too long. I didn't know what to say to her. My own emotions were in flux. When I finally surfaced, she was next to me.

"Oh, I was worried. You were underwater for a long time."

I didn't know what to say in the silence between us, so I just sort of half-nodded and half-shrugged. I coughed up some seawater.

"I'm sorry," Ren apologized again. "I just...I'm confused now. I was thinking you were gay almost from that first night we met. I guess I got used to that idea. At the time, it was easy. It made everything simple. We could just be friends. And now, if you're not—and, I mean, we've got this whole Adam and Eve thing going..."

"It's okay." I insisted. I was going to say something else, but what else was there to say? After the Flu, I suppose I never expected sex or romance to be an issue. I hadn't really had any desire to have sex since the Flu first started. I had too much else to worry about without sex complicating life. I certainly didn't expect her to just fall in love with me if she didn't want to, but now I was just confused. So, I just repeated, "It's okay. Really. No problems." I tried to smile, but I'm sure I didn't sell it well. Awkward. Creepy. Maybe a little heartbroken. No, a lot heartbroken.

"No. I owe you an explanation. That sounded horrible when I said it, and I need you to know where I'm coming from." Ren started wading back to shore. I followed because I didn't know what else to do.

Ren started to dress, pulling her clothes onto her wet body. "It has nothing to do with you, or who you are, or anything like that."

"It's fine." I kept saying. "You don't owe me any explanation. We're both free and independent people. You can hold your views. I can hold mine. We can still be friends and rely on each other. We don't have to do anything else--"

"Twist—" She grabbed my arm. She locked eyes with me. There was a dark intensity to them. She gestured at the bay, at the empty buildings, at the deserted streets. "Look around us. I got you, and you got me. That's it. There's no one else. If I got pregnant or something, I'd have to deliver that baby in a crumbling world with little to no medicine. You know what the mortality rate was for women giving birth in the olden days? It was like thirty-three percent. That means I'd have a one-outta-three chance to die during or after delivery. Plus, there's the whole emotional thing that sex brings. What if it changes who we are and what we have between us? We cannot afford to alienate each other. It's better to stay the way we are than risk everything." Ren cut off her rant and sighed. She lunged forward and latched her arms around my waist. She pressed her head into my chest, clutching me to her as hard as she could. I felt the world melt around me. I looped my arms around her. We stood in the sand, dripping wet, and just held each other. Few things in my life have ever felt so good. Ren's voice muffled against my chest. "I just can't take any chances on losing you, Twist. You're all I have."

The rest of the afternoon was very awkward. On the one hand, I felt like we had broken through an important door between us; we had opened up and shared. Cards were on the table, now. We had addressed the elephant in the room. On the other hand, I realized that our relationship had been previously based on the stance that she thought I had been gay. Gay Me was apparently a very different person to her than Not Gay Me. The revelation of my heterosexuality forced a very distinct wedge into our tiny, confined world, and that only served to magnify the unspoken fallout from abandoning King Francis back in Atlanta. Everything between us felt weird and wrong now. It was uncomfortable. It needled at me.

In silence, I drove the RV out of Panama City Beach and headed west. Ren sat in the passenger seat cuddling Fester in her arms like he was an infant. She idly stroked his chest and belly. His big, stupid head lolled over the crook her arm and he squeezed his eyes in pleasure. Neither of us said anything. It felt like the first day we started riding together, both of us trying to feel each other out, trying to gauge how we would behave, how we would react. The only difference was that Ren was not looking at me, was not trying to find things along the road to point out to force us into conversation.

The empty wasteland was painful when I was alone. I thought it would be better with someone else, but now I wasn't sure anymore. It was going to make for an awkward fifty or sixty years if we both lived a long time and never got over this. I pictured us in rocking chairs on the porch of an old farmhouse, still walking on proverbial eggshells and talking around the fact that I only saw her almost naked once because she thought I was gay.

We camped in the parking lot of a gas station in Pensacola. I let Ren set up camp while I worked on filling the tank. I noticed the gas didn't look right. I couldn't tell what was wrong with it, though. It just wasn't right. I hoped my filters would continue to work. We were so close to finding a home. We were so close to being done. I just needed the van to hold out another couple of days. Then, it could lock up and become a lawn sculpture. I'd convert it to my writing shed or a man cave on rusting rims. We would figure out a new life after that.

Ren was reading a travel guide about Louisiana that she'd plucked from the convenience store. "Madisonville is right next to Lake Pontchartrain, right?"

"Yeah. I figured it would be a good place to be. Big supply of fresh water."

Ren held up a finger. "Wrong, dude. Lake Pontchartrain is brackish. It has an inlet to the ocean."

"I thought 'brackish' meant unpleasant. I was going to make a purification system."

"It also means a mixture of fresh and salt water."

My face flamed in embarrassment. "Ooh. That means—"

"We ain't drinking that water." Ren consulted a map. "How about Houston?"

"What about it?"

"Lake Houston is just northeast of Houston. It will have land for hunting and farming around it. There is plenty of fresh water, plus we'd still be able to scavenge the city of Houston if we needed stuff. It's not too far beyond Louisiana. Maybe an extra day or two of travel."

It was a good plan, as far as I could tell. "I guess that's what we'll do, then." I had never considered living in Texas, but I guess there could be worse places.

"Tomorrow, we'll head to Texas." Ren closed her map and went back into the RV to throw it onto the passenger chair.

"Deal."

Ren put her bare feet on the dash. "You think we'll be able to find a nice house there?"

"Sure. Plenty of them, probably." That was true enough. I refrained from telling her that most of them might take a little elbow grease to get them up to par, but that was nothing we couldn't handle.

"What about a house with a fireplace? It's Texas. Might not be too many of them."

I thought for a second. "We can build an outdoor wood-fire oven. I've seen kits for them at Home Depot. They're made of concrete. They'll last a long time. We'll adapt. We'll improvise. We'll overcome. We can figure it out as we go." I settled into my chair next to Ren. She handed me a plate with steaming canned corned beef hash and a plastic fork. I ate without tasting the food.

We didn't speak. An hour passed. The awkwardness between us was sickeningly uncomfortable, like a hair shirt or thumbscrews. It was like we were on a bad blind date that we couldn't leave. Fester stalked his way out of the RV to nestle himself in Ren's lap. He might have been my cat to start with, but it was clear that while he enjoyed my company, he preferred Ren. At that moment, that bothered me more than anything else. I got antsy. I wanted to say something, but I had nothing to say. I didn't know what to do. I didn't know how to repair the gap between us. The jittery feeling in my gut worked its way to my legs. My feet started to itch. I had to move. I stood. It was an abrupt motion. It startled Ren and Fester. I scratched at what felt like bugs crawling on my scalp. I had to get away from there for a while. "I'm going for a walk. See what I can see. You be okay here alone?"

"Yeah, sure." Ren looked concerned, but she said nothing. "Do you want—" She stopped. I knew she had been about to ask if I wanted her to come with me, but she had reconsidered. She chewed her lower lip for a second. "Twist?"

"Yeah?"

"Be...be careful," Ren said. I nodded and started to walk away from the camp, but Ren called back. "Take a gun, at least. If something happens, shoot. I'll come running."

I didn't feel like I needed a gun. Part of me wanted to willfully ignore her like a petulant child. *You're not the boss of me!* I knew that would only lead to more discussion between us, her pleading and me protesting, and I didn't want that at the moment. I reached into the Greyhawk and plucked my gun belt from its spot. I didn't fasten it around my waist, like normal. I just threw the belt over my shoulder. I was wearing nylon basketball shorts and a pair of Adidas flip-flops. It wasn't the sort of look that said "bad ass gunslinger." If you're going to carry a weapon, you should at least look the part. Long pants. Boots. Look like you're ready for a fight. I looked like I was ready for a quick pick-up game of three-on-three. As an afterthought, I grabbed a flashlight, too.

I meandered through the beachfront properties, shining my flashlight into the windows. Most of the homes had suffered damage over the previous year. Windows were broken. Palmetto trees were toppled. The formerly manicured hedges and lawns had grown out of control. Chunks of siding or stucco were ripped from homes and lay on the ground to be slowly reclaimed by the Earth.

I walked north for maybe a mile, maybe a little less than a mile. I found a gated community with houses that easily would have been in the half-million dollar-and-up range before the Flu. Nice places, all vaguely similar in design and coloring, but different enough to not quite be cookie-cutter. The large, wrought-iron gate at the community's access road was no longer secured. Both halves had been opened, probably to allow ambulance access while the Flu was becoming epidemic. A few of the homes were looted. Most of them weren't. On a whim, I walked into one of the looted homes because the front door was wide open, propped open with a heavy iron doorstop. The house had been looted and destroyed. The looters had survived late into the Flu, apparently. They had put holes in most of the walls, smashing through the drywall with hammers, feet, or fists. They had smashed mirrors and picture frames. Carpet had been lit on fire and swaths of it burned. On one wall, someone had spray-painted *The Flu is a Government Lie Created to Get Away with Killing the Poor!* On a large entertainment center, a massive flat-screen TV had been shattered, the orange-handled claw hammer used to do it still hanging from the center of the broken screen. The house, without the damage, would have been amazing. The kitchen was large and open, the living areas equally so. It was a house that my parents would have willingly sold me to a pit-fighting ring to have, and we hadn't been even been anywhere close to poor. My parents worked to have a very distinct middle-class life. This was a high-end upper-middle class home, maybe even on the lower end of upper class.

I moved to the stairway and walked upstairs slowly. I didn't smell a lot of human death in the house, possibly because it had been well-aired out over the past year, but it didn't smell *right,* either. There was something unusual about the air. It smelled like feces and rot, but not the standard rot smells. It was different. It was something I had not smelled in my travels to that point.

The stairs exited at the second floor hall. A half-dozen doors were visible along the corridor. All but one was open. I moved to the first one, the only closed door, and tried the handle. Locked. That made it much more curious. I backed up and kicked the door police-style, planting my foot flat on the door just above the handle. The door cracked loudly, but didn't give. Two more kicks broke the doorframe. Beyond was a bathroom, a large, marble-tiled room with a standing shower, a toilet and bidet, a large pedestal sink, and a wooden armoire for storing towels and supplies. The bathroom's only window had cracked, a corner of it broken out. In the corner of the large shower was a dried corpse.

At this point, I was becoming so jaded to skeletons and mummies that I didn't even blink. They still weren't my favorite things to happen upon, but they didn't faze me like they used to. I crept over to the skeleton and knelt next to it. The skin had rotted from most of the skull, but there was still moldering flesh and tissue beneath the clothes. Judging from the clothes, this was likely the person, or one of the persons who trashed the house. The body was lying on its left side, head tilted to the ground. The sleeve of his jacket was rolled up on the left arm, a needle still stuck into the dried flesh at the crook of the arm. A lighter was on the floor of the shower, as well as a dirty, brown-stained spoon. Heroin. I guess it seemed a better way to go out than letting the Flu win. I wondered if that person had even been experiencing symptoms of the Flu. It might have been accidental overdose, too. But why here? There were a billion questions I would never get answers to, and this was one of them. I left the corpse to its resting place.

I went to the next room down the hall. There was a study filled with books. The smell of mold was heavy there. There were two small bedrooms. They lacked personality. Guest rooms, probably. At the end of the hallway, I peeked into the final bedroom. This would go down as one of the great regrets of my short, young life.

My flashlight caught eye-shine first, and then I heard a low, throaty rumble. I saw bones, the remnants of a small deer in a corner. Its head was bent back at a horrible angle and most of its body was missing. Dried tendrils of tissue extended from the carcass. I caught a glimpse of a massive animal curled on the king-sized bed in the room. It took up a great amount of space on that bed. I saw a lot of rusty orange fur intermixed with thick, black stripes. A tiger, a broad-headed, glossy-eyed Bengal tiger, had turned the bedroom into its lair.

My heart stopped for a moment. I clicked the flashlight off and backed out of the room. I took two steps backward, spun on the ball of my foot, and sprinted for the stairs. I was out of the house in a flash, my legs carrying me with speed that I hadn't known I possessed. Terror does a lot to help you run. Even in flip-flops.

The tiger followed, though. I'd disturbed its slumber. I had invaded its lair. And I had run from it. Of course it was going to follow. The tiger might have been a zoo escapee or one of the animals released by a keeper in the waning weeks of the Flu. It might have been one of those exotic animals trafficked to America by drug dealers or idiots with too much wealth and not enough IQ points. It didn't matter. It must have known humans, because it had been living comfortably in a home, and it had followed me. Maybe it thought I had food. Maybe it was just curious. I don't know. I saw animals in the wild on my travels. Most predators will run from humans. If you make noise, black bears will run. Wolves avoid people altogether. Coyotes fear humans. This tiger *followed*. It *knew* humans. That made it particularly dangerous. Was I food to it? A plaything? Or a provider?

The tiger was out the front door by the time I made it to the end of the driveway of the house. I made it to the street before the animal caught me. It was three hundred pounds of sprinting apex-predator. I couldn't outrun it. I felt claws slash my lower back and left butt cheek. It ripped through my flesh like tearing paper. White hot pain flashed through my body. There was so much pain that I couldn't even scream out. It was paralyzing. The tiger's broad head and shoulder smashed into my back and sent me sprawling face down on the asphalt. The skin on my knees and palms was shredded on the rough pavement. I couldn't get breath. I could feel blood seeping into my clothes. A steady stream of blood was seeping from my back to my sides. The tiger had veered to the left slightly after taking me down. I saw it out of the corner of my eye. It was rounding back on me. I fought to make my arms work. Every move hurt. The flesh on my back was shredded. The muscles had probably suffered some damage, too. My breathing got labored. A wave of cold fear rushed over me, the kind of fear that shakes you to the core of your being. I started to get light-headed and I felt a wave of nausea. Shock? I bit hard on the end of my tongue. This was *not* the time to pass out.

The gun belt was still looped over my left shoulder. I rolled to my right side, my right hand flailing, trying to catch the handle of the gun through some sort of miracle. The tiger snuffled lowly. Its head was down. It was moving slowly. It saw me writhing. It knew the game was almost over. Its massive head snuffled at my shoulder. I felt teeth start to sink into my shoulder. The power in the animal's jaw was immense. I felt my skin pop beneath its pronounced canines. I screamed out in pain. I think this scared the cat. It released my shoulder and backed up a half step.

I caught the pistol handle and somehow yanked it free of the holster. The tiger stepped forward, a massive paw reaching for me, steel-black talons bared. It slashed at my forearm, toying with me like a house cat would with a mouse. I felt my forearm tear open beneath its claws. I fired. Once. Twice. The first bullet clipped the animal in the rear leg. It leapt to the side. The second bullet hit it higher in the flank, near its rear hip. The tiger snarled and backed away. I fired a third time with a wobbly arm. The bullet flew wide, but the noise and sudden pain of the first two shots was enough to make the tiger retreat. It turned and ran, disappearing in the night in a flash of orange and black.

My body was shuddering involuntarily. I was hurt. Badly. Every move—even breathing—sent waves of crippling pain through me. Those stories about people gaining superhuman strength or determination when they were injured—that wasn't happening for me. I think I might have even pissed myself. There was so much blood seeping to my groin that I couldn't be sure. I was getting cold and weak. A mile, in the grand scheme of the universe, is nothing. It is an inconvenience. At that moment, it was about a mile back to the RV, back to Renata, back to my only chance to get help before I bled out or went into shock. It might as well have been interstellar travel. It was an insurmountable distance in my condition. I came to terms with a cold reality: I was going to die.

Death was not scaring me at that moment, though. I think I was ready for it. I had been ready for it since the Flu first started knocking off wide swaths of the world's populace. I had made my peace with death. I was willing to go. But, then I thought of Renata. I thought of her trying to make it in this world without me. I did not doubt that she could—she was tough. She was a Brooklyn girl. She would be fine. But, I realized that I selfishly did not *want* her to live without me. I wanted to be there with her in this world, even if it meant only being near her, and never *with* her. Near her would be enough. I did not want to abandon her. I needed to keep living.

I had twelve more shots in the semi-auto. I squeezed off three more into the night sky. I would have done more, but the strength in my hand failed. Three was all I could muster. Renata hearing those shots was my only hope. I dropped the gun. I remember laughing, thinking of the absurdity that she would hear the pistol shots so far away. She was near the ocean with its constant static noise of waves. There was wind. There were other sounds in the night, dogs and insects. There was no way she would hear those gunshots. It had been a slim chance, at best. I did not want to resign myself to death, though. The will to keep fighting reared up inside me. I absolutely *did not* want to die.

The MagLite lay six feet to my right. Using my right leg to propel myself, I was able to rock my body across the pavement to the flashlight. It took more effort and energy than I thought it would. I could feel myself getting weaker by the second. I bounced and scraped along the pavement. I extended my hand, grabbed the heavy handle, and thumbed the button. The bright, white light lit the darkness. I pointed the light down the street toward the campsite, toward Renata. Then, I let my head drop to the pavement. The ground was still warm from absorbing the sun during the day. It felt good, not too hot. Pleasant. I started to get sleepy.

I tried to fight unconsciousness, but shock and blood loss took over. I felt sick and cold all at once, a wracking shudder ran through my entire body. I started seeing amoeba-like blobs of black swimming across my vision. The pain in my back and shoulder lessened, and then it left me entirely. Comforting darkness blanketed me. I closed my eyes and let it.

I only remember bits and pieces for a while after that, little flashes and fragments of memory and experience. Some of them felt so strange that I think they were dream-state hallucinations. Some were definitely real.

Bigfoot tending to my wounds was likely a hallucination. I remember clearly seeing an ape-like visage up close, a friendly, rubbery Sasquatch face smiling benevolently. The shaggy mop of ape-fur around his leathery face smelled of violets and summer grass. I felt thick, heavy fingers prodding at my back and sides. "You'll be okay," Sasquatch said to me. "I will make sure of it." I tried to thank him, but he swirled into darkness in a whorl of black fog and disappeared.

The RV headlights roaring down the road toward the MagLite's beacon. That felt real, at least *more* real than Bigfoot did. They looked like the eyes of an angry monster, brilliant and blinding. For a moment, I was scared, but then my body and brain told me I was too hurt to be scared. I relaxed and decided the monster could kill me if it wanted. I would not fight it anymore.

Renata going into full emergency room nurse-mode was definitely real. I have vague visions of her leaping out of the cab, rushing for the First Aid kit, and falling to her knees by my side. There are sound bites and flashes of vision lodged in my memory. Gauze. Iodine. Ren sniffling back tears. Ren yelling commands at me. *Don't go. You stay here with me!* Swearing—mine and Ren's. A fire. Boiled water. Volcanic, white-hot pain as Ren scrubbed the wounds trying to clear out whatever manner of toxic infestation the tiger's dirty claws might have put into me. There was the warmth of my own sticky blood running down my sides. I remember being dragged into the RV. For a petite, diminutive woman, Ren somehow muscled me into the camper with incredible strength. Did I help her? Did I stand and walk with her support, or did she lift me? I can't remember. After that, there are great gaps of darkness. I woke at one point and found myself lying facedown on my bed, my head propped to the side so I could breath. I tried to roll over, but lightning bolts of pain kept me facedown. I felt feverish and sweaty. Sick. Sicker than I had ever been in my life. I was immune to viruses, but not bacteria. Why was I so sick? Did I throw up? My stomach felt empty. My mouth tasted like death. I worried about what the bile from my stomach would do to my teeth. I let the darkness come back.

It was two days before I remember waking up and being fully conscious, fully aware. Even then, I was not well. I was sick, feverish. I was hot and cold all at once. The blankets I had on my legs were simultaneous too heavy, too hot, and not warm enough. Everything on my back hurt. My left ass-cheek felt like a hunk of rawhide leather, stiff and unwilling to bend. I was lying on my bed. I would have thought that I would have needed to pee, but I didn't. I realized that I didn't feel quite normal *down there*. My first instinct was that the tiger got my penis. Let me tell you—that was a blast of panic the likes of which I had never experienced. If you need a reason to suddenly be a hundred-percent conscious, just pretend a man-eating beast got your junk. You, my friend, will be *wide a-friggin'-wake*. After a few seconds of self-examination, I realized there was a tube coming out of my urethra. Renata had put a catheter in me. I didn't know where she'd gotten a catheter, but there were plenty of hospitals out there. I am sure she knew what she was doing.

I was naked beneath a sheet on my bunk. I could feel thick, heavy bandages on my back. The RV was swaying, and I could hear the sounds of the engine and tires-on-road. We were traveling. I was suddenly aware that I was thirsty. My throat, my tongue, my lips were dryer than desert air. I was thirstier than I have ever been in my life. I felt weak from thirst. I tried to call out, but it came out a croak. I tried to summon wetness from my salivary glands by kneading my tongue into the roof of my mouth until I was able to approximate something close to speech. It was weak and feeble, but I was able to call her name. "Ren."

She heard me. The brakes immediately locked up and the RV lurched to a hard stop. The sudden change in momentum hurt. I groaned involuntarily. I heard the transmission shift to park. I heard the seatbelt being unbuckled. I could not look back over my shoulder, but I could feel her coming. She was at my side in an instant. "Twist? You there? You awake? How do you feel?"

I licked my lips. I coughed. I felt the bed move slightly as she knelt on it. She rolled me to my side and placed a bottle in my mouth. I was able to suck down some water, lukewarm, but clean and wet. It made me cough. Coughing hurt. The muscles along my left side were torn and sore. "Feel okay." I grimaced. Any hope of being cool and stoic went out the window. I was in a bad way. "No, that's a lie. I feel bad, actually. Everything hurts."

"I don't doubt that," she said. Ren laid me back on my stomach. She started looking in my eyes with a penlight. "You got ripped the hell open by some kind of big animal."

"Tiger."

"Really? A tiger did this?" Ren shook her head. Her tongue made a clicking noise. "Amazing. You lost a lot of blood and you had a fever." Her hand cupped my forehead. "You still do. You're very warm." She left the bed and returned with pills. "I would have given you something intravenous, but it was all expired or stored incorrectly because of the lack of refrigeration. I couldn't risk it. I made do with a little saline solution to help you get back some fluids. That stuff will keep for a long while." She put the pills in my mouth and made me take more water with them. I swallowed them, but they felt like large chunks of gravel in my throat. I coughed and struggled to get them down.

"Where are we?" I choked the words out.

"The panhandle of Mississippi, almost to Louisiana. We stayed an extra day in Pensacola to get you travel-ready."

I nodded. I tried to picture the location on the map in my head, but the whole Mississippi/Alabama/Louisiana area blurred into a single lump in my brain. Was it Alabama, then Mississippi, or the other way around?

"You scared me." Ren started to laugh, but it came out as a half-sob. She spent several minutes composing herself. I could hear her sniffing. She used a corner of my sheets to wipe her eyes. I felt her fingertips touch my right shoulder. They were warm and soft, but toughened by a life of surviving. "I mean, I didn't think you were going to die. You would have if I hadn't found you, but once I found you I knew I could save you. I just…couldn't stop thinking about what I would do if you died."

"You'd adapt. You'd make do."

Ren's voice was just above a whisper. "No. You do not get to die on me. Not now. Maybe in sixty or seventy years, we can discuss it, but not now. I need you too much." Her voice cracked with emotion. She sniffed again. "Please swear to me you won't try fighting a tiger again."

I felt a corner of my mouth curl into a smile. "No promises."

She punched my shoulder gently. "Jerk." Even the light jostling hurt, but I didn't complain. Her hand stayed on my shoulder, gripping it lightly.

I shifted my body a bit and felt fire burning down my back and on my left side. "How bad is it?"

"Bad enough," she said. "Mostly flesh wounds. A little bit of muscle tearing. The tiger got you good, sank its claws deep into your back muscles, but it didn't hit anything vital. You're going to be sore for a long time. Going to take a long time to heal. Want some painkillers?"

"Hell, yes." I remembered Doug and his painkillers. *Hit me again, dealer. I only have a five and a three showing.*

Ren got up from the bunk and came back with another bottle of pills. "Just take one. It'll knock you out for a while."

I swallowed the pill. It could not start working fast enough. I tried to tighten the muscles in my back, but the flash of pain made me yelp. I gritted my teeth and turned to look at Renata's face. Her cheeks were tear-streaked. I reached up and ran my thumb over one of her cheeks. She grabbed my wrist and held my hand on her face.

"Twist, I'm sorry--"

I cut her off. "No, I am sorry. This is my fault. I was angry and stupid, and I should not have gone off alone."

"No, I am sorry. I was stupid. I was confused. This is on me."

I started to protest, but she pressed a finger to my lips. "No talking, now. Your job is to just rest. Get better. I can handle things for a little while. Okay?" She leaned down and pressed her lips to my cheek. I inhaled. She smelled like violets and summer grasses. Was she Bigfoot? It felt good to have her face that close to my face. I did not want it to end.

It was then I noticed Fester. He was curled up in what I called the "snail pose." He was a lump with his head up and his back curled like a snail's shell, but his paws completely tucked under him. He was staring at me with concerned eyes.

"He never left this bed, except to eat and use his box," Ren said. She ran a finger over the cat's head. He closed his eyes and purred loudly. "Wouldn't even come sit by the fire with me at night."

At that moment, I felt a swell of love for that stupid, semi-traitorous cat. I should have known he would not have forsaken me. I laid my head back on the bed. "Hot in here."

Ren laughed. "Hot everywhere. It's Mississippi." She sat on the bed next to me. She reached out a hand. I felt her fingers lightly caressing the back of my neck. It was soothing. The endorphins her touch gave me helped bury a lot of the pain. Or was it the pills? Maybe both. I let my eyes close. That's the last thing I remember that day.

If it was the last thing I ever remembered, I would have been okay with it. I felt loved. Cared for. I felt hopeful. I felt like the future was broad and expansive, an unwritten book. I felt whole again, even if it was a new shape for feeling whole, it was still a feeling of being whole for the first time in more than a year.

Best of all, I did not feel alone.

CHAPTER FOURTEEN

The End of the Road

It took almost a week to cross Louisiana. With only Ren able to do all the work, we spent a lot less time on the road. She had to clean my wounds, change my bandages, and give me drugs to fight off infection and pain. She had to pump all the gas by herself. She was not used to it. She fatigued a lot faster than I did. It took her longer. The gas was also going south (no pun intended) in quality. The world's remaining supply of gasoline was quickly turning gelatinous. The time of the internal combustion engine was coming to an end. The future was looking painfully rustic and pioneer-like. Maybe that was a good thing?

We did swing through Madisonville because I insisted. Ren helped me struggle into the library where I had intended to live when I first set out from Wisconsin a lifetime ago. There on the wall in the entry, I wrote a message to anyone who might have seen my message back in Sun Prairie and traveled to Louisiana looking for me:

> *Moved to Lake Houston, Texas.*
> *Come find us. We are surviving.*
> *We are still alive.*
> *—Twist and Renata*

I was mostly bedridden for four more days. In that time, Ren spent a lot of time keeping the wounds on my back moist beneath the bandages so the scabs wouldn't form too quickly. There were no stitches because the tears were too ragged. There were no clean edges to join. I would have scabs for a while, and eventually the wounds would turn into ragged scars. The muscle damage hurt more than the skin damage. The skin damage burned a bit, and it itched where it was healing, but the small tears in the muscle *hurt*. I don't know of a better way to explain it other than that. A deep-set ache made every motion, every breath a chore.

Ren pulled the catheter, since I was awake and able to deal with that business on my own, with a bit of assistance. Ever had a catheter pulled out of your junk? It's not a great feeling. It burns and it feels like your bladder is being yanked out through your urethra. All in all, given a choice between yanking a catheter or having chocolate cake, I'm just saying--always take the cake. Once the catheter was out, and I stopped screaming, I started laughing.

"What's so funny?" Ren demanded.

"A couple of days ago, you and I were embarrassed because I saw your boobs."

"Yeah?"

"And you just stabbed a tube into my junk and then ripped it out. You've cleaned bedpans for me. If you don't find that hilarious, check your pulse, lady."

Ren tried to be angry at me for a moment, but she couldn't. A half-smile curled on her mouth, and she punched my shoulder. "Jerk."

At the end of the fourth day, I was feeling better. I numbed up with a couple of hydrocodone pills, and I actually sat up on my own. Every move was painful, but I was able to grit my teeth and get through it. That was the first step. It was important. After that, it would be a long, slow expansion toward getting back to normal, but I would recover. Nothing would be easy in the next few months, but I would recover. I would eventually be fine. I would have some bad-ass scars, to be sure—but I would be fine.

That whole time I was bedridden, I didn't think about *surviving*. I only thought about *living*. That was enough. I just worried about continuing to live, to breathe, to take in air and let it back out. Simple. Easy. Just exist, and keep existing.

I replayed the confrontation with the tiger over and over in my head. I remembered the base level, lizard-brain panic. I remembered scrambling for the gun and shooting. I remembered the agonizing crawl for the flashlight. There was no conscious thought in that time, only panic. Only an animalistic desire for self-preservation, a sheer, unfettered will to live. I had zero desire to die during that whole exchange. I had been prepared to accept it, but I did not *want* it. It would have been really simple to just let death win, too. All I would have had to do was just stop fighting. I had been hurt. I didn't want to fight. I had wanted to just lie there, but I fought. I could have just let shock take over my body, and I could have just lay there and bled, but I didn't. I fought. This made me think about the stormy early June night in Wisconsin where I'd thought about taking my own life. I hadn't. My body had not wanted me to die. No matter what I felt about the existential dread that plagued me, no matter how meaningless life felt, no matter how many pieces of logic I could stack up to justify my own death in the coming wasteland, at heart, at a base level where thought and logic did not apply, I *desired* to live.

Over the days it took us to cross Louisiana, all I did was concentrate on that fact. I *wanted* to live. I *wanted* to be alive. I *wanted* to experience everything this life could offer, this strange post-societal existence in which I was trapped. It was a brave new world, but not in the Aldous Huxley sense. It was hopeful. There was unlimited potential hampered only by my will and sense of adventure.

I wanted to laugh. To love. To risk. To be safe and sheltered, but to face the wild unknown. I wanted to know what tomorrow might reveal. I wanted to know what next month, next year, and the next decade might present to me. It might be rough, but as long as I wasn't tiger food, I could face it. I *would* face it. I could take the chunk of my brain that made me dwell on sad things and the meaninglessness of existence, and try to retrain it to be positive, to think of the future, and make myself a life. What was done was done, and nothing I could do could change it. There was only the present and the future. There was only now, and what came next—whatever that might be.

And I looked forward to it.

We crossed the Louisiana/Texas border in the late afternoon. We stopped at a Flying J Travel Center just outside of Orange, Texas. Ren was still driving, as I was still crunching painkillers to function. She made up camp while I stood next to the van and swung my left leg back and forth, trying to rebuild some of the damaged muscles in my buttock. Every kick hurt, but I just told myself that pain was only a symptom of being alive. Alive was good. Alive was positive. There was potential in Alive. I would handle the pain.

Ren built up the fire. We looted the Travel Center together, me limping heavily and leaning on a cane. We found a backroom that was still stacked with bottles of water. It was the post-viral apocalypse equivalent to finding a cache of money hidden in a well. Ren hauled the water to the RV one case at a time while I sat and felt worthless because I couldn't even lift a case of water at that moment. Ren rooted through a couple of nearby homes and rooted out a massive aluminum pot, one of those twelve-gallon beasts that an Italian restaurant would use to make the day's marinara. We filled that thing with water, let that water boil, and then used the hot water to take actual showers using a camp shower bag. It was a rare treat. The soap and water stung my wounds, but it was a good kind of sting.

Ren scrubbed my wounds with scalding water and opened them afresh (which hurt like blue blazes), but they bled bright red blood. Healthy blood. And they only bled--no pus, nothing gross. The infection was gone. That was a good sign. She repacked the wounds with clean, fresh bandages and pronounced my recovery on track.

We sat together by the fire that night and listened to the crickets and the cicadas. There were fewer of them now. Fall was coming. It had to be sometime in mid-September. Maybe even late September. In Wisconsin, I could tell the seasons by the trees and the fact that the mornings would get colder. In the South, all the mornings were warm, as warm like late summer days in Wisconsin. All the leaves were still green. I couldn't tell anything about the time of year anymore. Being in the South was going to throw off my ability to keep track of the passing of time. Maybe that's a good thing.

The wedge that had been driven between us that day at the beach was still there. It didn't feel quite as big, but it was still there. At least, it still felt like it was there to me. I laughed. I tried to joke. Ren talked some. There were some prolonged pauses in the conversation. There was still a strange distance between us. We were circling each other like magnets of the same polarity, spinning in circles near each other, but never touching—we were just keeping a safe, respectful distance between us, but I felt like the distance was shrinking. I think we both had confusing emotions that we needed to learn to control.

Ren sat in a chair by the fire and flexed her toes in the heat. She chewed on her lower lip for a while. "We'll get to Houston tomorrow. There is going to be someone alive there, you know. At least one person, maybe more." Ren shrugged. "I don't know if we'll find them. Houston is big. Not New York-big, but still pretty big."

"In some ways, it's bigger. Houston is more like Madison or Milwaukee than New York. New York is condensed. It builds upwards. Madison and Houston build outward. They sprawl. Houston is like that. It covers a lot of ground."

Ren stopped chewing her lip. She looked over to me. "I hope they'll be friendly. And not insane."

"Me, too," I said. "I wonder if other people are traveling around the country like we did. I wonder if they're looking for us."

"There are." Ren's tone wasn't hopeful; it was definitive. She was dead certain on that fact. "They might never find us, but there are people out there. They are looking."

You don't really appreciate how big this country is until you're trying to find needles in the haystack. America is massive. Sure, if you have a good car and a supply of No-Doz, you could drive across it in four or five days. I think someone once did a speed drive from Los Angeles to New York in something like thirty-two hours. When you think about America like that, it doesn't seem all that big. It is big, though. It is grand and broad and majestic. There are hundreds of million miles of roads, hundreds of millions of homes. We were but specks of unimportant dust in the massive landscape, a pair of sand grains blowing across a vast, expansive prairie. I told Ren, "We'll build a big fire after we find a place to live. We'll burn it black so that clouds rise up. If people are within thirty miles, they'll see the smoke. They can come to us."

Ren's voice dropped to a low, serious tone. A grim, nervous expression settled on her face. "Can we really do this? Can we really be like Ma and Pa Ingalls in the Kansas Territory and just be self-sufficient? Can we make a life out of this place?"

I didn't know the answer to that. "We can try. I don't think we have much of a choice, otherwise. We can try, though. If we try hard enough, we will find a way to make it work. We will not only make a life, we'll make a *good* life. It won't be an easy life, but it will be a *good* life, I promise you that."

Ren stretched out a hand and rested it on mine. Her hand was warm and soft. At that moment, when she touched me, I felt sparks run up my arm and across my back. The sparks danced in my head. Ren leaned closer to me. "Thank you."

I turned to look at her. "For what?"

"For bringing me with you." She smiled. Her face was warm and sincere. At that moment, something unspoken passed between us. The wedge between us melted away, never to return.

I smiled back to her. For the first time in my life, the smile felt natural and unforced. I hope it looked like a real person's smile. "Thank *you*."

We lapsed into silence again. I felt like saying something more, but I didn't want to break the mood. Maybe we'd said enough. I could not ignore the fact that Ren's hand was resting on the back of mine, though. I turned my hand over so that she was no longer resting her hand on mine. We held hands. Our fingers interlaced. Ren squeezed my hand tightly. She made no attempt to pull it away. I didn't look over at her, but I knew what that squeeze meant. It said more than words ever could.

Lake Houston spread out before us, a long, shimmering expanse of water in the middle of the Texas prairie. We stood on the shore and watched a badling of ducks circling overhead and descending for a watery landing, their wings splashing water before transitioning into an easy, graceful float. We saw a herd of deer in a field nearby. They looked strong and healthy. They were thriving in the post-human world. I thought about the hunting rifle I had stored in the RV. Fresh meat would require killing. I was not a fan of the thought of having to take an animal's life, but I would cross that bridge when I came to it. In the drive through the Texas countryside, we had seen herds of cattle, mobs of horses, and loads of formerly domestic pigs gone feral in roving packs. The countryside was practically crawling with life. There was food on the hoof aplenty. And, since we were in Texas, I knew there wouldn't be any shortage of ammunition any time soon.

There were dozens of nice homes around the edge of the lake. Any one of them might be our new house. We had an outdoor brick oven kit lying on the mattress in the back bunk. We would build an outdoor fire pit and wood-fired oven. If we found a house with a hearth and fireplace, even better. Some of the homes had barns. We would need one of those, eventually. I wanted to capture a few horses and cows. We would require them in the coming years. I knew nothing about horse training, but that was why there were libraries. I would find books and teach myself. I would learn by doing, by trial-and-error. There were large, open parcels of land in the area, and many of the homes had expansive lawns. Lawns were a needless luxury now. Ren and I would turn them into large, sprawling gardens and vast orchards. We would capture chickens and raise them for eggs. If we could catch rabbits and pigs, we could farm them, too. We would reclaim the overgrown land. We would wrestle weeds from the ground, till the soil, and plant gardens. We would return our little patch of the world to an agrarian paradise. We would build our life.

"It's beautiful here," said Ren. She turned her face to the sun and inhaled the warm prairie air. "I mean, it's not Brooklyn, but I think I can be happy here."

"Happy is a state of mind," I told her. "You can be happy anywhere as long as you set your mind to it and *decide* to be happy."

Ren smiled at me. Her smile thrilled me. She said, "*We* can be happy here." She leaned up on her tiptoes and kissed my cheek. I turned my face, and we found each other's lips. I put my hand on the back of her head and the kiss extended from a peck to something much longer and sweeter. Her hands ran gently over my shoulders. I cradled the small of her back. Time stopped for several seconds, a blissful and welcome break from reality.

When we parted, Renata turned and climbed into the RV. "C'mon, Twist." She shut the passenger-side door and leaned out the window. "We traveled enough for this lifetime." She nodded her head toward the houses on the west side of the lake. "It's time for you to take me home."

I smiled at her and turned back to the lake. It was beautiful there. The flat prairie stretched for miles. There were plenty of homes we could scavenge for supplies and wood until we could turn the land into a working, sustainable farm. There were animals we could capture and domesticate. It wouldn't be easy, but it would be *worth* it. We wouldn't be stuck in a weird, half-life existence, struggling to live out of a library or a cramped RV on odds and ends we found lying in the wreckage of the world. We would have a home. A *real* home. I looked to the woman I loved. The smile on her face lit my entire world.

I think this is what Doug had been trying to tell me. He wanted me to *live*. To feel like life was not an inconvenience, but rather a gift. He wanted me to not worry so much about living day-to-day, and to start worrying about doing something more than merely existing in a state of desperation. He wanted me to have joy. To have love. To have a bit of something beyond being in the moment. I stood on the shore a moment more. I hoped my parents were proud of me, wherever they were. I hoped Doug could see where I was, and what I would accomplish. I hoped he was proud of me, too.

I limped back to the RV and climbed into the driver's seat. I started the engine. I looked at Ren, and she looked at me. She placed her hand on my shoulder. I shifted into drive and let the Greyhawk roll slowly back to the road. The future stood before us like the lake, bright, wide, and shining.

It's Thursday, I think. I'm not sure.

Honestly, it doesn't even matter. The apocalypse wasn't a cruel dream. The Flu was real. Almost everyone I have ever known or loved is still dead.

However, the world looks less vacant and barren than it did. I am no longer alone. I found a woman in New York and she came to the South with me. We sought many long, empty roads for possible survivors of a catastrophic viral apocalypse who might have wanted to help us rebuild civilization, but found no one, so far.

We know there are people out there, though. We hope they will find us. If not, she and I are prepared to carve out a good life together.

We will succeed.

This is the continued journal of my daily life.

My name is Twist. I'm nineteen, and heading toward twenty. I still miss Big Macs, television, indoor plumbing, and going to the movies.

~~And I am still alive.~~

And I am actually living.

Acknowledgements

When I first wrote *After Everyone Died*, it was really just a response to my growing contempt with the post-apocalypse fiction genre. Everything I was reading was about panic, or warring factions of armed militia-types, or putting children in gladiatorial arenas to fight to the death (*which is seriously messed up, when you think about it*), or—of course—zombies. When I really thought about the apocalypse, I figured Cormac McCarthy probably had it right in *The Road*, but his vision was so bleak and brutal. I wanted to know what would happen if you just plucked an average, beta-male type kid out of his suburban life, and forced him to keep living with no further advantages. I did not really want him fighting others for survival. I did not want to see a large group of people trying to rebuild a town. When I really thought about it, in a good viral apocalypse, boredom and isolation would be the biggest enemies. Humans are social animals. Take that away from us, and we can be driven to madness. That interested me more than any sort of violence or action. I wanted to write a small, quiet, intimate look at a life after the fall of humanity. It was not an exciting vision, but I felt it was truthful. One of my favorite writing teachers, Dr. Emilio Degrazia, used to say, "It doesn't matter what you write, as long as you tell the truth about it." And I felt this was as truthful as I could tell it.

When I started submitting *After Everyone Died* to agents and publishers, the ones that actually read it said the exact same thing, every single one of them: *we want more action and characters in your book about loneliness, boredom, and isolation.* They all had a well-defined formula for post-apocalypse novels, and they were not going to deviate from it. It made me realize that my personal, intimate vision of the apocalypse probably wasn't going to sell many copies for larger publishing houses. I do not blame large publishers. Their job is to sell stories they feel the majority of the public would like to read. I freely admit this book series is probably not for everyone. I thought for a while about changing the story to suite their given demands, but I realized that to change it would be telling a very different story, a story that had been told many times before, and I did not want to tell that story. Others had already done it better than I could. I was not willing to compromise on what I viewed as the reality of the post-apocalypse world, so I knew I would have to step out on my own to do it.

I had no idea what would happen. I had no idea if people would like the book at all. I had no idea if anything I did would work. One universal truth about writing is that a writer should only write books that he or she wants to read. I did that, and then I just had to hope that others wanted to read that book, too. I believed in the story and hoped for the best.

Turns out, I made a good decision.

After Everyone Died was my seventh novel. It has outsold all my other books combined ten times over and then some. This book has easily been my greatest success. At last count, I was over 15,000 copies sold (*mostly the Kindle eBook version on Amazon, but a fair amount of hard copies sold, as well*) and heading toward 20,000. Not to mention, over 5,000 free downloads during a promotional venture on Amazon. I ended up with over 100 reviews on Amazon (*so far*), and that means *AED* was included into some of Amazon's promotional materials, which helps more than you would realize. By some book-selling metrics, that Little Book That Could became a best-seller. I could officially put "author of the best-selling novel…" after my name.

And that's not nothin'.

I could not have done any of this without you, the readers, though. Without people believing in the book, enjoying the book, posting reviews on Amazon (*especially posting reviews—you have no idea how much they help authors. If you like a book—any book—please, post a review*), and telling friends about it, it would not have gone anywhere.

I could not have written the sequel without seeing the positive response in the reviews and the kind emails requesting more. Those emails meant the world to me. I appreciate so much that someone would take time out of his or her day to send a quick note to me on Facebook or Twitter. Without people pestering me for more, I honestly don not know if this book would have been completed. During the first draft process, I had become stuck around 15,000 words in the manuscript with that *"What's the point?"* malaise writers so often get when staring down the barrel of three hundred or so empty pages. I had put this book to the back burner and started working on other projects, but the occasional nudge from random strangers made want to finish this book. It made me *need* to finish. It was very gratifying to know that someone out there connected with the simple little melancholy isolation story I wrote and wanted more. We all need some help occasionally, and I will be eternally grateful for those who wrote those notes and helped me finish this book.

When it comes to the people I know personally, I have to start by thanking my cover designer, Paige Krogwold. She is a fiery little elfin sprite with attitude, but if you had to be stuck in the apocalypse with someone, she would not be a bad choice.

I must thank my editor, Ann Hayes. Ann is a true friend, and although she is sometimes too blonde for her own good, she is still one of the smartest and kindest people I know. If you needed someone to ride shotgun in your RV while you're out scavenging the crumbling ruins of a dead society—Ann is the person you want having your back.

The wonderful Mary Holm needs a special thank you, as well. She's probably one of the nicest people I have ever met, and she offered to give a read-through of my manuscript, pointing out all my bonehead typos along the way. Truly, if this book is any good, I owe a debt of thanks to her.

There are always people lurking in the background who might not have anything to do with the book itself, but who are always willing to help in any way they can, even if it is just by distracting you from myriad torments of decay and rot. People like Ryan Spindler, Jack Quincey, Ethan Bartlett, David Johnson, Veronika Garrett, Dusty Miller, Josh Upton, Chris Koterba, Andy Cerney, Fran Cohen Brown, Nancy Gray, Carol Kaufman, Jennifer L. Miller, and Steve Kittleson are those sorts. As is Eric Larson, and all the good people at TeslaCon. In addition, my sister, Erin, sits among those who willingly brave the newly fallen lawless world in search of corned beef and cans of tuna. If anyone is going to be wearing a suit of armor and shouting orders to an invisible raccoon after society crumbles, it will be her. Just do not ask her to garden or make any sudden movements around her.

Many thanks to Maddy Hunter, Alex Bledsoe, Kathleen Ernst, Jerry Peterson, Craig Johnson, Doug Moe, and all the other writers in and around Madison who have let me attend their book events and have shown me how selling books should be done. Even with their stellar examples, I still will not likely be successful at hosting a coherent promotional event, but I enjoy how you all handle it with grace and style. Also, I have to thank everyone at Mystery to Me on Monroe Street in Madison. That is my "home" bookstore. They have always been very kind and supportive to me (*please return their support by buying books through them!*) and for that I am very thankful. I do not think I could what I do without their help. I sincerely hope the viral apocalypse spares you all, but if it docsn't, I will gladly dig your graves and mark them with fieldstone.

And of course, I have to thank my parents, who made me read when I was growing up, and made me want to write. I have to thank my wife, who does not complain when I read at the dinner table. And my daughter, Annika, who continues to be a large part of the reason I still try to chase my dreams—even when they are painfully out of reach.

Lastly, and most importantly, if you bought a copy of *After Everyone Died*, I thank you most of all. You are the reason this sequel even exists. Should you ever need to hide from Bigfoot, you are all welcome to lie on the floor of my RV in terror anytime you want.

I'll even bring the S'mores.

I know that some people will want to know whether there will be a third book in the Survivor Journals, or not. The short answer: *I hope there will be.* I will have to let readership speak to that. If there is enough demand, I have more stories to tell. I have the third book mostly outlined in my head. I would like this series to be a trilogy, at least. If *Long Empty Roads* does not find readers as well as its predecessor did and things end with this book, I shall be at peace with it, though. I have greatly enjoyed this venture, and I have grown to enjoy very much writing from Twist's point-of-view. If you want more, please, please, please—tell friends, write and post reviews, and make unreasonable demands of your local libraries and bookstores to carry this book. It will help more than you think, and I will be grateful.

Sun Prairie, Wisconsin
November 2017

About the Author

Sean Patrick Little lives in Sun Prairie, Wisconsin. He writes a lot. He watches too much TV. He plays guitar and bass badly. He has two cats that annoy him a lot. He has a dog, a walleyed, big-eared Heeler/Corgi mix, who demands constant belly rubs. He has a wife and a child.

That child has recently become a teenager.

Please send help.

You can follow Sean on Goodreads, Twitter, Tumblr, and Facebook if you are interested in keeping up with his upcoming projects. He is not hard to find.

He's not terribly exciting, but he enjoys the attention all the same. Since he had to give up eating wheat and sugar, tiny rations of attention is all that keeps him going anymore.

Facebook: facebook.com/seanpatricklittlewriter
Twitter: @WiscoWriterGuy

Other Books by Sean Patrick Little

The Centurion: The Balance of the Soul War
The Seven
*Longrider: Away From Home**
*Longrider: To the North**
*The Bride Price**
*Without Reason**
After Everyone Died

The TeslaCon Novels
Lord Bobbins and the Romanian Ruckus
Lord Bobbins and the Dome of Light (coming 2018)
Lord Bobbins and the Clockwork Girl (coming 2018)

All books are available a eBooks on your favorite online retailers. Hard copies can be ordered online or, preferably, through your favorite independent bookstore. Remember: local stores need your support more than major online retailers do.

*E-book only

Publisher's Note

The world of publishing grows more and more competitive every year. It is harder and harder for small press and independent books to compete in a crowded marketplace. There is a mountain of books published annually and only so many readers and so many hours in a day—not to mention the almost insurmountable competition from all the various electronic screens that beg for attention.

If you enjoyed this book, please help spread the word about it. Tell all your friends. If they buy copies and like it, ask them to tell their friends, and their friends' friends, and so on. Word of mouth is always the best sales tool.

If you are a creative type, doing things like posting fan art on social media, participating in message boards and plugging the book, doing cosplay and posting photos, or making models of things in the book is greatly appreciated. Use hashtags to make sure people know where the inspiration for the image originated and to what it relates. Anything that extends the reach and audience of the book is always a positive and always appreciated. Support the things you enjoy.

To further aid the cause, you can politely ask your local library to purchase a copy and ask your local bookstores to carry it, as well. Every little bit helps.

If you enjoyed this book, please leave a kind review on major websites like Amazon or Goodreads, or any of your other favorite book retailers. Link to the book on your Facebook pages or Twitter accounts. Good, honest reviews help more than you know, and we truly appreciate every review. The more positive reviews the book gets, the farther the reach of the book spreads.

If you have a bookstore or work in a library and want one of our authors to speak, or you would like to host a signing, please let us know. If we can make it happen, we will.

And if you really enjoyed this book, please let the author know. A kind word is sometimes the job a writer needs to keep working. That goes for any book you've enjoyed, ever. Most writers are on Twitter nowadays. Or they have email addresses or some other way to contact them. If you send them a message, they will see it. They might not reply, but they will be grateful.

You should probably also do the same things for anyone important in your life in general: your grandmother or grandfather, your parents, a favorite teacher, a friend that has been there for you—it really doesn't matter: If someone has done something that you have appreciated, please let them know.

Spread some positivity in this world. It will do you, and others, more good than you might know.

With sincere gratitude,
Spilled Inc. Press

CPSIA information can be obtained
at www.ICGtesting.com
Printed in the USA
FSHW020709230620
71458FS